Pineapple
Christmas

A Pineapple Port Mystery
Book Twenty-Three

Amy Vansant

Vansant Creations, LLC / Amy Vansant
Annapolis, MD
http://www.AmyVansant.com
http://www.PineapplePort.com

Editing/Proofreading by Effrosyni Moschoudi & Meg Barnhart

CONTENTS

CHAPTER ONE

It doesn't make any sense. I waited all night for someone to find the body and sound the alarm.

Nothing happened.

How could they not have found the body?

It's *impossible*. I left it in the middle of the room. Someone *had* to see it.

Now, it's morning, and everyone's acting like nothing happened. I ask where she is, and they say she's *sick*.

I know she's a lot worse than *sick*.

Why would they cover up a murder?

I see the two older ladies at both exits from the room like they're guarding. Someone's coming down the stairs. It sounds like they're struggling, grunting—maybe, carrying something heavy? I can't see.

Hm.

Later, with my mind spinning about so many things, I sneak upstairs, back to the room where I'd left her.

She's gone.

They *did* find her.

The dolls bunched in the corner stare at me as I gape slackjawed at where I'd left the body.

How could I have planned for this?

I go through the house searching for the body, trying not to look panicked. It *has* to be in the house—the storm outside is *raging*. I haven't seen anyone walking around bedraggled and wet. I haven't seen watery footprints on the floor. No one has gone outside.

The body has to be *in the house.*

It *can't* go missing.

That would ruin the whole *point.*

As I search the house, I realize I've skipped the kitchen. Where could someone hide a body in the kitchen? In the oven? Under the sink? Then, in desperation, I look—and spot the walk-in freezer.

I'd forgotten about that freezer.

I notice a padlock on the door.

That wasn't there before.

That's it.

Of course.

They put her in the freezer.

I smile.

I know where the key to that padlock is. I'd seen that lock in the utility drawer while looking for a pen.

I open the drawer and find the key in the back.

Ha!

I unlock the padlock and open the freezer door. I don't see anything at first, but then I spot her on the ground, hidden behind a row of white buckets, tucked underneath some low shelving.

A sigh of relief escapes me.

This will do just fine.

I'll leave her here.

And later...

Come see my secret.

I smile. The world is in order again.

It's beginning to look a lot like Christmas.

CHAPTER TWO

A Few Days Ago

Charlotte exited the Charlock Holmes Detective Agency headquarters with Declan on her heels. He paused to lock the door— she kept walking. Heading for the car, she glanced over her shoulder as she rounded the corner of their tiny office building and saw Declan had almost caught up. She held up the envelope in her hand for him to see.

"We should stop at Blade's—*oof!*"

The wind knocked out of her lungs as she smacked into something soft *and* solid. Something that shouldn't have been lurking around the corner of the building. It smelled too much like the lily of the valley to be a *wall*.

She bounced into Declan's waiting arms. Luckily, he'd caught up when he did, or she would have landed on her rump.

"*Whoa*," he grunted.

Charlotte blinked at the grinning figure standing before them. Mariska—the woman who'd raised her after her grandmother's death—stood with her hands outstretched like a benevolent angel beckoning her to heaven. Her cheeks glowed more pink than usual, and she seemed winded—probably because Charlotte had just bounced off her.

Mariska's eyebrows tilted with worry.

"Are you okay?" she asked. "I'm sorry. I was walking fast. I didn't see you until it was too late."

Her arms remained reaching toward Charlotte, palms up. She seemed frozen in that position.

"Are you getting ready to catch a pass?" asked Charlotte, finding her feet with Declan's help.

Mariska snorted a laugh and lowered her arms. "No, this is my *ta-da* pose. Guess what?"

Mariska vibrated with giddy excitement as she waited for an answer.

This worried Charlotte to no end.

She winced. "Do I have to?"

Mariska sucked in a deep breath and blurted her surprise.

"You're going to Victorian next weekend!"

Charlotte scowled.

"I'm *going to Victorian*?" she repeated.

Mariska nodded so hard her curls bounced.

"Yes, both of you!"

Charlotte exchanged a look with Declan.

"You're *going to Victorian*," she told him.

He nodded. "Awesome."

She returned her focus to Mariska.

"Quick question—how exactly does someone *go to Victorian*?"

Mariska chuffed. "Remember that Victorian Christmas package I signed up to win?"

"No."

"Oh. Well, I did, and I won as many as six people!"

Charlotte's eyebrows raised.

"You won six people? I'm pretty sure that's not legal."

Mariska rolled her eyes.

"Let me start over."

"That would be good." Charlotte motioned to Mariska's legs. "Another quick question—do you know you're in your pajama bottoms?"

Mariska glanced down at the loose cotton pants dotted with snoring cartoon sheep.

She nodded. "I was ready for bed when I found out. They just called. I rushed right over here."

The Charlock Holmes Detective Agency office lived in a tiny

building on the edge of Pineapple Port—the fifty-five-plus community where Charlotte had grown up. She'd been *grandfathered in* by her grandmother's death. Mariska, her grandmother's best friend, lived across the street—which put her within pajama-walking distance to their office.

Charlotte nodded. "As long as you're aware and not losing your mind. Go ahead. Sorry to interrupt."

Mariska took a moment to gather her thoughts.

"There's a Victorian bed and breakfast, not that far from here, near Orlando. The new owner ran a big giveaway for opening weekend. I won the giant Christmas package—tickets for two rooms and up to six people."

"Wow," said Declan with no actual enthusiasm. His tone said both *Congratulations!* and *Kill me now!* Charlotte fought to keep from giggling.

Oblivious, Mariska clapped her hands together. "I know it's so *exciting.* I hardly ever win these things."

"How does this work? Two rooms and six people?" asked Charlotte.

Mariska dismissed her confusion with a wave of her hand.

"I asked them about that. Each room has a trundle. I think they said *up to six* in case someone with kids won."

Charlotte nodded. *Kids.* That made more sense.

"Me and Darla and you two," said Mariska. "We don't need the trundles."

"What about Bob and Frank?" asked Declan, invoking the names of Mariska and Darla's husbands.

Charlotte side-eyed him.

Nice try.

Did he think he could get out of this that easy? Did he think Mariska would gasp, suddenly remembering she had a husband?

She knew neither of the husbands wanted to spend a holiday weekend at a Victorian bed and breakfast. They'd rather clean their gutters. Heck—they'd rather scoop their eyes out with melonballers.

As expected, Mariska pouted.

"No. Frank has to work, and Bob's sciatica is acting up—"

Charlotte nodded.

I bet.

Mariska slapped her hands to her chest, one on top of the other.

"Thank *goodness* I've got you two to use the other two spots—"

"Thank goodness," echoed Declan just loud enough for Charlotte to hear.

"—you two are even *better*," continued Mariska. "We'll have more fun without those two *grumps*."

Charlotte sniffed.

There it was. The guilt trip, to ensure they didn't say no, too.

"Wait, is it *this* weekend?" asked Declan.

Charlotte could almost hear his mind whirring as he searched for an excuse as to why they couldn't go.

Mariska nodded. "Yep. They're going to pick us up in a bus tomorrow afternoon."

Declan remained silent. Charlotte couldn't think of a good excuse either. No one needed a detective this close to the holidays. They were as slow as weekend beach traffic.

She offered a tight smile. "I'll check our calendar—"

Mariska shook a finger at her. "Don't *check*. You're *going*."

Charlotte nodded.

And that was that.

Before she could find another objection, Mariska turned and raised her hands into the air like she'd broken the tape at the end of a marathon.

"I *won*."

Charlotte wasn't sure if she meant the Victorian vacation or her bid to bring them along.

Without another word, Mariska headed for home, tush twitching in her sleeping sheep cartoons.

"Did we just agree to go to a Victorian Bed and Breakfast?" asked Declan.

"No. It's better than that. It's a *Christmas-themed* Victorian bed and breakfast in the middle of nowhere."

He groaned, and she patted his arm.

"If it makes you feel any better, I don't think we ever had a choice. You knew when you married me I came with baggage."

He chuckled. "A whole *neighborhood* full of baggage."

They returned to the car without Mariska serving as a linebacker.

"I'm going to setup the rolling puppies when we get back," mused Charlotte.

"The what?"

"I bought a Christmas decoration for the front yard—a bunch of puppies in Santa hats rolling around, tangled in a garland. I thought it was cute and funny."

"Ah. Well, I'm all for cute and funny. I married you, after all."

"*Aww...*" she said, chuckling.

He grinned at her as he pulled away from the curb and then furrowed his brow.

"Hey, what were you saying earlier about Blade?"

She straightened. "Oh, *thank you*. I almost forgot. If you stop at his house, I'll give him his check."

She held up the envelope containing the paycheck for their part-time employee.

He nodded and made a slight detour to head for Blade's. Blade had worked full-time at Declan's Hock o'Bell Pawn Shop downtown. After the shop burned down, Declan retired from the pawn-shop phase of his life to join Charlotte in their burgeoning private detective agency. The agency couldn't afford Blade full-time yet, but luckily, he had a healthy savings account and wasn't too worried about money.

Must be nice.

Blade had turned his love of taxidermy into a profitable side gig. He didn't stuff the animals but *zhuzhed* them up with costumes and props. His stuffed critter enhancements had been one of Declan's most popular items. He couldn't *give* those creepy things away until Blade showed up.

Declan drove to downtown Charity, where Blade lived near Main Street. The local houses and shops blazed with holiday lights.

Charlotte loved this time of year. Although they were in Florida and it never snowed, the residents of Pineapple Port went *crazy* at Christmas with lights, inflatable Santas, plastic reindeer, and every other possible holiday decoration. Every year, Mariska and

Darla took her on a traditional golf car tour of the neighborhood to see them in all their tacky glory.

Once, two Pineapple Port residents had made the national news *wrestling* in a big box store over the last inflatable snowman.

Charlotte had been *so* proud.

From the day after Halloween until January tenth, astronauts could see Pineapple Port from space.

Charlotte saw twinkling red and green lights covering Blade's house, too. As they exited the car and neared the front door, she cocked her head as the sound of music caught her ear.

"Do you hear Christmas music?" she asked.

Declan nodded. "It's definitely coming from Blade's."

She knocked. No one answered.

"He has to be in there. The lights are on, the music—is he having a party?"

Declan sniffed. "Do you smell something burning?"

Charlotte thought she'd smelled something and took a better whiff. Her eyes widened.

"I *do*."

She tried the knob and found the door unlocked.

"Open it slowly. Don't feed the flames," warned Declan.

She creaked open the door. The sound of Bing Crosby singing *Winter Wonderland* grew louder.

"It's safe. Sorta," said Charlotte, entering the living room of Blade's small downstairs apartment.

It seemed the big guy had made some *enhancements*.

Multicolored holiday lights dangled around the room, tacked to the shiplap walls, dipping as they crossed the ceiling from one side of the room to the other. A frenzied-blinking Christmas tree dominated one corner.

"That tree needs a seizure warning label," muttered Declan.

A fog of smoke hung in the room, adding to the disco feel. The smell of burnt *something* filled their nostrils.

"Blade?" called Charlotte. "Bla—"

She stopped when she realized they weren't the only guests at the party. Faces peered at her through the smoke.

She pointed. "Is that—?"

"We're surrounded," said Declan as he moved toward the kitchen—the source of the smoke.

Charlotte remained in the living room as her eyes adjusted.

Wow.

She knew Blade was odd, but she wondered if the man spent *too* much time alone.

In front of her, a stuffed raccoon wearing a jaunty, holly-covered vest stood on a wooden chair with a tiny teacup in its paw, toasting their arrival. A family of squirrels occupied one corner of the sofa, each with a red scarf wrapped around its neck. One clung to a red sled headed to nowhere. A turkey wearing a pilgrim outfit moped in the corner like a petulant teen. A mouse with a wine glass and spectacles sat beside a tutu-clad chipmunk, seemingly deep in conversation.

Even the deer head on the wall wore a Santa hat. Charlotte moved in to examine what turned out to be a red-painted golf ball stuck to its nose.

The living room table boasted bowls of snacks and a small charcuterie board of meat and cheeses.

Charlotte shook her head.

Is Blade having a party with his stuffed animals?

"This is like the Teddy Bear's Tea Party gone horribly wrong," she said.

Before Declan could cross the threshold into the kitchen, Blade appeared, wearing a green elf costume with a pointy hat, striped stockings, and metal bells on his toes that jingled as he entered the living room. He had a wooden spoon in his hand covered with some dark substance.

Declan stopped to keep from running into him, which was a good idea. Blade was *enormous*—it would *hurt* to run into him. Declan was tall at around six-three, and Blade *towered* over him, besides having a good hundred pounds on him.

It wasn't only Blade's size that made him stand out in a crowd. The man's impressive blond mustache rounded his mouth and drooped to his chin on either side. He wore his long, dirty-blonde locks in a ponytail, which started just below his elf hat. He almost always wore a tee shirt with knife-themed art on the front. She couldn't see today's design beneath the festive green vest.

Thanks to him, the Charlock Holmes Detective Agency also provided bodyguard services.

Blade gasped at the sight of them.

"What are you two doing here?" he asked in his baritone.

"Did we come at a bad time?" drolled Declan.

Blade glanced at his spoon.

"No, I, uh...I burnt my chocolate. I was making peppermint bark."

"Uh-huh." Declan eyed the stuffed animals in the living room. "Is there anything you want to talk about?"

"Talk—?" Blade followed Declan's gaze to the living room. "Oh. Yeah. That probably looks a little crazy, huh?"

Declan nodded. "It looks a *lot* crazy, buddy."

Blade offered them a sheepish smile.

"I just put them there. I don't have a lot of room. They're gifts for people. The mailman, the lady at the bakery—"

"And *your* costume?" asked Charlotte.

He shrugged. "I signed up to hand out toys at the hospital—I was trying it on to see if it fit."

Declan nodded. "Ah. So you're *not* having a party for your stuffed animals?"

Charlotte could see Blade blush even through the haze.

"Naw..."

A white creature as tall as Blade's knee appeared beside him. Charlotte jumped, slapping her hand to her chest before recognizing Blade's cat, Johnny Walker. The white cat had no front legs and walked on his hind paws as if he'd been born to do it.

When what looked like a small child entered the room with a cat's face, it tended to catch people off-guard.

"That *cat*," said Charlotte. "Got me again."

Johnny Walker collapsed and began licking his belly.

Blade motioned to the taxidermy.

"They *are* pretty good friends, now that you mention it. They never complain about my cooking."

His chuckling trailed, and he looked away.

Charlotte frowned.

Blade seemed sad.

"What are you doing for the holidays?" she asked.

The big guy shrugged. "Nothing special. I usually make myself a turkey. A little one."

Charlotte nodded and looked at Declan. He scowled, sensing she had an idea.

"Didn't Mariska say she could invite up to six?" she asked.

"Ooh, *right,*" said Declan, nodding his approval.

Of course he liked the idea. It meant he'd have a playmate for the Victorian vacation.

He turned to Blade.

"How'd you like to go on a trip to a Christmas-themed bed and breakfast this weekend?" he asked.

Now, it was Blade's turn to scowl with confusion.

"I don't get what you're layin' down," he said, his bushy blond eyebrows furrowing.

"Mariska won a trip, and she has room to invite another person," explained Charlotte. "We're going—do you want to come?"

Blade straightened, coming dangerously close to hitting his head on the cased opening between the living room and kitchen.

"*Really?*"

She nodded. "It's this weekend. I know that's short notice. Are you free?"

"And don't feel like you have to go," said Declan. "We know Christmas-themed Victorian weekends aren't everybody's cup of tea—but you'd be doing me a favor. Right now, it's me, Mariska, Darla, and Charlotte. I'm outnumbered."

"Even though that's a *dream,*" said Charlotte.

He smirked. "Of course."

Blade's eyes opened wide. "I think that sounds right *on.*"

Charlotte snorted a laugh.

"That makes one of us."

"Thanks, brother." Blade smacked Declan's shoulder, sending him stumbling forward. He threw out a foot to catch himself.

"No problem."

"Is that why you came over?" asked Blade.

"Oh, no," said Charlotte, holding out the envelope. "We

brought you your check."

"Oh, thanks," said Blade, taking it. He motioned to the sweating charcuterie board.

"Want some meat?"

CHAPTER THREE

"You're sure you don't mind that we invited Blade?" asked Charlotte as they stood outside Mariska's house, waiting for the bus taking them to *The Outback Inn, previously known as the Timeless Inn.*

Darla had joined them. She was Charlotte's backup mother in the neighborhood—and Mariska's best friend. Mariska had been the one who made sure she had food and shelter. Darla was the one who taught her how to pick a lock. All the basics covered.

Mariska shook her head. "The more the merrier. I wish I'd won a *hundred* tickets."

"Ooh. That would be something," said Darla, smirking at Charlotte.

Mariska eyed Declan and giggled when he winked at her.

"Speak of the devil," said Declan, nodding toward Blade as the big man parked and exited his pickup with an army green duffel bag slung over his shoulder. He wore a tee shirt featuring a raccoon wearing a blue bandana riding a motorcycle with a knife between its teeth. The raccoon had an eye patch for good measure. Beneath the art blazed the phrase, *Fur, Fangs, and Full Throttle!*

Charlotte had no idea what that meant, but it was classic Blade-wear. The man had more knife-themed tee shirts than Mariska had chicken statues in her kitchen, which was saying something.

Mariska's chicken obsession had made Christmas and birthday gifting easy—though she'd recently shifted her alliance to sea turtles. No chickens this year. Pass the word.

Blade lumbered over, his grin pushing his mustache wide.

"Hey everybody," he said.

"Hi, Blade," chimed the group.

A door creaked, and all eyes shifted to Mariska's house. Her husband Bob stuck his balding dome outside.

"*Mariska*," he called. "Hypothetically, if someone wanted to find their favorite whiskey tumbler, where would they find it?"

Mariska glared. "*Hypothetically*, someone isn't supposed to drink whiskey."

Bob nodded.

"But, *hypothetically*, someone *might* have some buddies over and might *hypothetically* have one or two."

Charlotte's dog, Abby, poked her head out at Bob's knee level. He shifted his foot to block her from escaping. He was on babysitting duty. Charlotte questioned if she'd made the right choice.

"Is my husband *hypothetically* one of these buddies?" asked Darla.

Bob sniffed. "I refuse to answer on the grounds he'll be pissed off if I do."

Mariska and Darla exchanged a look. Darla shrugged.

"It's behind the bar where it always is," said Mariska, relenting.

He shook his head. "I looked there."

She dismissed him with a wave and turned away.

"You looked the way *you* look. Try looking the way *I* look."

Bob scowled and waved to everyone before disappearing back inside.

Mariska tilted back her head to stare at the sky.

"That man will be the death of me."

Darla chuckled and pretended to hit Blade in the stomach with rabbit punches.

"Hey, big guy. How have you been?" she asked.

Blade pretended to block and then pursed his lips at her. "Good. How's Frank?"

She shrugged. "Same ol' same ol'. Driving me crazy."

"I bet the Victorian bed and breakfast has never seen anything like *him* before," Charlotte whispered to Declan, her eyes on Blade.

Declan laughed. "Safe bet."

They heard an engine and turned to see a rusted, half-sized bus headed their way. As it pulled up in front of the group, Charlotte noticed someone had blacked out all the windows. She pointed them out to Declan.

"That's not ominous or anything."

"I'm more disturbed by the logo," said Declan.

He had a point.

Someone had painted *Casey's Bus Service* on the side of the bus in what looked like a child's scrawl. It felt a little like their ride went straight to Bonkersville.

The blue bus stopped, and the door cranked open. A young man with short red hair smiled down at them.

"All aboard the Timeless Inn Express," he said.

"Do you mean The Outback Inn, previously known as The Timeless Inn?" asked Charlotte.

He shrugged. "Sure."

"That's reassuring," murmured Charlotte as they boarded.

She climbed the stairs and noticed the seating was different than she'd imagined. The first three rows followed the usual bus seating arrangement, but behind those rows, bench seating lined the outside wall of the vehicle, giving it a limousine feel. One final bench ran along the back.

A small disco ball hung from the ceiling in the 'lounge' area. Someone, presumably Casey with the lousy handwriting, had painted the inside midnight blue and dotted it with realistic stars.

"*Wow*," said Charlotte, putting her small suitcase in an overhead luggage rack.

"I know how we're going to dinner on our next big night out," said Declan behind her.

Charlotte laughed as she dropped into her seat.

"I'm sittin' in the back," said Darla, heading directly for the disco ball.

Mariska followed Darla.

Declan sat beside Charlotte.

Blade sat across the aisle from Declan and Charlotte behind the driver.

The driver jerked the door shut.

"Are you Casey?" asked Declan as they pulled away.

The young man nodded.

"I am. This is my bus."

"Been doing this long?"

Casey shrugged. "I bought Bertha here for seven hundred dollars, fixed her up, and I've been driving for about six months now."

"Good for you," said Declan.

Casey nodded. "It worked out great. It ain't easy to get work after prison."

Charlotte's attention shifted from the window to the driver.

Wait, what?

Casey was the proverbial icing on the cake. She'd already been wrestling with the idea of this trip—she suspected the inn would be full of creepy Victorian dolls, and *she did not like dolls.*

Dolls and clowns were her two bugaboos.

Now, the driver taking them to Creepy Doll Land on the Crazy Bus was an ex-con?

Maybe it was a good thing they'd brought Blade.

Should I ask him what he went to prison for?

She looked at Declan, and, reading her mind, he shook his head.

She nodded to let him know she understood.

Yeah. Maybe better to get to the inn and *not* upset the driver, who may or may not be a murderer.

They drove thirty minutes east—at least, Charlotte assumed it was east. The blacked-out windows made it hard to tell. About halfway through the trip, Casey flipped a switch, and music and glittering lights filled the back half of the bus, much to Darla and Mariska's delight. Darla did her best *Saturday Night Fever* imitation, and the ladies giggled.

"Were they drinking this morning?" asked Declan, twisting to watch.

Charlotte shook her head.

"You'd think. I'm afraid this is just their natural state of being."

After another fifteen minutes, the bus slowed, and Charlotte saw a long stretch of fence through the front glass. Casey turned to eek through a bus-sized gap in the fencing onto a dirt road.

They bounced along this road for some time.

Through the front window, Charlotte saw little more than open fields, the occasional lonely palm, or clump of trees.

"This place really *is* in the middle of nowhere," she muttered, looking at her phone. She had zero bars.

"I don't see a house," agreed Declan.

Charlotte leaned to whisper in his ear.

"Hopefully, we're not going to Casey's killing shed."

Declan snorted a laugh.

Charlotte longed for Monday when she'd be back home with Declan and Abby—safe and sound. She was sure they'd have a good time over the weekend, but it wouldn't hurt for it to be a nice *memory*...

They drove through a small forest, the bus's suspension groaning as they bounced in their seats. Once through the trees, a large Victorian-style home appeared in the distance. Charlotte felt the tension in her shoulders release.

Whew.

She recognized the building as the one she'd researched online after Mariska's invitation. The giant home's pastel paint, corbels, and gingerbread details gave it a dollhouse-like feel. A wide porch wrapped around the front and disappeared on either side. Christmas lights had been strung along the porch frame, though they were nearly invisible in the daylight. Red ribbons and bows wrapped each post. Rocking chairs, stained glass windows, and a holiday wreath awaited.

Declan pointed to the turret on the right side of the building.

"That's where the dolls drag you at midnight."

She smacked his leg.

"Oh, come *on*. Why would you do that to me?"

Laughing, he put his arm around her. "Don't worry, Freakshow. I promise to remove all the dolls from our room."

"*Thank you.* You'll have to look around, though. They *hide*."

He chuckled. "Now you're freaking *me* out."

The road turned to gravel and led to a large parking area in front of the home. The bus stopped.

"Here we are," said Casey, opening the door. He tapped a bucket taped to the front of the dash. "Tips appreciated."

They piled out. Mariska, the last to leave, had barely stepped out of the vehicle when the door shut behind her, and Casey roared away.

They watched the bus bounce into the distance.

"He left fast," said Darla.

Charlotte never thought she'd miss that bus, but she immediately did.

She noticed a few nearby palms had unlit lights wrapped to the top and sighed.

Christmas. Think *Christmas.*

As she scanned the area, something struck her as odd. It took a moment for her to put her finger on it.

"There are no other cars here," she noted.

Declan made a quick three-sixty turn.

"You're right. That's weird. I guess they keep vehicles in the back?"

Charlotte walked to peer down the side of the house. She didn't see anything there or in the back. It didn't look like cars regularly drove over the lawn there.

"Did we get dropped at someone's house? Are we sure this is the right place?" she asked.

She and Declan both looked up the road.

Walking to the *main* highway would take them half a day.

Door hinges creaked, and they turned.

A tall woman with short spikey hair exited the inn and clomped down the porch stairs in thick rubber-soled boots. Behind her, a skinny young man wearing a Santa hat on his impressive head of hair followed with a granola bar in one hand and what looked like an empty, lidless shoebox in the other.

"Here we go," said Mariska.

The woman wore khaki shorts, a white tee shirt, and a festive green holiday vest. The vest looked like the one Charlotte had seen on Blade the day before.

Could there be two of them?

The woman wore a wide-brimmed leather hat, which reminded Charlotte of the Australian outback, except for the giant holly-laden bow pinned to the side.

Charlotte elbowed Declan to get his attention and whispered.

"Does she look Australian to you—"

"G'day, mates," said the woman as she stopped before them and tipped her hat.

"Yes," said Declan without looking at Charlotte.

"Moy name is Bindy, and I'll be your host for the weekend. I'm happy to have you with us."

The group waved and shared hellos.

As Bindy put her hands on her hips, she pushed open her vest, and Charlotte noticed the woman's tee shirt featured an octopus. The creature held a different weapon in each tentacle—a gun, a knife, brass knuckles, a grenade...Charlotte couldn't see them all, but she got the idea. The words, *I've got you covered* ran along the bottom of the picture.

She scowled.

That was...*reassuring?*

"*Bindy.* I've heard that name before," mused Darla aloud.

Bindy hooked her mouth to the right.

"Yeah, that famous Croc hunter's daughter's name is Bindi, but she spells it with an i. I spell it with a Y." She ran her forearm across her nose before adding, "It's more feminine that way."

Charlotte looked up at Blade.

"Do you have that tee shirt?" she asked.

Before Blade could answer, Bindy held up a hand.

"I'm going to need you to pay attention to me for a second there, mate."

"Sorry," said Blade and Charlotte in unison.

Bindy offered Blade a saucy smirk. She didn't seem to notice Charlotte was there at all.

Charlotte looked at Declan, but he was too busy brushing his finger at her, making the international symbol of *shame on you.*

She rolled her eyes.

"Now, before we go in, I'm going to need you to put all electronic devices into the box my assistant Munch has here," said Bindy, continuing.

The young man beside her took another bite of his granola bar and thrust the shoebox toward them.

"Our *phones*?" asked Charlotte.

Bindy nodded. "Yeah, the Outback Inn is a digital detox zone. They don't always work out here anyway, but we take them to keep everybody honest—like the contract says."

"The *contract*?" asked Declan.

Charlotte looked at Mariska, who avoided eye contact.

"I filled it out for all of us," she mumbled.

"Looks like we're at the right place," said Declan.

Bindy heard him and nodded.

"Yeah, nah—it *was* The Timeless Inn, but I bought it, and now it's The Outback. We're still switching over the marketing and whatnot. You'll be out of touch with the outside world for your stay."

"And that's a good thing?" asked Darla.

Bindy tucked in her chin as if she were shocked by her comment.

"Yeah, no worries. You'll see. *Relaxing.* You can't buy this kind of relaxation."

"No, you win it," said Mariska triumphantly.

"I think it's a great idea," said Blade, dropping his ancient flip phone into the box.

Charlotte realized she'd never seen him *use* a phone.

"Yeah? Do ya?" asked Bindy, locking her gaze with his.

Munch held out the box as they each dropped their phone inside. Charlotte surrendered hers to the box and noticed Blade and Bindy *still* staring at each other.

"What is *happening*?" she whispered to Darla, nodding to the two.

Darla shook her head. "I don't know. It's like watching lovesick sasquatches meet in the wilderness."

Charlotte moved a step closer to Mariska.

"You didn't mention the *no technology* aspect of this trip," she said.

Mariska frowned. "I *forgot*."

"Uh-huh."

Darla huffed as she placed her phone into the box.

"*I'll* suffer the most. I won't be able to see my funny videos all weekend."

Charlotte chuckled. "Oh, poor thing. No cat videos? How will you survive?"

Mariska giggled. Charlotte turned to poke a finger at her.

"And *you*—I know what I'm getting you for Christmas. I'm going to drive you to the middle of the Everglades, push you out of the car, and *drive away*."

Mariska gasped. "Oh, you're terrible. It's not my fault. I just *forgot* to mention the phone thing."

Charlotte scoffed. "You did not *forget*. You thought we wouldn't come if we knew, and you were right."

Bindy spoke before Mariska could close her gaping mouth to retort.

"Aw, right, folks. Follow me."

She turned and marched back up the stairs and into the house. Munch rushed to follow and held the door open for the others.

"Ready?" Declan asked Charlotte as they headed up the porch stairs.

Charlotte smirked.

"No worries."

CHAPTER FOUR

Pineapple Port

Sheriff Frank knocked on Bob's door. Bob answered, wearing rubber elf ears cuffed over his own. Frank pretended not to notice because he knew *noticing* was the only thing in the world Bob wanted him to do.

"Eh? Huh?" said Bob, turning so Frank could better see the ears.

"What time's the party starting?" asked Frank, ignoring the ears as he pushed past him into the house.

Bob closed the door. "I dunno. It's early, but they left about two hours ago, so I'm getting pretty antsy. You too? What are you doing here so early?"

Frank bent to pet Charlotte's soft-coated Wheaten terrier and Bob's white mutt, Izzy. He battled through the attentive dogs to the open sliding door leading to the lanai, where he and Bob always did their best drinking.

"I invited Seamus, too," added Bob as Frank took a seat.

Frank groaned. "Why? That loudmouth gets on my nerves."

Bob sat in the chair beside him.

"Yeah, well, that loudmouth owns a bar, and when I invite him over, he always brings a bottle." Bob leaned to cock an eyebrow at Frank. "Unlike some *sheriffs* I know."

Frank snorted. "Yeah, yeah. He's okay, I guess. He's just a pain in the neck sometimes."

Bob shrugged. "You look at him and see a *pain in the neck*. I look at him and see *free booze for life*."

Frank poked a finger at his friend.

"You know what? I should arrest you for murder. You *squeeze to death* every penny you get your hands on."

Bob chuckled. "That's a good one."

Frank smirked and then straightened as another thought occurred to him.

"*Speaking of cheap*—I don't care what you give Seamus, but don't give *me* the cheap bourbon tonight."

"I'd never do that," said Bob, gasping with dramatic horror.

"Uh-huh. I don't mean the *actual* cheap bourbon that I can see. I mean the cheap stuff you pour in the *good* bottle. I'm telling you now, I'm not falling for it."

"Maybe not the first glass," muttered Bob.

Franks scoffed. "None. *Never*."

He watched as Bob started to play with one of his elf ears. He knew he wouldn't last long.

He'll ask me in three, two, one—

"Aren't you going to say anything about my ears?" asked Bob.

Frank swallowed his grin and shrugged.

"What about them? They look normal to me," he said.

Bob side-eyed him and plucked them off to toss them on the nearby table.

"You saw them," he muttered. "You're messing with me."

Frank looked at his phone.

"Did Mariska call you?" he asked.

Bob shook his head.

"No. Why?"

He shrugged. "Darla usually calls when she gets to wherever she's going, but I got nothing."

"They're probably napping after all the tea and scones. Oh, hey, you never said—why are you here so early? Did you want to start drinking now? It's early, but you could talk me into it—"

Frank shook his head. "No. I want you to come help me set up my Christmas decorations."

Bob pouted. "*Really?*"

"*Yes*. I have most of it done already. I just need you to hand me up the lights while I hang them along the eaves. I want to show you this funny thing Darla bought, too."

Bob put his hands on his thighs and stood. "*Fine*. If I do a little work, I feel less guilty when you start drinking."

Frank stood and slapped him on the shoulder. "Exactly. That's what I was thinking."

Bob grimaced as he headed to the door.

"Maybe *guilty* is the wrong word. What I mean is—I hear less of Mariska's voice in my head."

They crossed the street to Frank's house, where Frank opened the garage door to retrieve his ladder and the Christmas lights. He needed to get this chore done. If he didn't, Darla would ask him what the heck he'd been doing the whole time she was gone, and he'd have to *think of things* to tell her.

It was easier just to *do the things.*

He set up the ladder and turned to find Bob untangling his most unruly ball of string lights. He watched with interest.

"You're good at that," he said.

Bob glanced at him. "Thanks."

His tone said he thought Frank was teasing him.

"No, I'm serious. You're like an idiot savant at untangling lights."

Bob eyed him. "*Thanks*. Be sure to tell Mariska. She's been trying to find what I'm good at for years."

He shook out the last bit and wrapped it neatly around his arm, hand to elbow.

"What's the funny thing you wanted to show me?" he asked as he looped.

Frank scowled. "Hm? Oh, I forgot. It's over—"

He fell quiet, pointing at a fake Christmas tree propped against the house near the front door.

Bob's eyebrows bounced upward. "A naked tree. I gotta say—not that funny."

Frank walked to the tree and moved aside the branches to look behind and around it.

"It had a Grinch on it," he said, finding nothing.

Bob wandered over. "A Grinch? Like, the Dr. Seuss guy? The green one?"

Frank pressed his lips together and scanned the yard.

"*Yes*—Darla bought this thing—a giant cut out of the Grinch. You tuck it into a tree, and it looks like he's sneaking away with it."

"I don't get it," said Bob.

"Well, no wonder. It's because you can't see it, *Bob*. Someone took it."

"Someone stole the *sheriff's* decorations?" teased Bob.

Frank glared.

Bob had a talent for getting on his last nerve—probably worse than Seamus. He was just more used to Bob.

"Yes. The sheriff's been robbed. Ha ha. *Hilarious*," he said.

He stabbed his fists into his hips and scowled at the empty tree.

"When did this happen?" he asked aloud.

"I don't know," said Bob.

"It was a rhetorical question."

Bob shrugged. "It was also just *a question*, but I don't know."

Frank rubbed his forehead and imagined himself leaving the house that morning. He'd left a couple of times. He'd gone to work for a bit and come back and then left for Bob's—could he have not noticed all those times?

"I'm trying to remember if I saw it before I came to your house. I put it up yesterday. I bet someone took it last night, and I didn't notice this morning."

"Makes more sense. I mean, to steal it at night."

"But that means Darla didn't notice either—" He huffed. "—but that's not all that strange if she had things on her mind."

"Like tea and scones," said Bob.

Frank nodded. "I wonder if I'm the only one they robbed or if someone went through the whole neighborhood? We should ask around."

Bob squinted at him. "I agreed to hand you lights. Now you got me canvassing the neighborhood?"

"We'll take the golf cart. You won't have to walk."

Bob huffed. "*Fine*. Do I go with this?" He held up his arm to display the wrapped lights.

Frank frowned.

"No. Let's hang these quick and then go," he said, heading back to his ladder.

"Okay. Goodie," said Bob, following.

Frank found his staple gun and stewed as he hung the lights. Now, he had a thief in the neighborhood *and* had to worry about Darla.

He *hated* it when she went somewhere without him.

God help him if she ever found out.

CHAPTER FIVE

Charlotte and the rest of the group entered the Outback Inn's large foyer. A check-in desk sat to the right, and to the left, stairs led to the second floor. Carved ivy encircled the ornate banister's newel post, and a glowing holiday garland snaked around the spindles.

The smell of pine and cinnamon filled Charlotte's nostrils. The place smelled like Santa's body spray.

An oversized faux cowhide with four legs splayed out at each corner covered the center of the floor. At least, Charlotte *hoped* it was faux. She wasn't sure. Maybe steers came that enormous in Australia. Either way, the hide was an interesting choice.

A table made from a wagon wheel sat in the corner. A mounted crocodile head wearing a Santa hat stared down at them from behind the check-in desk. More traditional Victorian bed and breakfast *accouterment* remained scattered around the room, like the doilies on the back of an oversized padded chair and the porcelain figurines in Victorian dress running along a shelf.

The renamed Outback Inn suffered from split personalities. Charlotte wasn't sure which was winning yet, though the crocodile head probably meant Australia had the lead.

What could the Victorians throw up against a croc? Smallpox, maybe?

"You should feel right at home here," said Charlotte, pointing out the taxidermy to Blade.

Blade nodded. "He could use a pipe. *Whoa—*"

Blade wobbled and placed his foot awkwardly to the right. Charlotte saw he'd narrowly missed stepping on a ridiculously large fawn-colored rabbit that had skittered out from behind the desk, flushed out by Bindy as she moved back to check them in.

"Watch the rabbits," said Bindy as she opened a sign-in book.

"That's not a rabbit. It's a *horse*," said Charlotte.

Bindy chuckled. "They're Flemish. They can get up to four feet long, but these finished growing closer to two feet."

Charlotte marveled at the size of the creature.

"My dog likes chasing rabbits, but I think she's met her match with this one."

"The former owner has a long history of Flemish rabbits. These came with the property."

Bindy leaned in as if she were about to share a secret.

"But between you and me, they had German names, and every time I tried to pronounce them, I sounded like I was gargling marbles. I renamed them—Bunno, Wombat, Dingo, and that's Thumperoo. He's my smallest."

Charlotte's eyes widened. "He's the *smallest*?"

Bindy nodded. "Hey, what do you call a row of rabbits walking backward?" She paused and, when no one answered, continued.

"*A receding hare line.* Get it?"

She hooted to herself.

"And what's *his* name?" asked Declan, motioning to a giant stuffed bird in the corner. The thing stood nearly five feet tall and had a black body, blue neck, and red wattles.

"That's the biggest, angriest chicken I've ever seen," said Mariska.

"It's like a turkey on steroids," said Darla.

"That's a cassowary," said Bindy. "Deadliest bird in the world. Each of its three-toes has a four-inch claw like a curved *dagger*. They can slice a man open with a single swift kick." She swung her hooked finger to imitate a claw tearing through the air. She grinned and added, "Not that one, though. He's dead."

Blade moved closer to inspect the bird.

"Nice job on the taxidermy," he said. "Could use a hat, though."

"I don't disagree," said Bindy, turning the book to face the guests. "Give me yer names in the book here so I can check you off my list."

While the others signed the book, Charlotte wandered into the next room. The parlor didn't disappoint and, not to be outdone by the foyer, featured its own eclectic mix of décor. An ornate gold-framed mirror hung over a Victorian fainting couch, and a whiskey barrel served as a table for a lamp made of antlers.

A black rabbit slowly hopped to her, and Charlotte crouched to pet it. It was a little bigger than the last one. She would have assumed it was a dog at first glance if it hadn't been for the ears.

"You're too big. I feel like I'm in some kind of alternative universe," she said to it, stroking the soft fur. It seemed to enjoy the attention.

"That's my second biggest—Wombat," Bindy called out to her. "Careful—if you're a pushover for pets, you'll never get rid of him."

"I signed us both in," said Declan, joining.

"Thanks. Look how big this one is," said Charlotte as her eye fell on a pair of crossed Samurai swords on the far wall. "This place is *crazy*."

She'd decided the inn was an even split between Victorian and Outback, but the samurai swords meant she'd have to start all over.

The only thing the décor pieces had in common was that Christmas decorations draped over everything. Garlands stapled to the wall ran along the moldings. An enormous tree sat in the corner of the parlor, sparkling with lights and tinsel.

Darla sidled up to Charlotte.

"Getting decorating ideas?" she asked.

Charlotte tittered. "How does Mariska find these places?"

Darla shook her head as she petted the rabbit. She couldn't ignore it—it started rubbing against her ankle the moment she entered the room.

"It's a gift," she said. "I'm just glad Frank didn't come. He would have *killed* me."

"Okay, everybody, let's go see your rooms," called Bindy from the desk as Blade signed in.

Bindy plucked keys with bunny-shaped charms from the wall behind her, preparing to show the guests to their rooms.

Charlotte, Declan, and Darla rejoined Mariska and Blade in the lobby.

"She's something else," said Darla.

Mariska nodded but didn't appear to be listening. She also wasn't cooing over the giant rabbits, which Charlotte found odd until she noticed what *had* stolen Mariska's attention.

"Are you seeing what I'm seeing?" Mariska asked, pointing to Blade.

Charlotte watched as Blade rushed to gather their bags before Bindy could reach them.

"I can get those," Bindy said, rounding the desk.

"No, ma'am. I've got them," he said, bowing a little.

Bindy stood back and smiled at him almost coquettishly, which, on her gruff expression, struck Charlotte as comical.

"Are they *flirting*?" asked Declan.

Bindy headed up the wide staircase with the giant following in her footsteps like she were the Pied Piper.

The other four exchanged looks.

"Crikey," said Darla. "Oi think she's stolen his haart."

Charlotte winced as if she were in pain.

"Was that supposed to be an Australian accent?" she asked.

Darla scowled. "It was a *perfect* Australian accent."

Charlotte laughed and headed for the stairs.

"It sounded like a Dickens character, post-stroke," she said over her shoulder.

The others followed up the stairs.

"Yer all on the third floor," said Bindy, rounding the second-floor landing. The landing had a small sitting area and a view of the check-in desk from the balcony railing.

"Is there an elevator?" puffed Mariska as she paused on the landing.

"Nah, the place was built in eighteen sixty-six by Leopold Zeitz. They didn't have elevators then," said Bindy.

Declan patted Mariska on the back as her friend leaned on her knees, searching for breath.

"You going to make it?" he asked.

Mariska straightened and nodded as she continued.

"They didn't have air conditioning in eighteen sixty-six, but *you have air conditioning*," she called up to Bindy.

"This is the middle of Florida. If she didn't have air conditioning, she'd have dead customers littered all over the place," said Darla, starting the next flight of stairs.

"I'll look into adding an elevator once I make my money back on the purchase," Bindy called down. "Check back to me at half past never," she laughed.

Mariska found her wind and mounted the stairs.

"I better bring everything I need for the day when I come down to breakfast because I can't do this more than once a day," she panted.

"You don't need anything except me," said Darla.

Mariska snorted a laugh.

Once they reached the third floor, Bindy motioned to the first room on the left.

"You'll be in here, Miss Mariska and Miss Darla. You go ahead, get settled, and meet us downstairs out back when you're ready. We're having brunch."

Mariska sucked in a breath.

"Oh, I *love* brunch," she said.

Darla nodded. "That's how we'll get you down the stairs. I'll bring bacon to the room to get you back up."

"I *love* bacon," said Mariska.

"We know," said Charlotte.

Blade left the ladies' suitcases inside their door and rushed to follow Bindy to the next room. Declan had to bounce to the side to avoid being clipped. He glanced over his shoulder at Charlotte and smirked.

"This is you, then," said Bindy, stopping at the next room's door. "Elke, the previous owner, is across the hall, and I'm at the end."

Declan walked inside to put his backpack on the bed. Charlotte started to follow and then stopped when her focus hit the far corner of the room.

"*No*," she said.

A pile of dolls sat in the corner, five feet wide and almost as high. There had to be twenty of them, most in red or green dresses, blondes, brunettes, and redheads. The collection ranged across decades—older ones with cracked faces and eyes that blinked mixed with newer models with unusually large eyes or other more modern tweaks. One poor girl had a unicorn horn.

"I can't say I love this either," said Declan.

Bindy peered into the room.

"What's that then?" she asked.

As her gaze fell on the dolls, she cocked her head.

"That's weird," she said.

"I'd say so," said Charlotte.

Something about the woman's tone struck her as odd, and she looked at her.

"Wait. What do *you* think is odd?" asked Charlotte.

"Those dolls," said Bindy. "I put them in the attic. How'd they get back down here?"

She looked at the ceiling and then back to the dolls.

Charlotte raised her hand to her mouth.

"Tell me you didn't just say that," she mumbled behind her hand.

Bindy shook her head like a wet dog.

"Yea, nah. No worries, mate. She'll be right."

Charlotte looked at her, expecting more, but nothing came.

"What does that *mean*?" she asked.

Bindy slapped her on the shoulder. "I'll have them moved. Don't you worry."

Charlotte looked at Declan and mouthed the words, *help me.*

Bindy turned to Blade, who stood with only his duffle bag over his shoulder.

"We only had the two rooms left. Yer staying in here with them?"

Charlotte, Declan, and Blade exchanged looks.

They hadn't thought this out.

Bindy nodded to the bed. "There's a trundle under there, but I don't think yer gonna fit on it."

Blade shrugged one massive shoulder.

"I can sleep anywhere."

"We invited him to join us. It's our problem," said Declan.

"We'll figure it out."

Bindy eyed Blade, pulling at her chin.

"Do you have a cot and a closet?" suggested Blade.

Bindy barked a laugh.

"Big boy like you? I don't think so. If you think Victorian rooms are small, you should see the closets." She scowled and then shrugged. "Tell you what. Put yer bag in there, and I'll figure something out for you. Come on down and join us when yer ready."

She slapped him hard on the arm and clomped back down the stairs in her rubber-soled work boots.

Blade set his bag down inside the room.

Charlotte smirked at him, and he arched an eyebrow.

"What?" he asked.

"I bet I know what bed she's going to put you in," she teased.

Blade rushed into the hall, flustered.

"I'm going to go down," he said without stopping, heading for the stairs.

Declan shook his head at Charlotte.

"Don't tease the poor guy."

"What? You didn't see the attraction going on there? I'm surprised we weren't all sucked into that vortex of lust."

Declan laughed. "*Vortex of lust?*"

As they left their bags and headed after Blade, Charlotte hooked a thumb over her shoulder back at their room.

"He might be sleeping with you if those things aren't gone by tonight. I'd rather sleep on the porch than under the watchful eyes of dolls, who move themselves from the attic."

Declan grimaced. "I'm going with you."

They trotted downstairs to find Mariska and Darla waiting in the foyer. Charlotte paused, and Declan continued out back to find Blade.

"Our room is full of dolls," she reported.

Mariska gasped. "Oh no. You hate dolls."

"I *know*," she said. "I told Declan he might be sharing the bed with Blade tonight."

"Is that why Blade walked by looking spooked?" said Darla.

Charlotte giggled. "No. That's my fault. I teased him about the attraction between him and Bindy."

"You're terrible," snickered Mariska.

The three walked through the parlor, dodging the black rabbit determined to trip them, and exited through the back door. Immediately to their left, a shaded rabbit hutch took up much of the porch. Inside, a white rabbit sat steadily munching on a treat. A giant rabbit-sized door led back into the house on one side and down into a small fenced-in outdoor pen on the other.

"Those rabbits live better than we do," said Charlotte.

They walked down the few stairs to a spacious yard, where a group sat beneath a pergola at a long wooden table covered with breakfast foods. Beyond the more manicured area sat a shed, a small barn, a large vegetable garden, and what looked like a small cemetery.

"Quite a setup," said Declan as the ladies arrived at his side.

"Pretty nice. Peaceful," agreed Charlotte.

Munch, the young man who'd taken their phones, walked around the table with a platter of donuts, offering them to the guests. When he thought no one was looking, he broke one in half and stuffed it in his mouth before setting the platter on the table.

"I think I know where he got his nickname," said Charlotte as she and Darla watched him gobble his treat.

"It would make a good nickname for Mariska, too," said Darla.

"I heard that," said Mariska.

"Have a seat, and I'll let everyone know our schedule," said Bindy.

The ladies sat near Declan and Blade, and Bindy began.

"First off, again, I'm Bindy. I'm the new owner."

She motioned to a matronly champagne-blonde woman sitting at the opposite head of the table.

"This is Elke. She's the former owner—she's been doing this for fifty years, and she's staying the weekend to help me get up and running. Lucky you—you get two hosts for the weekend."

Elke offered a tight smile and nodded to the group. Her gaze lingered on the glamorous-looking woman in her late thirties, maybe early forties, sitting across the table, but she looked away.

The younger woman looked familiar, but Charlotte couldn't

place her. Her outfit made her stand out—she wore a red blouse with tiny stitched green clumps of holly scattered across it, green capris, and a crown tucked in her updo hair.

Sure, it was Christmas, but the outfit seemed like *a lot.*

Bindy continued.

"I want you all to have as much fun as possible. We'll play games, and I've arranged a little treasure hunt to start. The Outback Inn has one rule—everyone stays unconnected. Outback is a place to get away from the world."

"I never said I wanted to get away from the world," grumbled a young redhead who seemed to have as much trouble taking her eyes off the crowned woman as Elke did.

More loudly, the redhead added, "Where *are* our phones?"

Bindy motioned to the house. "They're in Elke's time lock safe. That way, you aren't tempted to go looking for them. The safe doesn't open until eleven o'clock Saturday night."

A groan rose from the group.

"You did it to yourselves," scolded Elke, animating as if she'd dropped into an argument she'd already been having. "I used to keep them in a box, but people kept sneaking around, trying to steal them back. That's why I bought the safe."

The woman glared at each of them as if she'd caught *them* trying to find their phones. As her steely gaze fell on Charlotte, she felt compelled to look away.

Yikes.

Elke poked a bony finger at them. "This is for your own good. You have to learn how to appreciate what you have and not be trapped by all those *beep-boop* machines."

"I *appreciated* the phone I *had,*" muttered the redhead.

Elke shot her a look and then glared at the tabletop. The look on her face threatened to curdle the coffee cream.

Declan looked at Charlotte and mouthed the words *beep-boop machines?*

She stifled a giggle.

Bindy moved on.

"We should introduce ourselves since we'll be spending the weekend together. Let's start with you, Princess Daria."

All eyes turned to the woman in the crown. She tucked a piece of errant hair behind her ear. Charlotte noticed she wore more jewelry on her neck, fingers, and wrists than any meal at the *Middle of Nowhere Inn* required.

The woman pursed her full lips and nodded her head slightly.

"My name is Princess Daria Dalca, direct descendant of Prince Nicholas of Romania." She paused to smile. "You might know me as Princess Christmas. You can call me *Princess*."

The redhead stared at her with an odd expression. Charlotte couldn't decide if she hated the woman or was in awe of her. Maybe a little of both.

The bespectacled man next to her also seemed enthralled. He was handsome in an odd way. He was of medium build and in good shape, but his nose seemed too small for his face. Charlotte couldn't tell if the pair were a couple. They seemed to know each other but hadn't spoken.

Charlotte turned her attention back to Princess, her head cocking as she remembered where she'd seen her.

That's why she looks familiar.

She'd seen her online somewhere. Social media phenomenon Princess Daria had married a Palm Beach playboy. Together, they broadcasted their socialite philanthropist lifestyle across media platforms to entertain wannabees. That exposure, combined with Daria's Christmas obsession, earned her the nickname *Princess Christmas*.

The couple had split for all the *wrong* reasons when the playboy left Princess for a younger model. For her revenge, Princess joined the cast of a reality television show, where she aired her grievances against him to the masses—all while selling her signature dolls and high-dollar ornaments.

Charlotte had only seen that one news story about her. Still, it was enough information to wonder why someone like Princess Christmas wanted to spend the weekend at a bunny-infested anachronistic inn.

"You're probably wondering why I'd be here in such a *common* place," said Princess.

Charlotte straightened, surprised to hear her thoughts spoken back to her.

Why yes, I was just wondering.

Elke made a chuffing noise. Bindy scowled, both women nonplussed to be tagged *common*.

"I know who you are," said the redhead, oblivious to the objections of the others. "They probably hired you to promote this place to your Palm Beach circle of friends."

Elke glared at Princess, who glared right back at her.

Charlotte looked back and forth between the two of them.

What is that?

Princess turned to smile at the redhead.

"Yes, *exactly*," she said. "I have quite a bit of influence with——"

Elke grumbled something, but Charlotte couldn't make out the words.

Bindy cleared her throat loudly enough to cut the Princess short.

"Okay, introduce yourself, Mr. Brendan," she said.

The bespectacled, forty-something man with a dirty-blond man bun looked away from Princess to find everyone staring at him.

"Me?" he asked, placing a hand on his chest.

Bindy nodded. "Introduce yourself."

He offered a sheepish smile.

"My name is Brendan. I'm writing a book about Florida history, and this home has quite a bit of historical significance——" He frowned at Bindy and continued, "Though, I need to talk to you about some of the new pieces here——"

Bindy held up a hand. "Let's finish up the introductions first, eh, Brendan?"

She motioned to the girl with the red ponytail.

"Go ahead then."

The girl nodded. "I'm Estrella, but everybody calls me Strella. I'm Brendan's girlfriend, but I'm also a travel, health and wellness influencer. I had *no idea* I couldn't have electronics here." She scowled at Elke. "You better let me take some videos on Sunday——"

"Yeah, yeah," said Bindy. "Of course, but I can't have you breaking the rules *for now*."

Strella grunted her disapproval. "I also think I'm allergic to rabbits—"

Bindy motioned to a dark-haired woman Charlotte guessed to be in her early fifties. The woman nodded.

"My name is Iko," she said, "I'm no one special, but I've always loved the zen of this place. I am all about disconnecting, finding my inner peace, and meditation." She placed her palms together and nodded. "Namaste."

Elke rolled her eyes and pushed away from the table.

"I've got some things to do inside."

She turned on her heel and started back to the inn.

Bindy's attention turned to the Pineapple Port gang.

"The rest of you are my contest winners," said Bindy.

"I won the raffle," said Mariska, perking. "I brought my friends Charlotte, Declan, Blade, and Darla," she said, motioning to each as she said their names. "They're famous detectives."

Charlotte felt herself blush.

Mariska—always talking her up.

"I don't know about *famous*," she said, rolling her eyes.

They nodded and waved hello to the table.

Bindy smiled and, glancing at the inn, screamed, *"Munch!"* at the top of her lungs.

Munch stood on the back porch near the rabbit hutch, gnawing on what looked like a beef jerky stick. At the sound of his name, he came jogging over.

He looked at Bindy expectantly without saying a word.

"Bring out the drinks and hit the music."

He nodded and jogged back into the house. A moment later, Olivia Newton John's *Xanadu* played on the speakers hidden in rocks near the patio. Munch reappeared with flutes of champagne, which he passed out to the people at the table.

"A toast to a fun, relaxing weekend," said Bindy, holding up a flute. "And to Olivia Newton-John, may she rest in peace."

The group held up their glasses.

Some more enthusiastically than others.

CHAPTER SIX

Bindy stretched out her arm and made a sweeping gesture toward the property.

"I've hidden prizes all over the yard," she said. "The person who finds the most will win a special prize."

"Ooh, I can win *more*," said Mariska. "I'm good at winning things."

"I bet it's a free stay," Charlotte whispered to Declan.

"It's a free stay at the inn," continued Bindy, clapping her hands with unbridled enthusiasm.

The group didn't seem as excited as she was, except for Iko and Blade, who clasped his own enormous hands together.

"That would be great, wouldn't it?" he asked Iko.

Iko nodded. "So peaceful. *So* peaceful."

"What do the prizes look like?" asked Mariska. "How do we know if we found one? I like that bunny rabbit garden ornament over there, so I'm hoping that's one of the prizes."

Bindy looked at the garden rabbit and scowled.

"Um, no. Sorry. The prizes are in plastic eggs hidden all over the yard."

She held up a lavender egg.

Charlotte recognized the lopsided orb as the standard plastic Easter egg Mariska and Darla used to hide around the house for her to find.

Actually, they still did it yearly, though she'd begged them to stop.

Mariska and Darla gasped at the sight of the egg and looked at

Charlotte.

Mariska pointed. "Those are like the ones—"

Charlotte held up a hand.

"I know. I see that."

Mariska bounced in her seat. "Oh, this will be *fun.*"

Strella scowled at Bindy. "I don't know how to break this to you, but that's *Easter*, not Christmas."

"She wouldn't know. She's from Australia," said Princess dismissively.

Bindy shot her a scowl, but Princess pretended not to notice.

"We have Christmas and Easter in Australia," said Bindy. "We *have* an Outback. *We don't all live in the middle of it.*"

"You wouldn't know it looking at your brows," muttered Princess before glancing down at her own nails.

Bindy snapped her tongue against her eyetooth and rocked as if she were thinking about launching herself at Princess.

Declan leaned to Charlotte.

"Are all bed and breakfasts so dramatic?"

Charlotte shook her head with disbelief. She *wanted* to watch what happened next between Bindy and Princess but suddenly found it difficult to take her eyes off *Iko*, who'd started rocking back and forth, tapping her knuckles against her lips.

"You can't use eggs on Christmas," she said, her voice cracking. "You should have gotten little tree tins or maybe hollow Christmas balls or—"

She spoke faster and faster until Charlotte put a hand on her shoulder.

"Are you okay?"

Iko's gaze shifted to her, and she nodded. She took a deep breath and closed her eyes, mumbling, *"The universe will work it out. The universe is all-knowing..."*

Bindy held up a hand. "For the record, I know the difference between Christmas and Easter, but Elke had about a million of these eggs leftover from years of Easter egg hunts, and I thought they worked. I would have used red and green ones if I could have, but they only came in pastels."

Strella crossed her arms against her chest.

"That's because they're for *Easter*—"

Bindy swiveled to her and spoke through gritted teeth.

"*Crikey*. Let it *go*," she snapped.

Everyone froze.

Bindy held up a hand.

"Sorry, sorry. Didn't mean to lose my temper, but the eggs *aren't the important part*. The *prizes* are the important part."

She motioned to the yard with a limp wrist as if it were almost too exhausting to point.

"Go ahead and start looking. They're all over the yard and the house, but only on the first floor."

She picked up a roll of dog waste bags and ripped away one after the other, handing them to each person as she worked around the table.

"You can carry them in here," she said.

Charlotte chuckled and mumbled to Declan.

"Good thing she didn't give us Easter baskets. The place would *revolt*."

Strella held her bag up, lip curled.

"We're supposed to put them in *poop* bags?"

"Good luck with that," said Princess as she headed for the house, leaving her bag untouched on the table.

She made it halfway to the house before Munch appeared from nowhere and excitedly gestured back to the barn. Princess glanced over her shoulder, seemingly confused, and tried to get around him to continue her path to the house. As she did, Elke exited the house to talk to her. Princess glanced back at the barn again and rolled her eyes but ultimately allowed the pair to lead her that way.

Charlotte looked at Declan.

"What's that about?" she asked as Princess, Elke, and Munch passed them on their way to the barn.

Declan shook his head. "I don't know."

"They're biodegradable," said Blade, holding up his dog bag. "You thought of everything."

Bindy looked at him as if she thought he was teasing, but as her gaze fell on his sweet grin, she smiled back in a way that said, *thank you*.

She sighed and turned back to the remaining group.

"Take your drinks with you and have a poke around. The person who finds the most gets a special prize. *Have fun.*"

Strella scowled. "I didn't bring the right shoes for this."

Bindy closed her eyes and pinched the bridge of her nose but didn't say anything.

The rest stood from their seats.

"I'm not sure this is as relaxing as you hoped," said Charlotte to Iko.

Iko cocked an eyebrow at her.

"Are you kidding? This is *heaven* compared to work."

"What do you do?" asked Declan.

"I'm an air traffic controller." She raised her arm to pull down her sleeve, exposing a basketweave of fine scratches from wrist to elbow. "On the weekends, I work for my family's mobile cat-washing business."

Charlotte and Declan blinked at her.

"This is *heaven*," repeated Iko, walking away to start searching. "*Heaven.*"

CHAPTER SEVEN

Pineapple Port

Frank hit the brakes, and his golf cart slid another foot before coming to rest in front of a home with an extensive collection of Christmas decorations on the lawn.

"Whaddya think? These people are likely victims if we have a repeat offender on the loose."

"I think you're going to *kill* me," said Bob, catching himself on the dash. "That's what I think. Give me a heads up before you slam on the brakes, will ya?"

"Sorry. This looks like a good one, though, don't you think?"

Frank hopped out of the cart and tugged his waistband up. He could hear Darla's voice telling him he shouldn't be looking for missing decorations—he should be looking for his *butt* to help hold up his pants.

Darla. *Hm.*

He pulled out his phone and dialed her, but the call went straight to voice mail.

Strange. Maybe she forgot to charge it before she left.

He dropped his phone back into his pocket and marched to the door to knock. Nothing happened. Frank was about to leave when the door opened, and he found himself faced by an elderly man wearing navy blue cotton pajamas with green piping.

Frank glanced at his watch. It was eleven. Little late for PJs.

"Can I help you?" asked the man.

"Hello, Sir, I'm Frank Marshall," said Frank, reaching to

remove a hat that wasn't there. He cleared his throat.

"Frank Marshall," said the man.

Frank nodded. "Yes, I'm the sheriff in town, and I was wondering if you'd had any Christmas decorations stolen?"

The man nodded. "Decorations stolen."

Frank's chin tucked back in surprise that he'd be so lucky on his first try.

"You did? When?"

The man squinted up at him, though Frank wasn't particularly tall.

"When?" he asked.

"When did you have your Christmas decorations taken?" asked Frank.

"Christmas," he said.

Frank scowled. "You mean last year?"

The man shook his head. "This year."

"Okay—so, *recently*—but do you know the day?"

"Friday."

"Friday. Good." Today was Friday, which meant the culprit had been at it for at least a week. "Can I ask what they took?"

"Who?"

"The person or persons who stole your Christmas decorations."

The man put his hand on his chest.

"Me?"

"You?" Frank frowned. "*You* stole Christmas decorations?"

He nodded and held his hands as if waiting for cuffs.

"It was me. You got me."

Frank looked over his shoulder at the yard. There *were* a lot of decorations. Were they all stolen?

He'd gotten even luckier than he thought.

"Are you saying all these are stolen?" he asked to clarify.

"I love stollen," said the man, lowering his hands.

A dreamy smile slid across his expression as if he were remembering his wedding day.

Frank's brown knitted. "*What?*"

The man scowled back at him. "What?"

A woman approached from inside.

"Dad, what are you doing at the door? We told you not to answer the door," she said, putting her hand on her father's shoulder.

The old man frowned at her.

"I want stollen and coffee," he said, shuffling away, presumably to the kitchen.

"Sorry about that," said the woman to Frank. "His mind doesn't work like it used to."

"He's talking about *stollen*? The fruit bread?"

She nodded. "He loves it. Can I help you?"

Frank sighed and realized the old man had been repeating everything *he* said. He *hadn't* found the culprit on his first try.

Figures.

"I'm Sheriff Frank Marshall. We've had some reports of stolen Christmas decorations. Have you had any taken?"

The woman shook her head. "I don't think so. We're visiting for the holiday. My husband put up everything in my father's garage for the kids."

Frank nodded.

"Got it. Okay. If you notice anything go missing, please call the sheriff's office and let us know?"

She smiled. "Sure."

Frank nodded his goodbye and headed back to his golf cart.

"Did you crack the case?" asked Bob as he climbed in.

"No. I thought I had a confession, but it was a false alarm."

He pressed the pedal and tooled onto the main drag running through Pineapple Port. He wanted to get to the entrance and then make a more orderly path through the neighborhood so he didn't miss anything.

As he passed the clubhouse, a stout man appeared, walking quickly down a driveway, waving his arms as if to flag him down.

Frank stopped the cart more gently this time, and Bob gave him a thumbs up.

"You're getting good at this," said Bob.

"Shut up," muttered Frank.

He focused on the man, who put his hands on the roof of the golf cart on Bob's side and leaned to peer at him.

"I thought that was you, Frank," he said.

Frank nodded. "Hey Zac, what's wrong?"

Zac rolled his eyes. "Don't get me started."

"Okay, see ya," said Bob.

"No, wait—"

Zac stepped back and flailed his arms as if he were motioning to every inch of the neighborhood.

"I'll tell you what's wrong. All these Christmas lights. Especially my neighbor. He's out of control. I can hardly sleep at night."

Frank sighed. "The holidays will be over soon enough. There's nothing I can do. The HOA doesn't have any restrictions on Christmas lights."

"It won't be over soon enough for me," grumbled Zac. "I'm *blinded* coming back from dinner. They light up my bedroom—"

"Don't you have curtains?" asked Bob.

Zac sighed. "The damn cat tore them down. Don't get me started. You've got to do something. There must be *something*. Light pollution or something?"

Frank turned his palms to the sky.

"I'm sorry, Zac, but I can't tell everyone Christmas is canceled."

Zac's arm swung to his left.

"What about just my *neighbor*? Alistair over there, he's, *what?*—eighty years old?—and he's got his yard lit up like an amusement park."

Frank shrugged. "It's his yard."

"Well, it's not *fair*." Zac poked a finger at them. "You're no help as usual."

"Catch me next year," interjected Bob. "My New Year's resolution is to be more helpful next year."

Zac pointed at him.

"And *you*—don't get me started. *You're* just a jackass."

"Calm down," said Frank, eager to change the topic. "Hey, you don't happen to know anyone who had decorations stolen, do you?"

Zac scoffed. "*Stolen?* I should be so lucky someone steals Alistair's." He grunted and huffed a great sigh. "But yes, now that you mention it, Jenny Teacup told Nan she had something stolen.

Some stupid blowup thing. Don't get me started on those—I can hear the little air blowers running all night. I'm about ready to throw them all in the lake."

"I thought guys with bellies like yours were supposed to be *jolly* this time of year," said Bob, motioning to Zac's stomach.

Zac's eyes flashed with anger, and Frank hit the pedal.

"Okay, see you, Zac!" he called as they shot forward.

Frank looked over his shoulder and saw Zac at the end of his driveway sending them off with a one-fingered salute.

"Why do you have to poke the bear?" asked Frank.

Bob grinned. "He *is* shaped like a bear, isn't he?"

Frank chuckled. It was pretty funny.

"Who needs a Grinch? You can just put Zac in your tree," continued Bob. "But whatever you do, *don't get him started.*"

Frank barked a laugh and detoured to head to Jenny Teacup's house.

When they arrived he left Bob in the cart again and knocked.

"Hello, Frank, what are you doing here?" she asked.

Her smile dropped before he could answer.

"The neighbor isn't starting with us again, is he?" she asked.

She and the neighbor had been in a little bit of a war over the placement of a shed on the property line between them.

Frank shook his head.

"No, Jenny. I'm asking around about someone stealing Christmas decorations. Zac said maybe you have something missing?"

Her eyes widened.

"I *do*," she said.

Frank perked. "Yeah?"

"Come in. I just bought some mini donuts."

Frank entered, and Jenny didn't even have the door shut behind him before there was a knock. She reopened the door.

Bob stood smiling at her. He waved.

"Hey, Jenny," he said, walking past her to Frank. He hooked a thumb at the sheriff. "I'm his partner."

Frank frowned.

"You heard her mention the donuts," he muttered.

Bob grinned.

"I have powdered donuts. Come sit down," said Jenny, walking past them.

Bob fell in line behind Jenny as she led them to her dining room table.

Frank shook his head. The guy had ears like a bat when it came to free food.

"Have a seat. Do you want some tea? Coffee?" asked Jenny.

"Sure," said Bob.

"*No*," said Frank. "Don't trouble yourself. We can't stay. Tell me about your decoration. You think someone took it?"

Jenny nodded and placed her hand on a box of mini-powdered donuts on the table.

"It was so cute, too," she said with a sad sigh.

Bob's attention locked onto the donuts. She pushed them partially toward him and he perked, but, distracted by her thoughts, she stopped to continue, leaving her hand on the lid.

"It was a *surfing* Santa. It was inflatable, so we thought it blew away during that little storm we had last week."

She began to open the box, and Bob's hand reached out. She didn't notice. Instead, she winced and rested her hand, closing the lid.

Bob deflated again, much like an inflatable surfing Santa.

"But I *looked*, you know?" she said, focusing on Frank. "I went everywhere I thought that thing could have blown off to, and it wasn't *anywhere*."

"So you decided it must have been stolen?" asked Frank.

"Do you want me to get those for you?" asked Bob, motioning to the donuts.

Frank scowled at him.

"You don't have any camera outside, do you?" he asked.

"We *do* have a doorbell camera, but Surfing Santa was out of frame."

Jenny sat back, her hand still resting on the box as she continued.

"It's funny you showed up today because I was talking to Julie last night—you know Julie, down the street?—and now I'm *sure* someone must have stolen it."

This caught Frank's attention.

"Did someone steal something from her?" he asked.

Bob put a finger on either side of the donut box and tried to slowly pull it out from under Jenny's hand, but incensed by her story, she pressed on the box, holding it fast.

"*Yes.* That's just it. Julie had her Christmas flamingo string lights taken. Can you believe it? *All of them.* All with their little Santa hats on. They were *adorable.*"

"I guess she didn't have a camera on them, either?" asked Frank.

Jenny shook her head. "No. They were in her back yard. She doesn't have a camera back there."

Frank nodded. This was good. This was progress. He stood, eager to find other victims. Someone had to have this guy on camera. It was just a matter of time.

"Well, thank you. Sorry to take up your day," he said.

"No problem at all," said Jenny, standing with him.

Bob remained seated, looking up at them.

"But—"

Jenny and Frank moved to the door.

"Let me know if you find my surfing Santa," said Jenny as Frank left.

He nodded. "I will."

Frank walked down the path toward the golf cart, deep in thought. He glanced over his shoulder and saw Bob's shadow following him.

"You know, there's a theme here, I think," he said, musing aloud. "All the decorations taken so far are sort of funny. My Grinch, her surfing Santa, flamingo lights—all campy. And, it's funny—they only ever take one thing from each yard. They're being *selective.* I don't think it's a coincidence. There's a *pattern* here."

Frank got into the golf cart, and Bob sat beside him.

"You're awfully quiet," he said.

He was about to hit the gas when he saw Bob's throat bob.

"Look at me," he said.

Bob turned.

"Hm?"

White powder sprinkled from his lips.

Frank sighed.

"Did you take a donut when we walked away?"

Bob held up a mini donut. Sugar showered into his lap.

"Two. Want one?"

CHAPTER EIGHT

The Outback Inn

As they prepared for egg searching, Charlotte turned to address the rest of her Pineapple Port group.

"Want to have a little side bet?" she asked. "For bragging rights. Make things interesting?"

"You're on," said Darla.

"Teams?" asked Mariska.

Charlotte shook her head. "Every man for himself—or herself."

Darla nodded. "May the best Darla win."

The group wandered from the table with the others to start searching.

Charlotte walked with Declan.

"Did you notice Mariska and Darla walked off together?" she asked, glancing over her shoulder.

Declan shrugged. "*We* walked off together."

She scoffed. "Yeah, but we won't cheat."

He smirked at her. "Speak for yourself."

She chuckled and watched Iko heading toward a shed.

"Poor Iko," she said. "I don't know if unplugging for the weekend will be enough for her. She almost had a meltdown over the Easter eggs."

He shrugged. "I figure the universe will fix everything."

She snickered. "Ha. The universe has its hands full with this group. It seems like a lot is going on we don't know about. Bindy and Princess, Princess and Elke, Strella and just about everybody—"

Princess stormed past them with enough huff to make her and Declan stop. Elke strode by a moment later.

Charlotte winced as Princess reached the porch—she'd hoped to be the first to check the first level for eggs, and by chatting with Declan, she lost her chance.

Princess made a sharp right and followed the porch around the house.

Charlotte grinned.

Maybe she *didn't* lose her chance.

Elke reached the porch, watched Princess storm around the corner, and went inside.

That was okay. Elke wouldn't participate in her own treasure hunt.

"Hey, how about a side bet between you and me?" asked Declan, moving fast for the porch.

Oh no. Now he's headed inside—

Charlotte flexed to run after him, but it was too late. She scowled as he bounded up the stairs and rested a hand on the doorknob.

Too late.

"Backrub for the person who gets the most?" he suggested.

She pointed at him. "You're on."

Declan went inside—the first person there.

Charlotte growled.

Shoot.

She'd need a new plan.

She scanned the room, searching for the most potentially egg-filled area. The porch worked. There were plenty of nooks and crannies for eggs—in flowerpots, behind chairs and tables—all good places to start.

She trotted up the stairs and spotted a pink egg in the first potted plant she checked.

Ha! The porch is a gold mine...

She opened the plastic orb to find a chocolate coin inside.

Hm.

Chocolates? Really?

A little underwhelming.

She'd hoped the prizes would be a little more creative, but things could be worse. Chocolate was still chocolate. She unwrapped it and popped it in her mouth before moving on.

She needed to keep up her energy—a donut, fruit, and rye toast wasn't enough to last a whole treasure hunt, was it?

The coin was better chocolate than the ones Mariska used. She'd always suspected Mariska kept the same giant bag of chocolates and used it for a couple of years in a row.

She continued working across the porch, searching plants and finding an egg in each pot. She felt pretty good about her lead when she heard voices from around the corner, somewhere on the side of the house—two women in a heated argument.

She paused to eavesdrop.

Worried she'd be seen, she didn't peek around the corner. She wasn't *sure* but guessed the women to be Princess and Elke. It made sense since she'd seen Princess head this way, and Elke could have easily met her there if there was a door on that side of the house.

"You're leaving me no choice—" said the voice Charlotte thought to be Elke.

"I don't know who you think you are. I knew I shouldn't have come here," said Princess.

"You can't just leave—it isn't right—"

"*Get off me.* You've got a lot of nerve if you think I would do anything for you."

She heard a door slam and crept closer to peek around the house's edge.

The side porch was empty. She stepped out and confirmed the existence of a side entrance.

Both had gone inside—or maybe one of them had rounded the front?

She strode to the front of the house and peeked around that corner.

Nobody.

Drama over.

None of my business.

Plus, she needed to force herself to use the weekend to *relax.*

She needed to *avoid* reading intrigue into whatever petty dramas brewed between the guests.

Charlotte spun on her heel to return to the back yard. A sudden breeze sent a hair across her face to tickle her nose, and she turned toward the wind to see ominous skies to the east. She hadn't thought to check the weather. She felt her pocket for her phone and remembered it wasn't there.

Grr.

Brushing away the errant hair, she noticed stairs leading from the porch to the side yard. She detoured there to see if any eggs lurked behind the bushes. Something cold and wet hit her face, and she touched her cheek.

Rain?

She looked up at a single dark cloud rolling in from the northeast. This one had arrived early, like a scout sent to find a path for the larger storm.

Ugh.

All those daily things she did on her phone that she took for granted—like checking the weather—were impossible now.

She shook her head.

Peace and quiet?

What a stupid idea for an inn.

She spotted another egg nestled behind a rain spout and grabbed it to find a butterscotch inside. The candy made her chuckle. She'd received plenty of butterscotch as a child growing up in a retirement community, especially since Mariska's husband *loved* them.

"This one is for Bob," she mumbled, slipping it into her pocket as she moved on.

CHAPTER NINE

Darla watched Charlotte and Declan walk off and smacked Mariska's arm.

"Hey—what do you think about working together?" she asked.

Mariska rolled her eyes and giggled.

"*Duh.*"

Her conspiratorial grin faded, and she hooked her mouth to the right as if suddenly worried about something.

"But wait—" she said, touching Darla's arm to keep her near. "Who gets the big prize if we win? What if we both want it?"

Darla shrugged. "We'll share it."

"But what if it's a statue or something?"

Darla considered this.

"Then I'll keep it for six months, and you keep it for six."

Mariska nodded. "Good idea."

They shook hands with one hard pump.

Darla pointed to a large garden.

"The kids headed toward the house, so let's check over there."

Mariska agreed. "That seems like a cute place to hide them. And when we finish, you give me all the eggs you found, and I'll turn them in to win for us."

Darla sniffed. "Right. Or, you know, you can give me all of *your* eggs, and *I'll* win for us. Whatever works."

They eyed each other as they strolled the crushed shell path leading deeper into the yard.

"I found one!" yelped a voice to their left.

Darla saw Iko near a small shed. The woman held aloft a small purple egg.

Darla scoffed.

"*One egg.* You'd think she found the holy grail," she muttered.

Without exchanging a word, she and Mariska picked up their pace. They split up and meandered up and down the rows of the garden.

"Anything?" called Darla.

"Nothing," said Mariska, heading her way.

They left the garden and put their hands on their hips.

"I can't believe there aren't any eggs in there. I thought for sure it would be *full* of them," said Mariska.

Darla nodded and tilted her head as a thought occurred to her.

"Maybe, she didn't *want* us all tromping around her garden?"

Mariska looked at her.

"Hm. Now that you mention it, that makes sense."

"I found another one!" said Iko near a large flower pot.

"That one's got issues," muttered Darla.

"Where now?" asked Mariska.

Darla nodded toward the small family cemetery not far beyond the garden.

"There must be some in there, right?"

Mariska shrugged, and they headed that way.

"Christmas, Easter, and now Halloween. This place has something for everyone," she said.

"I bet there are eggs behind every stone," said Darla, stepping over the low iron fence surrounding the plot.

Almost immediately, she dipped and came up with an egg, holding it aloft for Mariska to see.

"Got one!"

Mariska held out a hand. "Help me over."

"It's a foot tall," said Darla.

"Just *help* me."

Darla held out a hand to steady her friend as she stepped over.

"Was that so hard?" asked Mariska.

"I think you meant *thank you*," said Darla.

She headed toward another tombstone, pulled an egg from behind it, and twisted it open.

"Ooh, this one has a butterscotch," said Mariska, unwrapping a candy as she spoke. "What did you get?"

Darla heard hard candy clicking against her friend's teeth as she wandered closer.

"Chocolate-covered mint," said Darla as sugary peppermint coated her tongue.

Heaven.

"We're going to weigh a thousand pounds by the end of this game," tittered Mariska.

Darla's attention fell to the headstone in front of her, and she compared it to the others nearby.

"They all have the last name Zeitz," she noted.

"I guess that's who owned the house," said Mariska.

"Is that Elke's last name?"

"I don't know."

Mariska cracked open another egg and thrust a chocolate-covered mint at Darla.

"You like those more than me," she said.

"Thank you, but we have to stop eating. If we don't get a move on, we're never going to win this thing, even working together."

Darla paused and then took the candy from her.

"I'll give you all the butterscotches I find," she added.

Mariska snorted.

"Why do you think I gave you the mint?"

Declan dashed into the inn feeling pretty pleased with himself. He'd beat Charlotte to the door.

Bwahahaha...

He didn't feel bad. He needed all the help he could get. She *always* won things like this.

He couldn't take full credit for coming up with the idea to race inside. Earlier, he'd seen a plastic egg behind a vase on a table in the parlor, though at the time, he'd assumed it was part of the place's odd charm.

He glanced through the window and saw Charlotte making her way along the porch. She wasn't going to come inside to challenge him. If he moved fast, he could clear the first floor before anyone else arrived.

Declan swept over the parlor, checking behind chairs and lamps to find three eggs filled with chocolates. He wasn't a big fan of candy, so he put them in his pocket and put the opened eggs in his green doggy bag.

Charlotte would have no problem finishing off the candy. He'd put one on her pillow tonight. Then she'd threaten him with bodily harm if he didn't cough up the rest.

He paused his search to stare at a stuffed otter standing on its hind legs in the corner. It wore a little vest and an Outback-style Australian hat. In its paws, it held a tiny pair of binoculars.

It looked *really* familiar, which, in itself, was weird.

"Is that the one I had in the shop?" he asked himself out loud.

He was about to inspect it when he heard footsteps on the porch outside.

Forget the otter.

He hustled to the next room. If this new person didn't know he'd already cleaned out the parlor, they'd waste valuable time searching while he ran through the other rooms.

Declan found himself in a small library. Bookshelves covered one wall, overstacked with books. Most were popular novels from over the decades. After taking everyone's computers and televisions, Elke *had* to provide people with other forms of entertainment. It would be cruel not to, and he imagined it kept people from revolting and carrying her away with pitchforks.

He spotted movement and turned to find the largest white rabbit he'd ever seen sitting on a loveseat, nose twitching.

"Hello there," he said.

The rabbit twitched.

"Rabbits and eggs," he mumbled to himself. "Does it get any more Christmassy than this?"

He turned back to the bookshelf, scanning it for eggs. He didn't see anything at first glance, and pulling out the titles to check behind them seemed like a waste of time. He moved on to open the roll-top desk against the wall, where he found a pile of envelopes—mostly bills.

This was obviously Elke's personal desk. There wouldn't be eggs in there. He closed the top and was about to move on when he noticed an area beneath the bottom drawer on the right.

Hm.

He'd seen desks like this before. He'd had them in his pawnshop. A woman who brought one in once showed him a secret drawer at the bottom, beneath the other drawers. The hidden drawer had no knob and looked like it was part of the frame, but if you hooked your fingers under it and pulled, it slid out.

He squatted to test his suspicion, even though the secret drawer was too shallow to hold an egg.

The bottom piece slid out.

Ta-da.

It gave him a little thrill to have found it.

Inside, he found a scattering of paperwork, a brass key, and a torn photo featuring a younger version of Elke. A spare elbow hung near the tear. Someone stood beside her, but that person had been torn away. The photo was in color, so it wasn't *too* old—but old enough to be a developed print, not the product of a photo printer.

Declan heard a thumping noise above his head and quickly tossed the photo back into the shallow drawer before closing it, embarrassed by his snooping.

He stood and looked up at the ceiling. Bindy had said the eggs were only on the first floor. Someone wasn't listening.

He heard voices in the parlor.

Better get going.

He was running out of time to stay ahead of the others. He scanned the room and spotted one last place to check—a decorative box.

Opening it, he found a yellow egg, grabbed it, and moved to the next room.

Blade watched the guests leave the big picnic table to explore the grounds for eggs. He strolled behind Mariska and Darla toward a nearby vegetable garden and stopped to watch them poke around.

"You don't look like you're trying very hard," said a voice behind him.

He turned to find Bindy.

"Naw," he said. "I'll let the other people win."

Bindy smirked. "It sounds like yer saying if you tried, *you'd* win."

He looked at the ground. "Naw, I didn't mean it that way."

When he looked up, he found Bindy looking at him as if she were waiting for him to continue, but he couldn't think of anything else to say.

"Man of few words, eh?" she said.

He shrugged. "I suppose so."

"Whaddya think of the place?" she asked.

He nodded. "It's real nice, Miss Bindy."

She chuckled.

"Just call me Bindy. I don't think anyone's ever called me *Miss* in my life. I had a couple of people call me *Mister*, maybe when I was young. I had short hair then, too, and was five foot ten in sixth grade."

She laughed, and he grinned.

She had a nice laugh.

"I know something about that," he said. "They used to call me all kinds of names as a kid—Stretch Armstrong, Bigfoot, Too Tall Bones, Not Yeti, Luke Skyscraper—"

"Rainmaker, Mile High Bindy, The Ostrich—" She chuckled. "Kids are the *worst*."

Blade looked back at the house. "How long have you been here?"

"Not long. In fact, I just signed the last of the *official* paperwork this morning. I was supposed to have everything done by the first of the month, but between you and me, Elke keeps finding reasons not to leave."

Blade nodded. "I guess if she's been here for a long time, it's hard to let it go."

She rolled her eyes. "I guess, but all she ever does is complain about the place. Then she asked if she could stay a couple of extra weeks—said the place she was moving to fell through. Next thing I know, she's here another week and then *another*. When the guests leave, you should hear the way we argue. It's like being a teenager in my mother's house again."

"So you don't know when she'll leave?"

Bindy scoffed. "She's not a big *sharer*. She promised to be out this coming Monday, though. That should be it. *Hopefully*. I dunno. I'm starting to think I've got myself a *squatter*."

He shrugged. "At least she's here to help out with the guests this weekend."

"Yeah, *roight*. She doesn't help. She mopes around, scowling at everyone and making them uncomfortable. I had a test group here last weekend, and she hardly said a word to them." She squinted. "It's weird because, every week, she *seems* like she's going to play hostess, and then the people show up, and she falls into some kind of depression."

"She didn't seem too bad today," offered Blade. "Little cranky, but not too bad."

Bindy nodded thoughtfully. "Now that you mention it, she is better today. She seemed pretty upbeat this morning, but now she seems kind of *angry,* which is new. I'm not sure angry is better than mopey."

"Well, hopefully, she'll be gone Monday."

"*Hopefully*. If not, I'll have to thunk her on the head and bury her out with the rest of them."

She nodded to Blade's right, and he turned to see a small graveyard in the distance.

Mariska and Darla were heading that way.

"They'll find some there. Glad they're out of my garden," said Bindy, checking her watch. "Well, I better make sure Munch started lunch for later. I inherited him with the place. He's a good kid, but I might go broke trying to feed him."

"He worked for Elke?"

She nodded. "Some kind of relative, I think, but he doesn't talk—some form of non-verbal autism, I think. He understands well enough, and he's a good worker."

She motioned to a barn standing at the back of the property.

"He lives there. She built it into the contract that I let him stay and work here as part of the deal."

"That was nice of her to look out for him."

She tittered. "Maybe for *him*. Maybe less for me. We'll see, I guess."

She rubbed her hand over her face and flashed him a sheepish grin.

"Listen to me. I'm complaining more than Elke. It's been a stressful couple of weeks. I'm sorry if I'm bringing you down. It wasn't my intention."

"Not at all," said Blade.

She clapped her hands together.

"Alrighty. I'm going to go check on lunch."

She turned to leave.

"I like your hair," blurted Blade as she walked away.

Inside, he groaned.

Where did that come from?

The whole time Bindy talked, he was thinking how much he liked her streaky-blonde, spikey hair.

She raised a hand to touch her head.

"Yeah?" She grinned. "Thanks. I like your mustache."

Blade felt his cheeks grow warm.

"Thank you."

She left, and Blade noticed the wind picking up. A drop of rain hit his head.

It looked like a storm was coming.

CHAPTER TEN

Blade wandered the grounds briefly and then returned to the table under the pergola. He spotted Charlotte heading his way with a bulging bag in her hand.

"Hey, are you done?" she asked. "Did you find any?"

He shook his head. "Naw."

"I don't blame you unless you have a thing for cheap chocolate. How's everyone else doing? Anyone else come back?" she asked, pulling another bag off the roll Bindy had left on the table.

"You're the first I've seen," said Blade.

Bindy exited the inn and headed toward them. Behind her, Declan followed with a bag full of eggs. The two of them arrived at the pergola.

"How's it going? Are you winning?" she asked Charlotte.

Charlotte shrugged. "According to Blade, I'm the first to get a spare bag, but it looks like my husband is hot on my tail."

"Well, he would be, wouldn't he?" quipped Bindy.

Blade snorted a laugh, and Bindy winked at him.

It made his stomach feel funny.

Darla arrived with a bag of eggs.

"Wow, you found a lot, too," said Charlotte.

Darla thrust out her hand, asking for a spare bag.

"I'm doing okay, I guess," she said.

"How's Mariska doing?" asked Charlotte.

Blade heard the suspicion in her voice. He

tilted to the side to peer around Darla and spotted Mariska hovering behind Munch's barn, watching them from afar.

He chuckled to himself. Darla and Mariska were cheating by working together, but they couldn't get anything past Miss Charlotte.

Bindy checked her watch and clapped her hands together. She did that a lot. It made Blade chuckle.

"I think I'll get those wandering dolls back in the attic fer you," she said.

Charlotte's attention shot to her.

"*Please* stop making it sound like they came down from the attic by themselves. You're freaking me out," she said.

Bindy laughed.

"I'll help you," said Blade, standing.

Bindy grinned at him.

"Okay. You can probably pick them all up in one go with those big, strong arms, eh?"

"Sweet banana pudding," muttered Darla.

Blade ignored her.

"I can try," he said.

Bindy nodded and headed toward the house. Blade followed. As they walked through the parlor, he spotted a familiar face and stopped to point at it.

"That's *mine*," he said.

Bindy turned. "What's that?"

"That's Oliver the Outback Otter."

Bindy followed his pointing finger to the stuffed otter wearing Outback gear. Her brow furrowed. "You have one, too? I imagined that was one of a kind."

"It *is* one of a kind. That's what I'm saying—I *made* it."

Her eyes opened wide.

"You *did*? You do taxidermy?"

He shook his head. "Not from scratch. I find old taxidermy and give them new life. I give them back their dignity."

Bindy smiled. "I guess I owe you a thank you then. I love that little guy. I bought him at a pawn shop closer to the coast. I remember it had a funny name—"

"The Hock o'Bell."

Bindy pointed at him. "That's it!"

"That's where I worked." He pointed to the back yard. "Declan owned it. He had a lot of taxidermy when I showed up, and that's when I got the idea. I thought it would help him sell it."

Bindy shook her head as they entered the foyer. She leaned behind the check-in desk to grab a handful of garbage bags.

"Small world, eh? I thought Declan looked familiar, and I guess that's why. I don't think I saw you, though. I would have remembered you."

Blade looked at the ground. What she said made him uncomfortable, but not in a *bad* way.

"It burned down," he said.

"What did? The pawn shop?"

He nodded. "Yep. Now I work with Declan at his detective agency."

"Right, the lady said you were all detectives," said Bindy. "That sounds like a cracker of a job. What do you do? Catch people cheating on each other, or find lost dogs—?"

"Murders, mostly," said Blade.

She gasped as they mounted the stairs.

"Really?"

"Yes, ma'am. Charlotte is a really good detective. She caught the Puzzle Killer."

Bindy stopped halfway up the second set of stairs to gape at him.

"*Naur*," she said, turning the word *no* into a four-syllable mashup. It sounded a little like she was swallowing her tongue.

"She's *that* Charlotte?" she said.

He nodded. "You've heard of the Puzzle Killer?"

Bindy continued up the stairs. "I have. I'm a bit of a serial killer aficionado. Australia's got a few of them." She grunted. "How about *that*? Charlotte, eh? Never mind Princess being sort of famous. Here I am in the presence of serial-killer-catcher royalty."

They continued to Charlotte's room on the third floor. The door was open, and they approached the pile of dolls—a three-foot-high pile of red and green dresses and frozen expressions.

Blade couldn't say he blamed Charlotte for wanting them gone.

Not only were they creepy, but it seemed the dolls had *moved* since the last time he saw them. When he first saw the pile, they'd been neatly stacked, faces in a row, like they were now, but they were lower to the ground.

Now, they seemed to be sitting on a little hill.

He assumed it was his imagination.

"You've got a lot of dolls," he said.

Bindy shook her head.

"They aren't *mine*. They belonged to Elke. She had them all over the house. Removing them was the first thing I did when I moved in—gathered them up and put them all in the attic."

"And then she moved them back?"

Bindy scoffed. "I hope so. If not, it means they moved on their own like Charlotte's worried about."

"Maybe Munch?" suggested Blade.

"Nah, I think you were right the first time. This is probably another of Elke's passive-aggressive revenge plots. You were spot on when you said she's having a hard time leaving. She didn't *want* to sell the place, you know."

"No?"

"Yeah, nah. She had to. She'd taken out loans over the years. Between you and me, she's up to her eyeballs in debt."

She handed him a trash bag and they tackled the pile, tossing dolls inside the bags. Blade moved one in an oversized red tutu, and the sprawling costume revealed another face beneath it.

This face seemed too large to belong to a doll—

Blade gasped and pulled back.

That's no doll.

"Bindy," he said.

"Feet," she said.

It wasn't the response he expected.

"Feet?" he asked.

She, too, had taken a step back and stared at the pile with the same alarmed stare he knew he had plastered on his face.

He pointed.

"I think that's Elke."

Bindy leaned over to get a better view of his side of the pile.

The *face* side.

She gasped.

"Elke?"

The two of them pushed away the dolls to uncover the rest of the body.

It was clear Elke was dead.

Bindy stepped back and put her hand on her forehead.

"How is this possible? She was eating brunch with us an hour ago."

"She didn't do it to herself, that's for sure," said Blade. "She couldn't bury herself under the dolls."

Bindy shook her head.

"Who? *How*? Someone *here*?"

Blade frowned and looked out the window to the front yard. There were no cars outside.

"Could someone have stopped by when we were out back?

She lowered the hand from her head.

"Naur. I mean, I have a camera on the road—I can look—but no one comes here on accident."

"Then, that means the killer is still here," he said.

She looked at him, jaw hanging, and pointed toward the back yard.

"That means it's one of *them*."

"We need to get the police," said Blade.

Bindy's eyes bulged a second time.

"We can't. There are no phones. No way to contact anyone—" She touched his arm. "Plus, it'll *ruin* me."

He wasn't sure what to say. He understood her concern, but the woman was *dead*—

He looked down at her hand on his arm. Her touch muddled his thinking.

"But—" was all he could force out of his mouth.

She straightened like someone had shot an electric bolt through her body.

"I've got it," she said. "You're *detectives. You* can figure it out. You said she beat the Puzzle Killer. This'll be *nothing*."

Blade scowled. "Even if we did figure out who did it, we can't *arrest* the person."

"Naur, but you can figure it out, and then we'll make a citizen's arrest, give the police all the information. If I had to refund this weekend's money—it would be quite a blow."

Blade didn't know what to do.

He sighed.

"Let me talk to Charlotte and Declan."

CHAPTER ELEVEN

Charlotte was on the front porch watching the storm arrive when she heard heavy footsteps headed her way. The rain was on them now, and she heard thunder in the distance. The treasure hunt was over. No one in their right mind stayed outside during a lightning storm in Florida. The Sunshine State was the *deadliest* in America when it came to lightning—and probably most other things, too—but she was only worried about the lightning right now.

Blade rounded the corner and headed for her.

"I should have known those footsteps were you," she teased. "It sounded like a rhino."

Her grin faded when she saw the look on his face. Something wasn't right.

"What's wrong? Is everyone okay?" she asked.

"Not everyone," he said grimly. "I need you and Declan to come with me."

"Just us? Is it Mariska? Darla?"

He held up a hand and moved closer to lower his voice.

"It's not one of us. It's Elke. She's dead," he said.

Charlotte gasped. "*Dead?*" She shook her head. "We need to call someone. Find a phone—"

"She didn't just *die*," he said. "Someone killed her."

Charlotte blinked at him. Every time she spoke, things got worse. She was afraid if she asked how he knew it was murder he'd tell her there was a man in a mask with a chainsaw running for them *right now.*

"We found her buried under the dolls in your room," he said, guessing her next question.

"Buried under—"

Charlotte gaped.

She didn't have to talk.

Things kept getting worse anyway.

"You've got to be kidding me," she said.

He shook his head.

She placed her hand against her cheek.

"I guess there's no chance she buried herself under the dolls and then took poison?"

"No—" He winced. "I didn't check to see how she died. I came right to you."

She sighed and tried to clear her head.

"Okay. First things first—"

The front door opened, and Declan poked out his head.

"I don't mean to be a nag, but you two really need to come in. That lightning—"

"I know, I know," she said, heading inside with Blade following. "We have worse things than lightning to worry about."

Declan scowled. "That sounds foreboding."

"It's worse than you think."

In the large foyer, she looked around to make sure no one was near and grabbed Declan's wrist. She used it to pull his ear closer to her mouth.

"They found Elke in our room, *murdered*," she said before tugging him toward the stairs.

His eyes bugged. "What?"

The three jogged to the third floor to find their bedroom door closed and locked. Charlotte knocked. No one answered.

"It's me," said Blade. "I brought Charlotte and Declan."

There was a pause, and the door opened, revealing a distressed Bindy. They entered, and she closed and locked the door behind them.

Charlotte walked toward the dolls, stooping lower as she spotted Elke's face peering through the dresses.

"How is this possible?" she asked.

"And more importantly, why?" asked Declan. "Why leave her here? Is it a message to *us*?"

Charlotte looked at him. "Why?"

He huffed. "I don't *know*. That's why I asked the question."

She stuck her tongue out at him and crouched to study the body, pointing out thin marks on the throat.

"Ligature marks," she said.

Declan lowered beside her.

"Does it look like *two* lines to you?"

"Definitely and—" she squinted at a mark on the side of Elke's neck "—does that look like a *Santa* face to you?"

Declan leaned closer, brow furrowing.

"It *does*."

"What does *that* mean?" asked Bindy. "Santa killed her?"

"I have no idea," said Charlotte. "I suppose it could be a coincidence that the impression looks like Santa—we might have Christmas on the brain—but, *boy*, it really does."

She stood with her arms crossed against her chest, staring at the dead woman in her room.

"And you thought the dolls were bad," said Declan, rising.

"Oh, they're still a huge problem," she muttered.

She looked at Bindy.

"We need to call the authorities."

Bindy shook her head. "We can't. There's no phone."

"You were *serious* about the time lock?" asked Declan. "I thought you were kidding—an empty threat to keep people from looking for their phones."

Bindy shook her head.

"What about *your* phone? Or a house phone?" asked Charlotte.

"There is no house phone. Elke had it removed, and mine—" Bindy winced. "I should have kept it but chucked it into the safe with the others. I wasn't thinking."

"But there's a vehicle here?"

"Naur. I think Munch has a bike—?"

"No one's going out on a *bike* in a lightning storm," said Charlotte as the thunder crashed outside. "How can you not have any kind of vehicle? What if someone had a medical emergency? There has to be *some* way to get help?"

Bindy nodded. "There's a code that overrides the timelock."

Charlotte perked. "Oh, *good*. Then we'll use that—"

Bindy shook her head.

"I don't know it."

"You don't *know* it?" repeated Declan.

She shook her head. "Naur."

"Then, who does?" asked Charlotte.

Bindy looked at Elke's body, and the other three felt their gazes pull toward it, too.

Charlotte closed her eyes. "Elke knew the code."

Bindy nodded. "Right."

"CB?" asked Blade.

"Naur. Her whole thing was the inn being a place to *unplug*."

Charlotte took a deep breath.

"This is a *nightmare*. I assume it's hit the rest of you that the killer must still be here?" She turned to Bindy. "I'm hoping this is the part where you tell me the killer came and went?"

Bindy offered yet another sad shake of her head.

"Not that I know. There's a camera on the road. I mentioned to Blade that I can check to see if anyone came down the road—"

Declan's eyes widened. "A camera? It must be connected to WIFI. Maybe Elke was more connected than she let on?"

Bindy shook her head. *Again.* Charlotte wanted to shake *her* for delivering such consistently awful news—except that Bindy was a tall, muscular woman, and she'd probably kill her.

Maybe literally.

"The cameras are hardwired," she said. "They're old-school short circuit television that tape to VHS."

"Is it occuring to you that you've taken this off-the-grid vacation a little too far?" asked Charlotte.

Bindy nodded. "It is. Yes."

Declan looked out the window.

"What about other directions? Could someone have come from another direction? *Not* down the road?"

"Naw. There's nothin' for miles around here."

"Oh good," said Charlotte. "So, you're saying that even if one of us was crazy enough to go out in the storm, we could walk forever before we found someone who could help."

"Basically."

Charlotte rubbed her face, thinking.

"Okay. So, I know it wasn't me or anyone in my group."

"How do you know?" asked Bindy.

"Believe me. The people in this room spend all their time fighting crime, and the other two couldn't keep a secret if Santa himself begged them to do it. If Mariska and Darla had killed Elke, they would've told everyone, apologized, and driven themselves to jail by now."

"If they had a car," mumbled Declan.

"Which they don't." She grimaced. "That means it has to be Princess, Brendan, Strella, Munch, or—"

Declan, Charlotte, and Blade looked at Bindy.

She slapped her hand to her chest.

"Don't look at *me*. I didn't do it. Why would I kill her?"

"You said if she didn't leave on Monday, you'd put her in the cemetery out back with the rest of her family," said Blade. He held up a hand, "Not that *I* think you did it."

"I was *kidding*," screeched Bindy. "I just bought the place from her. If I was going to kill her, why would I wait until *after* money exchanged hands?"

"When was it official?" asked Charlotte.

Bindy scowled.

"I told Blade—it all happened suddenly this morning. She'd been putting me off. We'd been proceeding like it was a done deal— me bringing my stuff here, planning the contest, all that. Then, two weeks ago, she told me the contract wasn't official because she missed a spot signing. My real estate guy confirmed it was true. I was *devo*."

"Devo?" asked Declan.

Bindy rolled her eyes. "*Devastated*. Elke said there were no worries—she'd get to it. I chased her around, and *finally*, this morning, she showed up with the signed paperwork and shoved it at me."

Her shoulders slumped as if she were exhausted by her own

story.

"I didn't care if she stuck it to my chest with a knife as long as it was *signed*."

"And that's when she said she was leaving on Monday?" asked Blade.

She nodded. "*Finally.* She's been a real thorn in my side, but I didn't kill her. If I had, I sure as shootin' wouldn't have put her under the dolls I told you I'd move."

"Unless you wanted us to find her," said Charlotte.

Bindy stomped her foot.

"I didn't kill her!"

"Okay, okay," said Charlotte, holding up her hands to soothe the woman.

Bindy seemed truthful. She probably *didn't* do it—after all, a way-too-realistic murder weekend would *ruin* her brand-new business.

She'd quietly stay on the suspect list, but they needed her help for now.

Bindy took a deep breath and put her hands on either side of her head.

"I'm sorry. I'm freaking out a little. Look. Let's get through the storm, and then we can take the bike down the road and get some help."

"We just have to hope no one else dies in the meantime," muttered Declan.

"I wonder how long this storm will last," said Charlotte. "Ooh, I know, I'll check the weather on my phone—oh *wait*—I *can't.*"

"You don't have to get sarcastic about it," muttered Bindy. She paused and added, "I just need you to keep this a secret from the others."

Charlotte scowled. "And just let the killer pick them off?"

Bindy huffed. "This isn't going to be a serial killer situation. Someone clearly wanted *her* dead."

"How would you know—?"

Bindy rushed to continue over Charlotte's objection.

"If you tell those people, they'll be in a panic. That won't help *anyone*. They might go off half-cocked into the storm or start killing each other."

Charlotte squinted.

"I don't think they'll start *killing* each other, but you have a point. If the killer thinks the body is still hidden, they might stay calm and wait out the storm with the rest of us."

"Maybe they've already made a break for it. We should take a head count," suggested Blade.

Charlotte nodded. "Good idea."

Declan frowned. "I guess we can keep watch tonight. Everyone sleeps on the second and third floors, right?"

Bindy nodded.

"We'll take turns in the hall to make sure everyone stays in their rooms. When does the timelock open, exactly?"

Bindy grimaced.

"Saturday night at eleven. The bus shows up Sunday morning to take everyone home."

Declan nodded. "We have tonight and tomorrow to figure out who did this and keep everyone safe."

Charlotte nodded.

"*Then,* we'll tell the police."

Bindy nodded enthusiastically and clasped her hands together.

"*Thank you.* Anything you need from me, just let me know."

"The people will have to talk to the police when we get the phones. They might still want refunds," warned Blade.

Bindy shook her head.

"By then, they will have *spent* their weekend. I don't *owe* them refunds."

Charlotte grimaced. "I dunno. They might not see it that way. Not after you let them spend the weekend trapped in a house with a killer, locked away from their phones—"

"And you capped off the event with an hours-long interrogation at the local police station," finished Declan.

Bindy frowned. "Yeah, nah. *Whatever.* I've got until Sunday morning to think of something."

"Great, it's settled," said Charlotte. "We just need to stay trapped here with a hundred creepy dolls, a dead woman, and a killer. You know, I had my doubts, but this is the *perfect* holiday getaway."

Declan nodded.

"Mariska really outdid herself this time."

Bindy scowled.

"What do you mean *you had your doubts?*"

CHAPTER TWELVE

Frank and Bob knocked on neighbors' doors for another hour, stopping at every home with a substantial Christmas display. Six people admitted to missing decorations. One assumed animals had dragged her lifesized stuffed Santa body pillow away to make a nest. In two cases, the homeowners hadn't noticed they were missing anything until Frank asked them to take a quick inventory. One woman was *livid* it had taken Frank so long to get back to her about her missing inflatable Santa on a dinosaur—she'd reported it to the sheriff's office a week earlier.

Luckily for Bob, she wasn't so angry she didn't offer them pie. Once Bob realized people sometimes offered visiting law enforcement pastry, he accompanied Frank to every door.

After an hour, Frank had six robbed houses, and Bob had had two donuts, a toasted croissant, and a slice of pumpkin pie.

"I'm full," said Bob, unbuttoning his shorts as they returned the golf cart to Frank's.

"Please don't do that," said Frank.

Bob ignored him. "I had no idea what a good job being sheriff was."

"Right. It's all about the treats. No danger *at all*."

Bob sniffed. "That's what I'm saying."

Frank pulled up at Bob's house.

"Get out," he said.

"You're not coming in?"

As Bob stood, his unbuttoned shorts slid down his non-existent hips, and he caught them just in time to rebutton.

Frank closed his eyes and took a deep breath.

"Are you not wearing underwear?" asked Frank.

"I'm a *commando*," said Bob, saluting.

Frank sighed.

"*No*. I'm not coming in. I'm going to go back to the office. That lady gave me an idea. There might be more reports of stolen decorations."

"I'm going to take a nap," said Bob, shuffling up his driveway.

"Okay. Good idea. I'll see you later."

Frank took the cart home and, after a proper lunch with a book propped in front of him at the kitchen table, he drove to the sheriff's office to work and check for other stolen decoration reports.

He found the complaint from the woman with the pumpkin pie at the top of the pile. Deputy Daniel had gone to her house to take her statement, but progress had stopped there.

After a hundred interruptions, Frank found a few thefts reported from Silver Lake, the neighborhood across the street from Pineapple Port. Those had taken place in early December, and each missing decoration was something goofy—a Santa with a pool floaty, a collection of elves riding flamingos—so they fit the pattern.

Someone with a sense of humor was making the rounds—there was no denying it now.

Movement caught Frank's eye, and he glanced up to see Daniel crossing by his open doorway.

"*Daniel*," he barked.

Daniel stopped and walked backward to peer into his office.

"Yeah, Chief?" he said.

"Don't call me Chief."

"Sorry."

Frank held up a folder. "Did you see these stolen decoration reports?"

Daniel hung his thumbs in his belt and huffed a sigh like he'd had to answer this question every day for fifty years.

"Yep. *Kids*," he said like a wisened old grandfather.

He was twenty-eight.

Frank scowled. "You *know* it's kids? You caught them?"

Daniel's mouth opened, chin hanging loose for a moment. He

scratched his neck.

"No. I mean, I *figured...*"

"You *figured*? So you wrote all these off?" asked Frank, shaking the folder.

The folder was full of expense reports, but it worked for effect.

Daniel frowned. "No. I mean, I took the statements, but there's no way—"

"Did it ever occur to you there might be a pattern here?" asked Frank.

"A *pattern*?" Daniel winced. "They're just decorations. People steal them every year—"

"Oh, I get it. We *ignore* crime now because *it just happens*?"

Daniel's cheeks colored. "No..."

Frank rubbed his eyes with the butts of his palms.

"Alright. Just—don't assume things are too small to tell me about in the future."

"You got it, Chief—*er*—*Frank*—" Daniel winced again. "—uh, *Sheriff*."

Frank waved him on, and Daniel continued on his way.

Frank returned to his research, noting the dates of the thefts. It seemed like one thing went missing each day. None of the thefts overlapped. He didn't have a theft for *every* day in December, but he had enough to suspect the gaps weren't *days off*. Those were days when people didn't know they'd been robbed or hadn't bothered to report it.

He couldn't remember a year when they'd had so many thefts.

Why would someone rob one funny decoration every day? The chances of being caught seemed greater when spaced out that way. It gave time for people like him to notice a pattern.

It didn't make any sense.

He printed out a list of the robberies, added his own list by hand to the bottom, and then grabbed his phone to try Darla again. Sometimes, when he bounced things off his wife, she helped shine a new perspective on the problem.

He listened to the ringing on the other side of the line.

"Hi, you've reached Darla. Please leave a message..."

Frank hung up. He didn't like not being able to reach her. He tried Charlotte with the same result.

Hm.

Maybe it had something to do with the enormous storm over that area. Charity would be catching the outer edges of it as it worked its way west.

He'd have to try again later. Maybe get Bob to try Mariska again, too.

Speaking of Bob—

He checked his watch. It was getting late. Tomorrow, he'd swing by the homes of the people he'd pulled from the system and see if they could offer insight on who might be responsible.

For now...

Time for bourbon tasting.

He drove back to Pineapple Port, parked at home, and walked to Bob's. As he sauntered up the driveway, he spotted two figures in Bob's lanai, each with a drink in hand.

Declan's uncle Seamus had come early.

Great.

Frank sighed. Seamus wasn't a *bad* guy, but he was younger than him and so naturally *boisterous* that it made Frank feel like he had to be *on*. Things were more relaxing with just Bob. Bob was more of a labrador of a man. Seamus was more of a terrier.

Frank put his fingers on the handle of the lanai's side door and took a deep breath.

Here we go.

Seamus grinned and stood as he entered, speaking before Frank could say hello.

"*Frank*—there you are, Boyo. We've been talking about your Christmas decoration problem, and we've come up with a grand idea," he said in his ever-fluctuating Irish lilt.

Sometimes, Frank could barely tell the man had been born in Ireland. Other times, Seamus sounded like a breakfast cereal leprechaun. He wasn't sure why the man's accent wasn't more consistent, but he suspected it had something to do with booze and women.

"Oh good," Frank said as he closed the door behind him. "My problems are solved."

"Yep, we've got the answer right here," said Bob, motioning outside.

Frank moved to the window and saw an enormous wooden structure sitting outside that looked like someone had sliced off the front of an open barn. Beneath it sat a rustic manger filled with hay.

"Where'd you get *that*? It looks like it weighs a ton," said Frank.

"I borrowed it from my neighbor," said Seamus.

Frank squinted at him.

"*Borrowed* it? Or will I get a report of it being stolen on my desk tomorrow?"

Seamus looked into his glass as if something fascinating floated there.

"He goes to bed early. I'll have it back before he wakes up," he mumbled.

Frank scowled and turned to Bob. It was too early in the evening to start something with Seamus. He'd need a drink first.

"So your plan is a giant empty *stolen* nativity scene?" he asked.

Bob nodded. "Half the plan. The other half is this."

He pointed to a Santa with his back turned to them. It stood almost four feet tall.

Frank eyed the giant plastic doll, feeling less and less like hearing the rest of this plan. It was exhausting to guess, and he had no idea where it was going.

"I'm going to need a hint," he said. "And a drink."

Bob leaned to an outlet near the Santa and inserted a nearby plug. The Santa sprang to life, glowing as it bent over to pull down his red drawers. The dropping drawers revealed a lower back tattoo that said *Merry Christmas*, as well as the top of the little man's butt crack.

He pulled up his drawers and then dropped them again, over and over.

"Whadya think?" asked Bob, looking pleased with himself.

"Wow," said Frank. "That's something."

"It's *cheeky*," said Seamus, snorting a laugh.

"It'll be *irresistible* to our guy," said Bob.

Frank scowled. "Because...?"

"Because it's *funny*. That's what the guy likes, right? You figured that out."

"We'll put it out front and wait for someone to steal it," said Seamus. "It's a *trap*."

"That's not half-bad," Frank said, pulling at his chin as he considered the possibilities.

He'd decided it was both a *stupid* and *not terrible* idea.

"That's what we thought," said Bob. "And guess where we're going to lay in wait?"

Frank poked a finger at the ground.

"I assumed in *here*."

Bob shook his head.

"*Nope*. There's no way this guy is getting away. Check it out. This is the best part."

Bob caught Seamus's attention and cocked his head toward the main house. He grabbed a trash bag lying near the drawer-dropping Santa.

"Where are you going?" asked Frank as Bob jerked open the slider that separated the house from the lanai.

Bob and Seamus left the room.

"Just hold on a second," Bob called over his shoulder.

Left alone, Frank moved to the bar and found himself a glass. He helped himself to the bottle of bourbon and then stopped to sniff the contents.

He scowled.

Cheap stuff. I knew it.

Next to that bottle of *bad* bourbon sat the *good* Irish whiskey Seamus had probably brought. The bottle looked too expensive for El Cheapo to have bought it.

Frank decided it would be a *whiskey* night.

He opened the nearly full bottle and poured himself two fingers. As he took his first sip, his eyes rolled back.

Mmmm...

Seamus might be a bit of a jackass, but he sure knew good whiskey.

Frank heard the slider moving and looked up as Seamus and Bob returned.

He sucked in a breath, and the whiskey grabbed the back of his throat when a drop hit his airpipe. Coughing, he slapped down his sloshing tumbler and braced himself against the bar.

"You're *kidding*," he sputtered.

Bob and Seamus grinned, strutting back and forth like models to show off their costumes.

They'd dressed as Mary and Joseph.

Seamus wore a dark brown robe with a rope belt. Bob, as Mary, had donned a blue robe. A long dark wig poked out beneath a white scarf on his head. In his hand, he dangled a swaddled doll.

"Impressed?" asked Bob.

"Not the word I'm looking for," wheezed Frank.

The two men sat and picked up their drinks while Frank caught his breath.

"You okay there, Boyo?" asked Seamus.

Frank cleared his throat as the spasms subsided.

"Yes. I'm *fine*." He took a careful breath. "But you two, I'm not so sure about. Why are you dressed like that?"

"We're going to sit around the manger," scoffed Bob, as if Frank were a fool for not realizing the plan on his own.

Frank squinted. "You're going to sit like that for *hours*?" he asked.

"You too," said Bob. "We decided to let you be a wise man."

"I'm *honored*," said Frank. "Aren't there supposed to be three of me?"

Bob shrugged. "We'll work with what we have."

"We don't have to hold perfectly still the whole time," Seamus explained. "We'll hang out until we see a car coming, and then we'll *freeze*."

Bob and Seamus both froze to demonstrate.

"No car," said Bob.

They moved their arms and pretended to be talking.

"*Car*," said Bob.

They froze.

Frank shook his head. "But *why*? Why can't we just wait here and look out the window?"

"We talked about that. This plan didn't come from nowhere,"

said Bob.

"No. I'm sure it's very well thought out," drawled Frank.

Bob side-eyed him and continued.

"We decided it would be better to be *close*, so if they drive by and run out to grab Santa, we'll be right there to act fast."

Frank took a sip of his whiskey.

"You're *insane*," he muttered.

He gave up arguing. He was outnumbered by enthusiastic idiots and already enjoying the warm glow of the whiskey.

The three men hung out in the lanai until it was almost dark. Once the sun and their inhibitions had dropped they headed outside to set up the nativity scene.

"This thing *does* weigh a ton," said Frank as they shuffled to the front yard with the main structure.

Seamus grimaced and stretched his back.

"Yeah, in hindsight, we maybe didn't need this part. It took me and two bartenders to get it here."

"So you made your staff accessory to a crime," said Frank.

Seamus shrugged. "If you want to have such a narrow view of it."

"Go put your costume on, Frank," said Bob. "We'll get the manger and set up the baby."

Frank hesitated and then shrugged.

Eh, what the heck.

He'd told himself there was no way he'd dress like a wise man and sit around the manger, but after drink and a half into the evening, the idea didn't seem as crazy as it had an hour ago.

Frank went inside and found the trash bag that once held all the costumes in the bathroom. He donned his sparkly wise-man outfit and returned outside.

"Is it me?" he asked, holding out his arms.

"It's *perfect*," said Bob. "Did you grab the box of frankenfurter?"

Frank held up a small plastic box he'd found and said the word *frankenfurter* in his head.

It didn't sound right, but it didn't sound *wrong*, either.

The three of them knelt around the manger, from which Bob

pulled out a bottle of whiskey and three glasses. He doled them out and poured a round before sliding the bottle back under the hay and doll.

"We should maybe rent ourselves out like this for Christmas parties and stuff," said Bob.

The men nodded in agreement.

Seamus paused his glass at his lips and lowered it.

"Hey—your wives aren't mad at Jackie, are they?" he asked, invoking the name of his on-again, off-again girlfriend and Pineapple Port resident.

"No. Not that I heard," said Frank. "And I probably would have had to hear it if mine was."

"Not Mariska," said Bob. "Why?"

Seamus shrugged. "Oh, you know how the ladies gossip. We didn't get invited to this bed-and-breakfast thing, and one of the other ladies suggested to Jackie it was a *slight* and blah, blah, blah."

"Mariska only had a few tickets," explained Bob. "She might have gotten around to asking you two, but Charlotte and Declan wanted to do something nice for that big guy."

Seamus nodded. "Blade. Yeah. I figured. You know how it is with the ladies—gossip and drama."

"Don't I know it," said Bob. "Hey, did you hear about Tommy?"

The other two lowered their glasses to pay attention.

"No, what happened?" asked Frank.

"Gerry said he was cheating at golf."

Frank scoffed. "Tommy? I don't believe it."

Bob shrugged. "I don't either, but his sciatica has been acting up, and maybe he feels like he needs to make up for it? Otherwise, that rich guy he plays with might dump him, and he'll lose access to that fancy course."

"Is it his back? I heard it was his hip. I heard he strained it stealing oranges from his neighbor's tree."

"I heard he did it dating that widow down the street, if you know what I mean," said Bob.

Seamus shook his head. "No, he's got a girl."

Frank clucked his tongue. "I don't know. He's got that new

Corvette, and you know how that goes."

The men nodded, and Seamus sniffed.

"Anyway, I'll tell Jackie it wasn't a slight." He sighed. "Those ladies and their *gossip*."

The men fell quiet, nodding slowly to themselves.

"Nice night for this," said Frank, staring up at the stars.

Bob looked past him. His head cocked.

"Hey, is that someone at your house, Frank?" he asked.

Frank squinted down the street. Someone in white was wandering around his front yard.

He rose to his feet. "What the—?"

Seamus stood and put a hand on his arm before he could head for home.

"Wait, Boyo, let's do this right," he said.

Frank scowled at him. He could never decide how he felt about being called *Boyo,* but he didn't imagine it would stop. Knowing Seamus, the man would probably do it twice as much if he objected.

"I think I know how to approach a suspect, *thanks*," grumbled Frank.

Seamus nodded. "Aye, but there's three of us. Let's take advantage of our manpower."

Frank eyed Bob in his Mary costume.

"I assume you're using the term *manpower* loosely."

"I'm saying let's surround him. Give Bob and me a second to get into position, front and back, and then you approach him dead on."

Frank nodded as he watched the man in white make a loop around his yard.

Checking out the decorations, no doubt.

"Okay. I see what you're saying. Sounds like a good idea. He might make a break for it, but he won't get far. He looks drunk."

Seamus slapped Frank on the shoulder hard enough to send him forward a step.

"Aye. It'll be good to have us there. He might be belligerent. You know how drunks get."

Frank stepped around the manger to keep from falling over it.

"Okay. You two go ahead," he said.

Seamus jogged down the street, his robe flowing behind him.

Once he found a spot to set down his glass, Bob headed off behind the neighbor's house and popped up closer to Frank's to cover the escape route from that angle.

Seamus gave Frank a thumbs up from down the street. Bob saw this and mimicked him with his own signal.

Frank straightened his wise man frock and strode toward the man wandering his yard.

You're in trouble now, buddy. We've got you surrounded.

"Hey," he called when he was close.

The man didn't respond. He picked up Frank's garden gnome and turned it around in his hands.

The nerve.

The man was *shopping*. It made Frank *livid*.

"*Hey*," he barked again as he reached his driveway.

The man ignored him a second time.

Frank walked up as the trespasser continued to ignore him, eyes fixed on the ground.

Frank saw red.

He put a hand on the man's shoulder to stop him from shuffling past him. As soon as he touched him, the man's eyes bulged, and he screamed in Frank's face.

Screamed.

Frank whipped away his hand and stumbled back. He wasn't ready for *that*. His heart pounded in his chest as the trespasser screeched a second time. The man's arms went rigid at his sides, and his fingers balled into fists. He panted, eyes wide, gawking at Frank.

Seamus and Bob ran from their positions.

"What did you do to him?" asked Bob as the man continued to pant, expression frozen.

Still stunned, it took Frank a moment to respond.

"Nothing," he said, finally. "I barely touched him."

"He's wearing pajamas," said Seamus. "Look at his eyes. It doesn't look like he's *seeing*, does it?"

"He seems young to be losing it," said Bob.

Frank nodded. The man looked like he could be in his late fifties—just a kid in Pineapple Port terms.

"Jason!"

Three of the four men turned toward the voice. The one that might be *Jason* did not.

A woman in pajamas rounded the corner of the house at the end of the block and jogged toward them, waving her hands.

"Don't touch him! Don't touch him!" she called.

"Little late for that," muttered Frank.

She reached them and hovered near the man.

"He's sleepwalking," she said.

The other three opened their mouths, all thinking the same thing.

Oh. That makes sense.

The man suddenly collapsed to sit on the ground, his head hanging.

The woman crouched near him and gently put her hands on his shoulders.

"Jason, are you okay?"

The man looked up and seemed to recognize her face. He looked like any man in his pajamas sitting on the grass of a stranger's front yard, looking up at his wife.

"Dee?"

"It's me, sweetheart," she said.

He took her hand. "Where am I?"

He looked around and noticed the three men standing nearby. He put his free hand over his mouth.

"Oh no. I got out, didn't I?" he asked.

She nodded. "I didn't know you'd already fallen asleep. I didn't have the door locked yet," said Dee.

Frank leaned in to help the man to his feet. The man took his hand and rose to his feet. He looked mortified.

"Thank you," he said. "I'm so sorry. I sleepwalk—"

"No problem," said Frank.

The couple fell quiet. They were *staring* now.

Frank realized the couple had passed the sleepwalking incident and moved on to wondering why they were wearing nativity costumes in the middle of the night.

"Christmas play," he said.

The man nodded.

Frank had a passing thought and figured it wouldn't hurt to ask.

"You don't steal Christmas decorations in your sleep by any chance, do you?"

The man shook his head.

"No?"

He looked at his wife for confirmation, and she shook her head.

"Nothing like that," she said.

Frank nodded.

They ended the awkward exchange with waves and walked their separate ways.

"Is it me, or does a lot go on out here when I'm watching TV in the house?" asked Bob as they returned to the manger.

"It isn't you," said Frank.

CHAPTER THIRTEEN

The Outback Inn

Charlotte stared at Elke's body in her room. It had been bad enough to think she'd be sleeping in a room full of dolls. Now she'd have to sleep in a room with dolls *and* Elke's corpse?

That wasn't going to work.

There were a lot of problems in need of solving. Body in the room, guests wondering where Elke went, killer on the loose...

She looked at Declan.

"What are we going to do with her? Just cover her with dolls and pretend she isn't here?"

"We could put her in bed," suggested Declan.

"*Our* bed?"

He rolled his eyes. "No, *her* bed."

Charlotte nodded. "Oh. That makes more sense." She grimaced. "Still, I don't love the idea. I'm worried someone will walk in on her."

"We could lock her door?" suggested Bindy.

"Sure, but I also hate to move her at all. We'd be tampering with a crime scene." Charlotte tapped her knuckle against her lips and turned to Bindy. "Where does she sleep?"

"Across the hall."

Bindy opened the door and motioned across the hall. Her brow furrowed.

"Hold on," she said.

Her reaction drew Charlotte, Declan, and Blade after her, and they followed the few steps to Elke's bedroom.

Someone had pinned a note to the door in big, blocky letters written on a scrap of lined paper.

Not feeling well. Please do not disturb.

"Did you put that there?" asked Charlotte.

Bindy shook her head and pointed at the neat lettering. "That isn't her handwriting, either. I've been trying to decipher her notes all over the house. She writes *scripty.*"

"That looks like someone trying very hard to pen the most untraceable letter ever," said Declan.

Charlotte agreed. "No handwriting analyst would get any clues from that. It's too *by the letter.*"

Declan scowled at her pun, and she shrugged.

"I couldn't resist."

"Should I take it down?" asked Bindy.

"No, it might have fingerprints on it," said Charlotte. "And it works for us whether we decide to move her there or not. It'll keep people away."

"The note might be a good sign," said Declan. "Assuming the killer hung it, it means they took pains to make sure no one missed Elke, specifically. They probably aren't planning on killing more people."

"Unless they're just trying to keep us calm so they can pick us off one by one," mumbled Charlotte.

Declan, Blade, and Bindy looked at her.

"Well, aren't you Susie Sunshine," said Bindy.

Charlotte chuckled.

"On the upside, there's a bed for you now," she said, patting Blade's arm.

Blade frowned. "I thought we were putting her in her bed? We can't leave her under the dolls."

Charlotte shook her head. "No, we can't leave her there for two days. Even in the air conditioning, things will get ripe."

Charlotte had never been so happy about *decay*. Decay was an excellent reason *not* to sleep with a dead lady in her room.

Bindy nodded. "Even cooked chicken in the trash starts to smell after less than a day—" She winced. "Sorry. I didn't mean to say she's *chicken*—"

"What do you suggest we do with her?" asked Declan. "We can't leave her outside."

Bindy gasped and pointed toward the ceiling like an old-time detective solving a crime.

"I got it—we can put her in the freezer downstairs. There's a walk-in in the kitchen," she said.

"Really? That's a great idea," said Charlotte. "I don't think anyone would blame us. At least it'll look like we're *trying* to preserve evidence, and we *probably* won't go to jail for tampering with a crime scene."

Thunder clapped outside, and they all jumped.

"Can we keep everyone out of your walk-in?" Declan asked Bindy.

Bindy shook her head. "I can padlock it. I'll get the few things I need for the weekend out first."

"Good idea. I'm sure a health inspector would take issue with Elke sharing space with the ice cream," said Charlotte.

"I bet Elke never dreamed she'd be in her own freezer," mumbled Blade.

Declan scowled. "There's one other problem. How do we get her to the kitchen without anyone seeing?"

Bindy glanced down the hall to the stairs.

"Tell you what—I'll gather everyone in the sitting room downstairs. It's on the west side of the house. You go down the stairs and head east. The kitchen's there. The freezer's in the corner."

"That could work." Charlotte motioned to the men. "You two can carry her, and I'll be a lookout in case someone wanders."

"I like how you just got out of touching the body," said Declan.

Charlotte chuckled. "Bindy, do you have a camera anywhere? Something we could use to take a few pictures of her before we move her?"

Bindy frowned and then perked. "*Ooh*, I think I have one of those little disposables from a wedding reception I went to a while back. Let me go check."

Bindy jogged down the hall to her room and disappeared inside.

"What do you think? Are we covering our bases?" asked Charlotte.

Declan shrugged. "Freezer seems like our best option. We'll still lock Elke's door and leave the note to keep people from trying to talk to her. We can unlock it later if Blade wants to sleep in there."

"I don't want to sleep there," rumbled Blade. "It feels like bad juju."

Declan reached for the door, and Charlotte touched his arm to stop him.

"Don't bother locking it yet. We should go through her room and see if we can find something that explains why this happened. Bindy will have everyone on the west side of the house, so we don't have to worry about anyone wandering up here for a while."

Charlotte glanced back at their room and suffered a feeling of dread.

"If we're pretending we don't know Elke's dead, that means after we pull her out, we need to set the dolls up again," she said.

"Yep. So if the killer checks, it looks like no one's found the body," confirmed Declan.

She bit her lip, and Declan smirked, wiggling his fingers at her.

"Which means we'll be *sleeping with the spooky dolls*," he said in a scary voice.

Charlotte tapped his chest with her fist.

"That's just *rude*."

He laughed.

She turned her attention to Blade.

"How about we switch rooms? You can sleep in ours, and we'll take Elke's with the bad juju?"

Blade shook his head.

"No, thank you. I don't like those dolls any more than you do, and the juju in *that* room must be even worse."

Charlotte glowered.

"I might have to kill Mariska for this," she muttered.

Declan shrugged. "Hopefully the freezer's roomy."

Bindy returned with a small disposable camera in hand.

"Here you go. Sorry—had trouble finding it. My room is still a disaster since the move."

Charlotte took the camera. "We'll take photos while you arrange your meeting in the sitting room. Give us a heads up when we can head downstairs with Elke."

Bindy nodded and headed off.

Charlotte returned to their room and took photos of Elke from every angle. She squatted next to the body to take a few close-ups and checked one last time for evidence.

"I really don't know if we're doing the right thing," she mumbled.

"For a little more than twenty-four hours, we don't have a lot of options," said Declan.

She nodded. This was true. The storm was still howling. She'd sat through quieter hurricanes.

The Santa image on Elke's neck seemed even more glaring as she took a photo. She didn't know what the murder weapon was, but it was definitely Christmas-themed.

She was about to straighten when she noticed something in Elke's hair.

"This looks like hay in her hair," she said, pointing to it.

Declan leaned down to look. "*Hay?*"

"There's hay in the rabbit pen," noted Blade.

Declan nodded. "Killer rabbits. I knew it. Those rabbits have a vicious streak a mile wide."

Charlotte chuckled. "One problem with that theory is that the rabbits couldn't have buried her under the dolls."

Declan arched an eyebrow. "Are you sure? They're pretty clever."

"There's that barn in the back. Maybe she was killed there?" offered Blade.

Charlotte winced. "She *was* in there, but I saw her come to the house. I heard her arguing with Princess."

"You did?" asked Declan.

"Yes. Or, at least, I *thought* I did. I didn't *see* them. I saw

Princess walk around the side of the house and stayed to eavesdrop."

"Princess makes a good suspect then," said Declan. "And Elke *had* to be killed in or around the house. No one could carry her from the barn without being seen. There were people all over treasure hunting."

Charlotte agreed.

"What did they say? Could you hear?" asked Declan.

"The voice I thought was Elke apologized for something—I don't know what. She wanted Princess to look at something. But Princess—if it was her—was having none of it. She was angry. She said she wouldn't do *anything* for Elke."

"That sounds like they know each other better than we thought," said Declan.

"Which explains why they were eyeballing each other at brunch. There was a lot of tension there for two people who just met."

Blade scowled. "Didn't Princess say Elke hired her to promote this place?"

Charlotte laid her hand out flat and wobbled it.

"Kind of. She implied that. She asked people to guess why someone as *fantastic* as she would be *here* and admitted to having a lot of fans when Strella suggested she was here to promote the inn. She didn't exactly confirm that she was."

"Maybe she didn't like what she saw and threatened to pan the place. That would explain why Elke wanted her to see something more, and she wasn't into it," said Declan.

Charlotte crossed her arms against her chest, considering.

"That fits. We also know Princess was in the house during the hunt. Did you see anyone else come inside?"

Declan winced. "No, but I know someone *did*—I heard them come in behind me, but I was trying to stay ahead of them. I never looked to see who it was. I'm starting to think that was a mistake."

"That's at least one other person in the vicinity. That might be a good place to start when we question people. We should see who went in the house during the hunt." Charlotte smiled, feeling hopeful. "Whoever was behind you is probably our only other option. We're already narrowing down suspects."

Declan looked doubtful as his attention dropped to Elke.

"Don't forget about Munch. Did you see where he went? He might have come back into the house."

Charlotte's smile faded. "Hm. I see what you mean. Now, that's as many as three people in the house. And what about Bindy?"

Charlotte and Declan looked at Blade.

"Why are you looking at me?" he asked.

"Did you see her during the treasure hunt?"

He fidgeted. "Yes. We were outside talking, but—"

He paused.

"But what?" prompted Charlotte.

He frowned. "She came in here for a while and then went back outside."

Charlotte put her hand on her head. "Great. There's another one. Did you happen to see Iko or Brendan?"

"I saw Iko here and there, but she could have come inside, I dunno. I didn't see Brendan."

"So, long story short, it could have been anyone. One step forward, two steps back." Charlotte sighed and motioned to the body. "Let's pull Elke out of here and set the dolls up before Bindy calls for us."

Declan and Blade nodded and lifted Elke away from the dolls. They laid her gently beside the bed.

Charlotte searched the area where the body had been to ensure they weren't leaving behind any clues.

"Give me a couple of those pillows," said Charlotte, motioning to the bed.

Declan chucked her two pillows, and she used them to replace the gap where the body had been before restacking the dolls around them. She took her time.

"What are you doing?" asked Declan. "You look like you're playing Tetris with them."

"I'm putting them in an order I'll remember. That way, if someone moves them again, I can tell."

When she finished, she stood and wiped her hands on the bed.

"*Now*, what are you doing?" he asked.

Charlotte's nose wrinkled.

"I'm getting the creepy off them."

"Bad juju," muttered Blade.

Charlotte motioned to him.

"See? He gets it."

CHAPTER FOURTEEN

Charlotte left the room and hurried downstairs, pausing on the landing to look outside. The wind increased, and rain fell in sheets. She *really* regretted not checking the weather when she *had a phone*. Maybe there was a radio in the house somewhere to get a weather update.

All old houses had radios somewhere, didn't they?

At the bottom of the stairs, she heard Bindy gathering people in the large sitting room on the west side of the property.

"That's right. This way. Everyone to this big room here. I have some things to go over with you..."

Munch came in from the back porch, soaking from the rain, a plate of soggy donuts in his hand. He'd been cleaning up in the storm and looked battered.

He turned left to head toward the kitchen, but Bindy called out to him.

"Munch, you too. Come with me a second?"

He looked down at the plate and then back at her.

"Just put that down there for a second, mate," she said.

He huffed a sigh and did as told.

The others shuffled in the direction Bindy had led them. Darla looked to her left and spotted Charlotte in the foyer. Charlotte motioned to her, and she grabbed Mariska's arm to tug her in that direction.

Mariska seemed relieved.

"Where have you been? We were looking for you," she said. "Why do you look like that?"

Charlotte didn't realize their predicament was plastered all over her face, but if anyone could read her, it was these ladies.

"I'll tell you, but first, I need you to promise you won't gasp, yip, or make any noise."

"Promise," said the women in unison.

Charlotte scowled at how quickly they'd answered.

Suspect.

She looked to ensure no one could hear them and took a deep breath.

Best to just say it and get it over with.

"We found Elke upstairs. She's dead," she said.

The ladies gasped.

Charlotte grimaced.

"What did I tell you?" she hissed.

"You can't expect us not to react to *that*," said Mariska.

Strella, the last straggler in the parlor, turned to look, and Charlotte waved at her.

"That's *amazing*. You found a Snickers bar in one of the eggs?" said Darla loudly. "I *love* those."

Strella lost interest and followed the others.

"Nice cover," said Charlotte.

Darla grunted. "It worked, didn't it? So, what happened? Did Elke have a heart attack?"

Charlotte shook her head. "No. That's the problem. By the looks of her throat, she was strangled."

"*Strangled?*" echoed Darla.

"Were there ligature marks? Was her hyoid bone broken? How about her lividity?" asked Mariska.

Charlotte looked at her.

"You *really* need to lay off the true crime shows," she said. "But now that you mention it, there *were* ligature marks."

"I knew it," said Mariska, looking smug.

"No lividity—she's only been dead, like, an hour, and I don't know if they broke her hyoid bone. I'm not a coroner."

"Where did you find her?" asked Darla.

"Blade and Bindy found her hidden under the dolls in my room."

The women both gasped again.

Charlotte winced. Trying to reign them in was hopeless. She supposed if someone heard them, Darla could use the Snickers defense again.

"Under the dolls? Why?" whispered Mariska as best she could. She didn't really get the concept of whispering.

Charlotte shrugged. "We don't know. All we know is it must have happened during the treasure hunt."

"But who—"

The ladies looked toward the west side of the house.

"Oh *no*," said Mariska.

Darla nodded and poked at the ground. "We're the only people here. That means it's someone *here*."

"Right. That's the biggest problem," said Charlotte. "Whoever did it must still be here."

"Did you call the police?" asked Mariska.

"We *can't*. The phones really are in a time-lock safe. Bindy doesn't have another way to call anyone."

"She can't open the safe? There has to be an override," said Darla.

"There is, but only one person knew the code."

The ladies blinked at her and then said the name together.

"Elke."

Charlotte nodded. "Yep."

"What do you want us to do?" asked Darla.

"Like I said, Blade and Declan are going to carry her downstairs and move her into the kitchen over there." Charlotte pointed. "There's a walk-in freezer."

Mariska's nose wrinkled. "You're going to put her in the *freezer*?"

"It's the best way to keep her hidden and preserve evidence. We can't just leave her rotting away under the dolls."

"*Ew.*" Mariska chuckled. "And you were afraid of the *dolls* before—"

Charlotte held up a hand.

"Ha. We covered that. Anyway, we pulled her out and re-set up the dolls so the killer would think she's still there. That should buy us some time to figure out who did it."

"Should we tell the others?" asked Mariska.

"*No*," said Charlotte quickly. "That's just it. We aren't telling anyone."

"Because one of them *did it*," explained Darla.

"Oh, right," mumbled Mariska.

"We're going to have to interview everyone *subtly—*"

"So you don't want Mariska to help," quipped Darla.

Mariska scowled at her. "Very funny."

Charlotte continued, "We need to do one thing at a time. Bindy's keeping everyone in that big room so Declan and Blade can move her. You two station at the exits to help Bindy keep people in there. If someone tries to leave, tackle them if you have to."

The ladies nodded, their lips pressed tight with grim determination.

Charlotte started toward the stairs and then paused to turn back as her last words echoed in her head.

"Don't *really* tackle anyone," she added.

She started again and paused a second time.

"Unless you *absolutely* have to."

"Got it," said Darla, bouncing on her toes.

Charlotte could tell she was *praying* someone tried to leave so she *could* tackle them.

She needed to hurry.

She jogged to the third floor.

"Good to go," she called down the hall.

Declan and Blade exited her room, carrying Elke between them. Blade held her beneath her arms, and Declan supported her feet.

They shuffled down the hall with Charlotte leading the way. As they hit the second landing, Charlotte heard Mariska talking to someone.

She held up a hand, asking the boys to wait.

"She's not exactly a *waif*," grunted Declan.

"Sorry. Someone's coming. Give me a second."

She jogged down the stairs and peered around the corner. Strella stood at the north exit of the sitting room, talking with Mariska.

"I have to get my allergy medicine," she said.

She moved to walk around Mariska, who leaned in front of her. When she tried to go the other way, Mariska shifted that way.

"What is wrong with you?" snapped Strella. "*Get out of my way.*"

"I'll get it for you," offered Mariska.

Strella's expression twisted.

"What are you even talking about? You can't go into my *room.*"

"Strella, I really need you in here," called Bindy.

The woman stomped her foot like a petulant child.

"Look, this place is hopping with rabbits, and I have to *get my allergy medicine.*"

She pushed past Mariska.

Charlotte gasped.

Here she comes.

Mariska panicked and, for some inexplicable reason, warned them with a bird caw.

"*Ca-caw, ca-caw!*" she crowed.

Charlotte didn't have time to unpack that.

"*Back up!*" she hissed at Declan.

His eyes widened. "*What?*"

"Back. Up. *Quick.* Someone's *coming.*"

She pointed to the third floor.

Declan swore, and the boys grunted back up the stairs with Elke.

Charlotte saw a flash of movement and spotted Darla flying into the foyer to assist. She threw herself between Strella and the stairs.

Strella didn't stop.

She clipped Darla's shoulder and kept moving.

"Excuse *me,*" Strella snapped.

Behind her, Darla snarled and raised a fist. Charlotte snapped her fingers from her spot on the second landing. Darla looked up, fist still cocked, and Charlotte shook her head emphatically, eyes wide.

She mouthed the word, *no.*

Darla huffed and lowered her fist.

Strella reached the top of the stairs and noticed Charlotte there.

"Your friends are weird," she said.

Charlotte nodded. "No argument there."

"Bindy wants us in the sitting room. She's having a meltdown," she added, rolling her eyes.

Charlotte flashed a tight smile.

"Oh? Okay. Thanks."

She looked up and saw Declan and Blade hadn't quite made the turn to the third floor.

Panicked, she stepped in front of Strella, who nearly fell back, trying to stop in time to avoid walking into her.

"You're allergic to rabbits?" she asked.

Strella scowled. "Whoa—*what*? Yes. I *am.*"

"I mean," said Charlotte, continuing to block her. "Maybe, it's something else in the house? It could be the carpet freshener. I know I'm a little sensitive—"

Strella gritted her teeth. "Oh my *God,* can you please let me get to my room? What is wrong with you people? My nose is running onto my *face.*"

Strella dodged around her, passed the stairs to the third floor without looking up, and continued down the hall. Charlotte watched as she entered her room and slammed the door.

Whew.

She motioned for Declan and Blade to start down again.

"Hurry. She's getting medicine, but she won't be long."

They moved. They'd barely hit the landing when Strella's door opened again.

Charlotte spun.

No, no, no—how did she get it so fast?

"Back, back, back," she said to the boys, but it was too late. Their momentum couldn't shift fast enough, so they moved deeper into the landing, where little more than a sofa and a table sat.

Strella started down the hall toward Charlotte, who ran forward to meet her and give the boys more time to hide.

"Hey, that was fast. What kind of medicine do you take?"

Strella's eyes widened with annoyance.

"Why are you up here? Shouldn't you be downstairs suffering through this ridiculous meeting with the rest of us?"

She pushed past Charlotte and entered the landing. She stopped, head turning to where Charlotte knew Declan and Blade had gone.

Oh no. The jig is up.

She raced to the end of the hall to find Declan and Blade sitting on the sofa.

She didn't see Elke.

How?

She pieced it together only because she knew Elke *had* to be there. They'd laid the body across the sofa. An afghan, once folded over the back cushions, now draped across the corpse. Then, they'd draped *themselves* over the body to block Strella's view. Blade sat half on the poor dead woman's chest, his elbow propping him on the sofa's arm and his legs outstretched to run alongside Elke. Declan had draped himself similarly across the furniture but in the opposite direction so their ankles crossed.

To say their position didn't look natural would be an understatement. It looked like they were setting up for the strangest still-life painting *ever*. Their only advantage was that as odd as they appeared, no normal person would assume they were hiding a *corpse*.

Strella opened her mouth as if she were going to say something and then looked at Charlotte.

Charlotte smiled.

Strella rolled her eyes and headed for the stairs.

"*Freaks*," Charlotte heard her mutter.

"Tell Bindy we're coming," Charlotte called after her.

Strella stormed down the stairs without answering.

Charlotte released the breath she'd been holding.

Good to go.

"Okay, come on," she said, heading down the stairs.

The boys leaped to their feet and whipped the afghan off the body to hoist it up and follow.

They carried Elke down the stairs to the lobby and through a hall to the kitchen, with Charlotte leading the way.

The kitchen smelled like turkey, and there were containers and pots everywhere. It looked as if someone was in the middle of making a large meal, though she didn't see any actual food.

She opened the walk-in freezer's large door, and Declan and Blade laid Elke gently on the floor inside.

As Blade lowered Elke's shoulders, Charlotte saw a necklace slide from beneath her clothing.

A *locket*.

She knelt beside the body to snap open the charm. Inside, she found a small photo of a woman and a girl wearing a crown.

She unclasped the chain and stood with the necklace dangling in her fingers.

"Why are you stealing her jewelry?" asked Declan.

She clucked her tongue.

"I'm not *stealing* her jewelry. Look at this."

She held the locket out, and he took it to peer at the photo while Charlotte rubbed her arms. Freezers were *cold*. Who knew?

"Is it me, or does that little girl look like Princess?" she asked, bouncing on her toes.

"If the crown is any hint," he said, scowling at the photo. "It's hard to say, but it *does* look like a kid version of her."

He handed it to Blade, who shrugged.

"Could be," he said, handing it back to Charlotte.

"I think I've seen this photo before. Something close to it, anyway," said Declan. "It's hidden in a desk drawer in the library. I found it while I was looking for eggs. I'll show you."

Charlotte nodded. "Okay, let's put her somewhere where people won't see her if they happen to open the freezer door."

They rolled Elke against the wall beneath a low shelf and lined large white buckets in front of her to block the casual observer's view of the corpse.

Declan stepped back to admire his handiwork.

"That looks good," he said. "Even if someone comes here by mistake, they probably won't notice her."

"I hope not," muttered Charlotte. "I'll tell Bindy to go ahead and put the padlock on."

They shut the door.

"What now?" asked Blade.

Charlotte put her hand on Blade's arm to get his attention.

"I notice you and Bindy seem to have hit it off?" she said.

He paused a moment and then nodded.

"I think she's a cool lady. You want me to talk to her?"

"Sure, but I need you to *really* listen to her. I need you to remember—"

His brow furrowed as she continued.

"—she might be the killer."

CHAPTER FIFTEEN

Darla shook her head as she watched Charlotte, Declan, and Blade hustle into the kitchen carrying Elke. That woman had been sitting at the end of the table a couple of hours ago, and now she was on her way to the freezer.

Life is strange.

She walked over to where Mariska still stood guard.

"They're in the kitchen. I think we're good," she said.

"Whew. I let that one girl get past me—the little witch." Mariska scowled. "Now what?"

"Now, we need to interview people about where they were during the treasure hunt."

"*Subtly*," said Mariska.

Darla chuckled. "Right. Do you want me to get you a dictionary so you can look that up?"

Mariska glowered at her, and Darla laughed harder. A few of the people in the room listening to Bindy turned.

"Sorry," said Darla, holding up a hand.

Bindy looked at her, and when the others turned away, Darla flashed her a thumbs-up sign to let her know they'd completed Operation Hide Elke.

Bindy nodded and returned her focus to the group.

"Anyway, there you go, a short history of the inn. Munch, can you take a drink order from everyone, and we'll have a little mingle?"

Munch nodded and pulled a pad and pen from his pocket.

The group offered a light round of applause, though, from their expressions, Darla guessed they were most happy the presentation was over.

"That was all on the website," huffed Strella. "Every word."

"Pretty much verbatim," agreed Brendan. "But I never get tired of hearing the history of this area."

Strella rolled her eyes and asked Munch for a matcha tea. He scowled in a way that led Darla to believe there wasn't much chance she'd get one.

Darla noticed Princess sitting in the corner, staring at the ground.

"Her thoughts look a million miles away. I'm going to go talk to her," she told Mariska.

Mariska nodded. "Okay. I'll talk to Iko."

Darla strolled over to Princess, pretending to admire the trinkets around the room as she moved.

"Princess?" she said.

Princess looked up as if she were snapping out of a dream.

"Hm?"

"So, outside, you said you lived in Palm Beach?"

She nodded. "Uh-huh."

"And you're a real princess?"

Princess sat a little straighter. "Yes. Princess Daria Dalca, direct descendant of Prince Nicholas of Romania—*Princess Christmas* to my fans."

"Wow, I've never met a real princess before."

Princess's chin rose a little higher. "Well, now you can tell all your friends that you have."

"I will," said Darla. "Why don't you have an accent?"

Princess's chin lowered a notch.

"What?"

"If you're from Romania, why don't you have—"

Princess dismissed her comment with a wave.

"My family had to escape to America a long time ago. I grew up here."

"Oh." Darla nodded and took a moment to refocus on her mission.

Her naturally suspicious nature had her disbelieving Princess's story. She could tell questioning the woman's accent had annoyed her. Princess started to rock in her seat as if she wanted to leave.

Darla realized she was about to lose her and hadn't asked where she was during the treasure hunt yet.

Focus, Darla.

"How did you do on the egg hunt?" she asked.

Princess stopped rocking.

"I didn't play that silly game," she said with a haughty sniff.

Darla smiled to herself as she realized as long as she gave Princess a way to talk about her *princess-ness*, she was happy to stay and chat.

"That's too bad. I think we're—I mean, *I'm* in the running. I got lucky out by the cemetery."

"They hid eggs in the cemetery?" Princess said flatly. It felt more like a comment than a question. The tone confused Darla.

She pointed toward the back. "Yes. There's a cemetery in the back there—"

"Oh, I know," said Princess, looking bored.

She rubbed her finger under her eye as if checking her mascara and then wrinkled her nose as she looked up at Darla.

"I mean, I *saw* it," she added. "That's weird, isn't it—to have a cemetery in your back yard? Is that what *rural* people do?"

Darla had to keep her expression stony to keep from laughing. Princess was trying so hard to sound above the average person that she almost sounded like an alien asking how humans live.

"Not everybody has one," she agreed. "But I guess it isn't so weird with these old houses. Back in the day, people did it if they had enough land. Now, if I had one in *my* back yard, *that* would be weird."

Princess smiled but remained distracted. Darla felt like she was losing her. She needed to get to the point.

"What did you do instead of the treasure hunt?" asked Darla.

Princess looked at her.

"What do you mean?"

Darla frowned. The question did sound forced. She wanted to ask if Princess had been in the house during the hunt, but every variation of that question sounded strange in her own head.

"I think I saw you come this way when the hunt started," she said. "I guess you came inside?"

"Mm," grunted Princess.

Darla scowled.

What a noncommittal noise.

Was that a yes or a no?

Darla thought of a great way to pose her next question. So great that she bounced a little on her toes.

"So, you didn't *search* while you were in here?" she asked. "I was thinking the house would be full of eggs."

Princess's expression darkened. "Why would I look for eggs? *I don't even want to be here.*"

Princess spat the last sentence through gritted teeth.

Darla swallowed.

Yikes.

Princess stood, and Darla panicked. She still hadn't gotten any good information. She thought she'd found a way to corner Princess about being in the house, and she'd still found a way to answer without answering.

"It's nice not being connected to the outside world, don't you think?" Darla said quickly.

"*No*," said Princess flatly. She squinted at Darla. "Who are you again?"

"Darla. My friend Mariska won the weekend in a giveaway. A promotional thing Bindy did."

Princess grunted. She was about to leave when Munch arrived with his pad and pen, inadvertently blocking her escape. He mimed drinking a cocktail to let them know why he was there.

"Do you have iced tea?" asked Darla.

He nodded and wrote *iced tea* in careful block lettering on his pad before turning to Princess.

"You know, I think I'll make my own," she said.

Princess flashed Darla a tight smile and moved around Munch to walk away.

Darla sighed.

Shoot.

She watched Princess walk off and grimaced.

Was she supposed to let people go off on their own? She couldn't remember—did Charlotte want them to keep everyone in sight at all times?

She spotted Mariska holding a glass of champagne and headed over to her.

"How's it going?" she asked.

"They have *champagne*," said Mariska.

"I see that. How did your talk with Iko go?"

"Good. I talked to Brendan and Iko."

"Were they in the house?"

Mariska nodded. "Yes."

Darla tucked her chin. "Really? Did they say anything else?"

"Like what?"

"Oh, I don't know, like, *hey, did you see how I killed Elke?*"

Mariska scowled.

"*No.* They wouldn't be dumb enough to say that."

"Maybe not, but did you ask them if they *saw* Elke?" asked Darla, realizing *that's* what she should have asked *Princess*.

Dang it.

Mariska scowled. "Hm. That's a good one. You should have mentioned that earlier."

"Yes," muttered Darla, looking around the room.

"Where's Strella?" she asked.

Mariska took a sip of her champagne.

"I didn't see her."

Darla grimaced. "Were we supposed to make sure no one wandered off?"

Mariska's eyes widened. "Were we?"

"I don't know—that's what I'm asking."

"Oh. I don't know. If we were, we didn't do that."

Darla groaned.

"I think we might have messed up."

CHAPTER SIXTEEN

Charlotte entered the sitting room and spotted Mariska and Darla in the corner. A quick sweep of the room told her not everyone had remained sequestered there. Bindy, Princess, Strella, and Brendan were missing. Munch was there, handing Iko a drink.

She walked over to the ladies.

"They have *champagne*," said Mariska, holding up her glass.

"I see that. Where is everyone?" asked Charlotte.

"We were just talking about that," said Mariska. "Were we supposed to keep them *here* even after you finished your thing?"

She sighed. "No. I didn't say that, though I probably should have. I didn't know everyone would scatter so fast. How many places are there to go?"

She spotted a doggy bag of plastic eggshells sitting on a table and squinted at Mariska.

"Hey, I meant to ask you. Did you ever use chocolate coins from the same giant bag across multiple years?"

Mariska coughed. "Hm?"

"I said—"

Mariska turned and coughed again.

Charlotte scowled, suspicious that she had her answer.

Before she could confirm, Declan joined them and motioned Charlotte toward the library.

"I'll show you that photo," he said.

She nodded.

"Keep your eyes peeled," she said to the ladies before leaving.

Charlotte followed Declan into the library. He squatted to pull out a secret drawer at the bottom of a roll-top desk. He smiled up at her.

"Ta-da."

"How did you know that was there?" she asked, impressed.

"I've had desks like this at the pawn shop," he said, plucking a torn photo from the hidden drawer.

He handed it to her, and she pulled the locket out of her pocket to compare the two images.

"Elke's wearing the same outfit as in the locket—probably taken the same day. I suppose it's the girl who's torn off this photo, but I can't tell by this little piece of elbow."

She stared at the photo of the girl wearing the crown in the locket. She *did* look like Princess, and her dress was green with red lace trim—very much like something a future *Princess Christmas* might wear.

"If this girl is Princess, maybe they have a long history of not getting along," she said.

Bindy entered the room and cocked her head at the secret drawer.

"What's that now?" she asked.

"Secret drawer. Common in this desk model," said Declan.

Bindy grunted. "Neato."

Charlotte eyed Bindy with her open expression and casual air. She didn't carry herself like a person who just choked Elke to death, and if she wanted Elke dead, her timing was way off. Like she said—why kill her *after* they made their deal for the inn?

Sure, she might be annoyed the woman was hanging around longer than planned, but that was hardly a motive for murder.

Maybe if she was still here *next* Christmas...

Charlotte decided to treat Bindy as a friendly until she had a good reason not to. As the new owner, she knew more about Elke and the inn than anyone else. She could be helpful as an ally.

"We found this inside," said Charlotte, handing Bindy the photo.

Bindy gave it a look.

"That's Elke, I'm sure," she said, looking up as she returned it.

"Why is it torn?"

"We don't know. The other half isn't here," said Declan.

"We also found this locket around Elke's neck."

She held up the open locket, and Bindy squinted at it.

"That's Elke there, too."

"The girl—does she look like Princess to you?" asked Charlotte.

Bindy's squint deepened. "I suppose it could be. As a teenager, eh? Looks like a princess, doesn't she, with that crown?"

"Do you think Princess could be related to Elke?" asked Declan.

Bindy leaned back to eyeball him.

"I never thought about it. She didn't say anything. Neither of them did."

"Did *you* invite Princess to this weekend?"

Bindy crossed her arms against her chest.

"There's a funny story, now that you mention it. Elke told me *she* invited her, which I thought was strange because she hadn't been very helpful up to that point. In fact, up until this morning, I was worried she might try to tank things for me or even pull out of the sale. Like I said, I'd been proceeding on faith that she'd stick to her word. Like a drongo."

Charlotte didn't know the word *drongo*, but by the way Bindy muttered it, she understood it to mean *idiot*.

"So Elke invited her," mumbled Charlotte.

Bindy winced.

"Yes, *but* she said I needed to offer Princess money."

"So *you* paid her to be here?"

Bindy nodded. "One word from that woman, and I'd have bookings for a year. Unfortunately, I'm pretty broke right now. I only offered her a few hundred dollars."

"And she came for that?"

Bindy shrugged. "No one was more shocked than me."

"It's odd Elke knew how to contact her, don't you think?" asked Declan. "She didn't seem like the social media type."

Bindy shook her head. "I didn't think much about it at the time, but now..."

"She just got a divorce," offered Charlotte. "I'm pretty sure she needs money."

Declan dropped the torn photo back into the hidden drawer and shut it with his foot.

"I can't see the Palm Beach Princess needing money bad enough to come here for a couple hundred dollars," he said. "No offense."

Bindy shook her head. "None taken."

"Which makes me think it wasn't about the money," said Charlotte. "That little bit of cash was to make you *think* it was about the money."

"I don't understand," said Bindy.

"Neither do I," admitted Charlotte.

Declan frowned. "Maybe we should *ask* Princess what her relationship with Elke is."

"There's a novel idea," said Charlotte. "Except, if she's our killer, that might tip her off that we know. And if she isn't our killer, it might inspire her to look for Elke."

Declan frowned. "True. Plus, if we show her the locket as proof, and she knows Elke wore it around her neck, that could make for an awkward moment."

Bindy leaned in to murmur in a low tone.

"Speaking of Elke, I assume you, uh, *took her where she was going*?"

Charlotte nodded. "You can lock the freezer."

She nodded. "I'm on it."

The lights flickered, and the three froze, holding their breaths so that they wouldn't lose electricity. When the nearby lamp resumed a steady glow, Charlotte noticed Princess standing at the doorway with an empty glass of champagne. She seemed wobbly on her emerald heels.

Her gaze dropped to the locket in Charlotte's hand.

Charlotte grimaced.

Whoops.

CHAPTER SEVENTEEN

"What's that?" asked Princess, pointing.

Charlotte dropped her gaze from Princess to the locket in her hand. She glanced at Declan, who bobbed one shoulder.

No reason not to ask her now.

"We found this. It kind of looks like you in the photo. Is it yours?" she asked, holding out the locket.

Princess teetered over and took the necklace from her. She seemed pale.

She cracked open the locket, looked at the photo, and thrust it back at Charlotte.

"You think because she's wearing some cheap crown, that's *me*?" she asked, lip sneering.

"I guess not," said Charlotte. "I just thought it looked like you and Elke."

Princess scoffed and tried to take a sip.

"Yeah, well, it's not," she said into the empty glass.

She lowered the flute and turned it upside down to shake it before continuing.

"That looks like some girl that came in *second* in some stupid contest. I'm a *real* princess. That girl is playing make-believe," she muttered.

She swiveled to lock her squinty gaze on Bindy, who had just walked in.

"Where's that champagne guy?" asked Princess.

"Munch? Here, I'll get you more," said Bindy, taking her glass.

Bindy exchanged a look with Charlotte and Declan and walked out. Princess shot them an insincere smile and followed.

"Did you believe her?" asked Charlotte.

Declan shook his head.

"Not particularly."

"*Second* place," mumbled Charlotte.

Declan looked at her. "That seemed oddly specific, didn't it?"

She nodded as voices rose from the parlor. A bright white light glowed in that room.

"What's going on in there?" she asked.

They moved to the next room to find Strella had set up a makeshift recording area. A ring light cast diffused brilliance across her stage makeup. Instead of talking at a phone camera, she sat in front of a large decades-old VHS video camera.

Brendan knelt beside her, fiddling with a television on a roller cart. Charlotte felt sure it hadn't been in the room before.

Strella grinned at the camera.

"I never expected that the one and only Princess Christmas would be—"

She stopped as Charlotte and Declan entered. The smile dropped from her face. She leaned forward to stop the recording.

"Could you *not* interrupt my recording session?" she asked.

"What are you doing?" asked Charlotte.

Strella held out a hand toward the camera.

"Isn't it obvious? Can you get out of my shot, please?"

"You brought an old VHS camera with you?" asked Declan.

She rolled her eyes. "*No.* I found it in one of the rooms upstairs." She grinned at it as if it were a precious child. "Isn't it old school? I might be on to a new trend here."

"I don't understand—what are you filming *for*?" asked Charlotte.

She didn't get how the woman planned to use the material. Was she so desperate to *pretend* she had a phone?

Strella sighed.

"I'm capturing the moment *now*, and when I get my phone back, I'll *video the video*. It's so *meta*, and I won't lose the raw emotion of the moment."

Charlotte blinked at her.

"The *raw emotion* of being at a bed and breakfast?" she asked.

Strella scoffed. "*Yes*. Under these conditions."

"And with a *celebrity*," added Brendan.

Strella side-eyed him and then nodded.

"That too. My followers are going to *freak* over Princess being here."

"How are you going to play it back?" asked Charlotte.

"That's what I'm working on," said Brendan.

Strella flicked her finger in the direction of the television. "There's a machine. Brendan said the square thing goes in the machine."

"The square thing?" asked Declan.

She held up a loose VHS tape.

Charlotte smirked. Strella was younger than her boyfriend—in her twenties. She'd probably never seen a VHS.

As someone who grew up in a retirement community, Charlotte couldn't *imagine* her young life without VHS.

Brendan leaned back to show them that he was hooking a VHS player to the old television.

Charlotte noticed a cardboard box full of VHS tapes and crouched to shuffle through them. She found one that said *Christmas Pagent* and held it up for Declan to see.

He grunted.

"Is that hooked up yet?" she asked Brendan.

He shook his head. "In a second. I think I finally found the right cord."

"He's a genius with old stuff," said Strella.

He flashed her a smile.

Iko entered and watched Brendan work as she sipped what looked like tea.

"Do they have cable? Maybe we can at least get the weather," she suggested.

"I tried. I couldn't get anything but snow on this thing," said Brendan without looking away from his fiddling. "I'm hoping that, at least, it works for the tapes."

Iko moved closer to the ring light.

"What is that?" she asked.

Strella grinned. "It makes your face look *perfect*."

Iko grunted as if impressed.

Charlotte moved to the sofa and slipped the Christmas pageant tape behind the corner pillow and cushion. It didn't look like she'd get access to the VHS soon, but she wanted to look at that tape later. It didn't matter if Strella had control of the television for now. She wasn't sure she wanted everyone to see the tape, and the room was getting more crowded by the second.

"Dinner's ready, everyone!" called Bindy's voice from the other room.

Declan looked at his watch.

"It's only a little after three."

Brendan jumped to his feet.

"This is the best part," he said.

"What are you doing?" Strella asked him.

He motioned toward the dining room near the kitchen.

"Dinner."

"Can't you finish this first so I can see my footage?"

"We'll do it later," he said, walking off.

Strella growled as she stood to follow him.

"*Fine*. I'll finish later. I swear, I don't know why I even came here. This *sucks*." She shrugged, mood brightening. "Though, when my followers see my footage of Princess, I'll get, like, a *billion* likes."

Charlotte shot Declan a bemused look, and the couple followed Strella into the dining room. Charlotte was surprised to find an enormous Christmas dinner spread awaiting them.

"Wow," she said.

Mariska and Darla arrived to ogle the table.

"That turkey is as big as *me*," said Mariska.

"Look at the stuffing. I *love* stuffing," said Darla.

"So here you go, a Christmas feast for everyone, and tomorrow, you can help me eat the leftovers," said Bindy pointing to the table.

"That's my favorite part," said Blade.

"Mine too," said Bindy.

They held each other's gazes.

"We better eat *fast* before they're rolling around on top of it," muttered Darla.

Mariska snorted a laugh.

Princess entered and flopped into a chair at the head of the table. She held up her empty champagne glass, and Munch scurried to fill it.

"This stuff is crap," she said, taking a large sip. "But when in Rome—"

She paused and stared at the table.

"I used to go to Rome," she sighed.

"Someone's hitting it pretty hard," Charlotte whispered to Declan.

He nodded. "Like something upset her."

As the others found seats, Princess scanned the table with tired eyes, her gaze settling on the empty chair at the other head of the table.

"Where's Elke?" she asked.

Bindy cleared her throat.

"She isn't feeling well. She went to her room," she said.

Charlotte watched to see if that news hit anyone as strange, but no one seemed to care.

Princess smirked.

"What's the vegan option?" asked Iko, eyeing the table.

"The what now?" asked Bindy as she sat.

"The *vegan* option? I don't eat meat—"

Bindy tucked her chin and looked at Iko as if she told her she'd never seen the sun.

"Er…there's corn and whipped sweet potatoes?"

"Is there butter in the sweet potatoes or on the corn?"

Bindy scowled. "I don't know. I'll be honest—I didn't cook it. I had a chef prepare everything before you all showed up."

Iko looked horrified.

"What am I supposed to eat?" she asked, her voice strained.

"There's a salad," said Declan, reaching for a giant bowl of greens. He handed it down to her.

"I'm so sorry if I messed up. Did you *ask* for vegan?" asked

Bindy.

Iko huffed. "No. I just *assumed*."

Bindy grew visibly agitated, and Charlotte wondered if she had the *temperament* for dealing with guests.

"Why would you assume we'd have a vegan Christmas dinner?" she asked.

Iko slammed the side of her fists on the table hard enough that the silverware jumped.

"I don't know!"

Everyone froze and stared at her until her shoulder slumped.

"I'm sorry. I'm sorry." She took a deep breath. *"The universe is all-knowing. The universe understands..."*

Bindy sighed.

"I'm sorry, Iko. I'm mad at myself for not thinking about this. Why don't you come into the kitchen with me, and we'll see if we can find something you'd like?" Bindy stood and added, "Er, this would probably be a good time if anyone wants to say grace for themselves. If not, dig in."

"To Elke!" yelped Princess suddenly, holding aloft her glass.

She seemed almost in a panic that the attention of the room had shifted to Iko.

"To Elke," said the others.

Strella didn't hold her glass high, and Princess squinted at her.

"You too, *wannabe*," she sneered.

Strella's eyes widened with what looked like horror.

Her glass shot upward.

"To Elke," she said.

Princess smiled.

CHAPTER EIGHTEEN

After dinner, most people retired to the large sitting room. Iko and Brendan played a board game while Strella filmed herself on the VHS. Though she still appeared ashen after suffering Princess's disdain at the dinner table, she was determined to stick with her video plans.

Charlotte put off watching the Christmas Pagent video. She wished Bindy could organize another game outside so she could view the tape in peace, but the storm continued to rage. The old house creaked with every gust and rattled with every thunderclap.

She couldn't believe they still had electricity.

Even if Strella lost interest in that classic twentieth-century technology, the old television would be too big to cart away and watch somewhere in private. Even if Charlotte enlisted Declan and Blade's help, the cart looked like it was one jiggle away from collapsing.

She didn't think she'd get much sleep with the dolls in the room anyway. Maybe she could sneak downstairs in the middle of the night and take a peek at the tape.

Princess, having had too much to drink, nodded off around eight, curled in a cushioned chair. She took herself to bed when she woke up a little while later. With few distractions to keep them awake, the others wandered upstairs around ten.

That's when the Pineapple Port crew got to work. They'd keep watch over the inn for the evening to make sure the killer didn't sneak into someone's room and claim another victim.

Charlotte, Darla, and Mariska took the first watch. Charlotte guarded the third floor and the ladies the second, stationing themselves on the landing where they could keep an eye on the halls to ensure no one left their room.

At one, they switched places with Declan and Blade.

"I'm here to relieve you," said Declan when he arrived on the landing.

Charlotte looked at her husband, eyes dry and lids heavy.

"I think I might be able to sleep, even *with* the dolls," she said, giving him a hug.

She almost fell asleep, leaning against his chest.

"I survived," he said. "Though the dolls said they were waiting for *you*."

That woke her up. She smacked his arm.

"You are the *worst*," she said as he giggled.

She left him to shuffle to the room. Entering, she stopped to stare back at the eyes looking at her from the corner.

Nope.

She pulled the top cover off the bed and draped it over the dolls.

Better.

She had a nagging feeling she was making the dolls *mad* by covering them, but she shoved that thought aside and collapsed into the bed.

She opened her eyes a few minutes later and glanced at the clock at her bedside.

Five a.m.?

It hadn't been a *few minutes*. She'd *slept*.

Yay.

Charlotte sat up in bed and checked the dolls. They remained covered.

She turned and looked at the closed bedroom door. She didn't feel like she'd fall back to sleep, so she slid out of bed and uncovered the dolls. As she made the bed, she heard the door rattle, and Declan stuck his head inside.

"You're awake?" he asked.

She nodded.

"I checked in on you and saw you had them covered."

"That helped. I was tired enough to fall asleep the first time, but I think I'm done. Too much running around my head."

He grinned. "Great. This is *boring*. Want to hang out here with me?"

She motioned to the pile of scary.

"Or hang with the dolls? Yes, please."

She found herself staring at the pile.

"Did you notice anything interesting about these dolls?" she asked.

He glanced at them. "Where do I start? They're creepy, and they're in Christmas colors—"

"Right, *that*. Do you think they're always in Christmas colors, or did Elke dress them for the season?"

"I'm sure I don't know."

She crossed her arms against her chest.

"I'm wondering because I'm noticing they're also all *princesses*," she said, walking to them.

Each doll had something about it that implied it was a princess. A princess-style dress, crowns—some held scepters.

"Aren't all little-girl dolls princesses?" asked Declan.

She laughed. "I'm not the best person to ask, but I don't think so." She frowned. "I guess Elke collected princesses—but can it be a coincidence that *Princess Christmas* might be related to her, and all the dolls look like Christmas Princesses?"

Declan snapped his tongue against his tooth.

"It does seem unlikely."

She nodded. "Plus, something is clearly up with Princess. She was a train wreck last night. I'd bet good money she knows Elke one way or the other."

"But do you bet she killed her? She still seems our most likely suspect."

"By far," agreed Charlotte. "But I don't know."

She glared down at the dolls, hands on her hips.

"What are you doing? Waiting for them to confess?" he asked.

"Ha, no. I want to inspect them but don't want to touch them."

"Inspect them for what?"

"I don't know. I just feel like there must be something about them we're missing. If you killed Elke, would your first instinct be to put her in the corner of one of the guest rooms and pile dolls on top of her?"

"Ah, *no*—and don't forget Bindy said the dolls weren't even there earlier. It's like someone *planned* to leave her under there. They had to get the dolls out of the attic first."

Charlotte's nose wrinkled. "Ugh, I forgot about that. That makes this even weirder. And why our room?"

He leaned back to glance both ways down the hall and huffed a sigh.

"I don't know. And I can't think of a reason to leave her there, but I wouldn't strangle her either, so what do I know?"

Charlotte was about to comment when she heard a scratching from the doll pile.

She froze.

"Did you hear that?" she whispered.

"What?"

She held up a finger. "Listen..."

The scratching noise happened again.

"Hear it?"

Declan's eyes widened.

"What *is* that?" he asked. "It's in the pile?"

"*Yes*," she hissed.

She motioned to the switch on the wall.

"Turn on the light before I *freak out*."

Declan hit the switch and walked inside to stand beside her.

The scratching started again.

The pile moved. One of the dolls fell sideways.

Charlotte yipped and slapped her hand over her mouth.

Oh no no no...

"It *moved*," she said, pointing.

"I saw."

"Go. *Look*," she urged him, pushing him toward the dolls.

He placed his palm against his chest.

"Me?"

"Yes, *you*. You're the big, strong man."

"Since when do you need me to save you from anything?"

"Since *dolls*," she said.

He rolled his eyes. "It's probably a mouse."

She pressed her lips tight. "Is that supposed to make me feel *better*?"

Declan hovered his hand over the doll in the pile's center—the one that had *moved*.

"Ready—?" he asked.

She shook her head. "Not really."

Before he could snatch the doll, it moved again, popping up toward his fingers.

He whipped away his hand, and Charlotte stumbled back against the bed.

The movement in the pile intensified, and Charlotte was about to lose her mind when a rabbit's nose poked out from between two plastic Princess faces.

Air blasted from her lungs as if she'd been hit in the stomach.

"It's a *rabbit*," she said.

"How did it get back *there*?" asked Declan. "It couldn't have been under there all day."

"It definitely wasn't there when we re-piled the dolls. And aren't they supposed to stay on the first floor?"

"I thought so."

The large black rabbit jumped out of the pile and sent dolls scattering.

Declan knelt beside the pile and pushed away the dolls around the spot where the rabbit had appeared.

He pointed. "There's a *door* in the wall here."

"What?"

Charlotte saw a flap cut into the wall she hadn't noticed before. The dress of one of the dolls had stuck in the door, or she might not have seen it at all. When Declan moved the dress away and the flap fell closed, it lined up so well with the vertical stripes in the wallpaper that it was almost impossible to see the edges.

She dodged the giant rabbit as it hopped by.

"Do we have a flashlight?" she asked.

"Probably in my bag," said Declan.

He rooted through his backpack and came up with a small tactical flashlight. He handed it to her. Using her fingernail to pick open the flap, she shined the beam inside the wall.

"There's a staircase here that goes to the bottom floor," she reported.

"A secret bunny shoot?"

"Ha—maybe servant access they left just big enough for giant rabbits? I assume they didn't make the servants crawl through doggy doors, even back in the eighteen hundreds."

Declan shrugged. "Either that or she had some *really* clever rats living here, who built a whole city in the walls. Is it big enough for a person?"

Charlotte hooked her mouth. "Yes. Maybe not *you*, but I can get through the doorway and work my way down."

She shined the flashlight down the stairs and noticed something. She crawled in and worked her way down to it.

"What are you doing?" called Declan.

"Two seconds—"

The thing was a coffee can full of cigarette butts. As she moved to head back, something sparkled on the stair next to the can, and she picked it up.

It looked like a jewel.

"Finding anything?" called Declan.

She moved to the top stair and stuck her hand through the flap.

"I found this," she said, holding out her palm to show him a small red stone.

"A ruby?"

"Looks fake, but yes."

She put it in her pocket.

She was about to crawl out when she noticed a flash of red against the wall. She turned the flashlight toward it.

A face glowed back at her.

"Holy—"

She fell back, and the flap closed.

"What's wrong?" asked Declan.

Feeling silly, she held up a finger and picked open the door again to shine the light inside. Grimacing, she grabbed the doll and pulled it into the room.

"Another doll," she said, holding it up for him to see. "It scared the bejeezus out of me."

She brushed years of dust off the toy. Even though it was infinitely dirtier, it seemed fancier than the others in the pile. The crown was more prominent and had an oversized fake diamond in the center. The doll held a red and green scepter as large as a pencil. Across her body, she wore a sash that had wrinkled during its time in the bunny run. She smoothed it out to read it.

Princess Christmas.

She sucked in a breath.

"These dolls have to be Princess's," she said, showing Declan the sash. "She's *got* to be Elke's daughter."

Declan bobbed his head toward the open bedroom door.

"Elke's room is across the hall. Now would be a great time to poke around and find out."

Charlotte nodded.

"I'll get my lockpicks."

CHAPTER NINETEEN

"Why did you bring lockpicks?" asked Declan.

Charlotte shrugged. "I still have them in the suitcase from the honeymoon."

"Do you think anyone else brings lockpicks on their honeymoon?"

She laughed as she started on the lock.

"*No.*"

The lock popped open a few seconds later.

It wasn't a hard one.

They slipped inside Elke's small room to find it half the size of theirs. Declan quietly shut the door behind them.

"Looks like Bindy downsized her to get her out of here," he said, eyeing the largely empty space.

Charlotte agreed. The room didn't look personalized enough to be the one Elke had spent the last fifty years in.

Declan hit the lights and headed for the small closet. Charlotte moved to the bedstand and slid open the only drawer. Inside, she found the usual things someone might keep next to their bed—a package of dental floss, a jar of aspirin, tissues, a few pens, and a lined notebook.

She picked up the notebook and leafed through it to find it full of shopping lists and promotion ideas. She was about to return it when she noticed a page that looked more like a letter than a list.

"Look at this," she said. "She's asking someone for money."

Declan joined her, reading silently over her shoulder.

> *I know that we haven't been close in a long time and that you're embarrassed by me, but I need your help. If I don't find some money soon, I am going to have to sell the inn. I know you don't want our family legacy to die this way. Or do you? I feel like I don't know you anymore.*

The page appeared to be a draft. Scribbles and cross-outs ran throughout the text. Elke had clearly had trouble finding the right words.

"Looks like she was second-guessing how accusatory to be," said Charlotte.

Declan nodded. "Calling people names isn't usually the best way to get money out of them. Who was she writing to? Any names?"

"No. Sounds like family, though, if we take that line about the *family legacy* at face value."

"Probably Princess."

Charlotte nodded. "She's my best guess."

She turned the page, looking for more. Toward the back of the book, she found a Palm Beach address.

"Ah ha!" she said, a little louder than she meant to.

"Shh," said Declan, holding his finger to his lips with one hand and hooking a thumb toward the room next door. "You'll wake up Bindy."

"Sorry. Look." She held up the book for him to see. "This has to be Princess's address. Palm Beach?"

He nodded. "It *has* to be, right? I'd love to look it up, but, you know—*no phone.*"

"*So* annoying," agreed Charlotte. "I get the unplugging thing, but sometimes the Internet comes in *really handy.*"

"We're going to have to talk to Princess again. Maybe try to get her alone tomorrow. See if we can get her to open up."

"And *confess*," added Charlotte.

"That would be nice."

She lowered the book, scowling.

Declan eyed her.

"What are you thinking, Crazy Pants? You've got that look."

She chuckled. "Nothing *too* crazy. What time is it?"

Declan looked at his watch.

"Five thirty, more or less."

"Do you think it's too early to talk to her *now*?"

His brow knitted. "Princess?"

"Yes. I mean, if we knock on her door now, at least, we know she's alone. It might be the perfect time to talk to her. Especially since she's probably hung over—she might not have the energy to lie to us."

"She might also try to kill us."

Charlotte nodded. "*True*, but we can give it a shot?"

He shrugged. "What the heck. Why not? Worst case, she hates us forever for waking her up."

"I can live with that."

Charlotte put the notebook back in Elke's drawer, and they walked to the other end of the hall.

"She's in this room, right?" asked Charlotte, pointing to the door when they arrived.

Declan nodded. "I saw her come out of there to use the hall bathroom while I was on guard, pretending I wasn't on guard."

Charlotte grimaced.

"Here goes nothing."

She rapped lightly on the door, and they waited.

Nothing happened.

She looked at Declan and tried again, knocking a little louder this time.

Still no answer.

"Could she have gotten out?"

He winced. "When we were dealing with the rabbit door?"

Charlotte grabbed the knob and twisted it slowly.

Locked.

"I'm going to pick it," she announced, reaching for the pick still in her pocket.

Declan nodded his agreement. "Go for it. It's not like she can call the police on us."

"We should be so lucky."

"She's got to be in there. She might be a hard sleeper."

Charlotte snorted a laugh. "Particularly after last night."

She pulled the picks from her pocket to get to work. The lock popped, and she eased open the door.

The room was dark, and Charlotte paused to let her eyes adjust. She didn't want to throw on the lights and give the poor woman a heart attack.

"Princess?" she called.

She took a step inside and saw the bed was empty.

"She's not here," she said.

Declan turned on the lights, and she looked over the bedsheets, hoping for no evidence of foul play.

She didn't see anything sketchy.

She dropped to the ground to look under the bed while Declan checked the closet.

"Not in here," he reported.

"Nothing under here. Not even dust bunnies. Pretty impressive, really."

Charlotte noticed something familiar about the wall near the baseboard. She crawled closer and realized she'd found another secret panel.

It lifted, the same as the one in their room.

"Another staircase," she reported, opening the flap. "Do you think she got out this way?"

"That means she knew about the staircases—like family *would*."

Charlotte frowned.

"This isn't good. Where did she go? Did she leave to go after someone, or is this how someone got in and grabbed *her*?"

She sat back and slid her feet through the flap.

"What are you doing?" asked Declan, alarmed.

"I'm going to see where this leads. Maybe she hasn't been gone long, and we can catch her."

She glanced over his shoulder to find him standing with his hand on his head. She'd seen the look on his face before. He was weighing the pros and cons of arguing with her.

His shoulders slumped, and she knew he'd decided *not* to dissuade her from her plan.

She smiled.

His training is going so well.

"What do you want me to do?" he asked.

"Go downstairs and wait for me wherever this one lets out. I'm going to guess the kitchen? On your way down, double-check with Blade that no one has been on his level."

He nodded. "Fine. Be careful."

She grinned.

"*Always.*"

CHAPTER TWENTY

Pineapple Port

Following the sleepwalker excitement, Frank, Seamus, and Bob resumed their spots in the impromptu nativity scene at Bob's house. They discussed the highs and lows of the current National Football League season, the price of grass seed, and the *(insert expletive)* traffic during tourist season.

They'd started a deep discussion about hernias when Frank noticed headlights headed their way.

"Hey, here comes a car," he said, leaning for a better look.

The three of them froze as the car rolled up the street, moving slowly.

Too slowly.

"Something's up with this boyo," said Seamus from the corner of his mouth as the car paused in front of Frank's house.

"What was that? Why did it stop in front of my house?" asked Frank.

He frowned as the car rolled forward again.

"Get ready."

They held their nativity scene poses as the car pulled up to park in front of Bob's house.

"This is it," whispered Bob.

Frank didn't think the man in the car could see them very well. Only a smiley-face sliver of a moon hung in the sky, and the makeshift barn front under which they sat blocked the lights from the house. They didn't need to be *perfectly* still—which was good because Frank saw Bob swaying, and the whiskey bottle was sticking out of the manger.

A man exited the running car and started up Bob's driveway toward where they'd set up the drawer-dropping Santa.

"Wait—" said Seamus, tensing, readying to attack.

Bob wasn't listening.

"Freeze, sucker!" screamed Bob, jumping to his feet. As he stood, he forgot about the roof of the barn front, and he bashed his skull into the frame.

He dropped as fast as he'd risen.

Oblivious to Bob's distress, Seamus burst into a sprint and made a diving tackle—driving the flailing visitor off the other side of the driveway and landing on top of him on the grass.

The man wailed as they hit the ground.

Frank hadn't gotten further than his feet. He stood as little discs flew into the air around him like an attacking squadron of UFOs. He heard what sounded like a plate shattering against the cement.

"I got him!" called Seamus.

"Get off of me!" said another voice.

Frank snapped from his shock.

"Hold it there," he said, striding over to the men on the ground. By the house's porch light, he saw broken cookies scattered across the driveway, a smashed plate, and Seamus pinning Jenny Teacup's husband, Pete, to the ground.

Pete stared up at him, his eyes wide.

"Frank, what is this?" he asked.

Frank scowled. "*You?* You're the one stealing decorations?"

"*Stealing decorations?*" said Pete, his face red and spittle flying. "We're the ones who were *robbed,* for crying out loud."

Frank tapped Seamus's back.

"Let him up before he has a heart attack," he said.

Seamus stepped back, bouncing on his toes, looking ready to chase after the man if he made a break for it.

Frank held out a hand and helped Pete to his feet.

"What are you doing here?" he asked.

Pete brushed off his pants.

"Jenny asked me to bring you these cookies as a thanks for your help this afternoon."

"Cookies?"

"*Yes.* I was going to leave them at *your* house, but it was dark, so I thought I'd bring them to Bob so the animals didn't get them. His lights are on."

"Oh," said Frank.

That made sense.

Pete glared at Seamus. "All I got for my trouble was *skinned elbows.*"

"Sorry about that," said Seamus, though he didn't sound particularly sorry.

He looked ready to get back into the huddle and find out who the quarterback wanted him to smash next.

Frank turned to find Bob arriving on the scene, holding his hand on his head and staring with dismay at the cookies scattered across his driveway.

"Were they peanut butter?" asked Bob.

"Yes," said Pete.

Bob moaned and bent to grab one of the bigger pieces.

"They're still okay," he said, inspecting it before he put it in his mouth.

Frank's lip curled. "They're going to have plate shards in them, Bob."

Bob waved him off. "Little stomach bleeding never killed anyone." He held up half a cookie. "You want one? I brushed it off. Half of these are yours."

"*No,*" said Frank.

"I'll take one," said Seamus. "Let's take the rest to the manger."

Bob handed him a good-sized chunk, and he popped it into his mouth before smacking Frank on the arm.

"Wrap it up. We have to get back into place."

Frank gritted his teeth but returned his focus to Pete while the other two gathered a selection of cookie chunks.

"Are you okay?" he asked.

Pete nodded. "I'm fine, but what are you crazy people doing?

Why are you dressed like a—" He scowled as he eyed Frank's costume. "—what *are* you dressed like?"

"I'm a wise man."

Pete grunted. "Sure. Should I ask why?"

"We're running a stakeout to catch the decoration thief."

Pete blinked at him and then shrugged.

"Well, I admire your dedication." He glanced at the driveway. "You owe Jenny a plate."

Frank nodded as Pete returned to his car and drove off.

He returned to the nativity scene, where he flopped down in his spot.

"I don't know about you guys, but I don't feel like this is going well," he said.

Bob shrugged.

"Free cookies."

CHAPTER TWENTY-ONE

The Outback Inn

Declan checked the hall bath to ensure Princess wasn't there and then jogged to Blade's floor, second-guessing himself with every step. He shouldn't have let Charlotte go down the secret staircase by herself.

He rolled his eyes.

Like I've ever been able to stop her once she got an idea into her head.

She *had* made a good point—they did need to know where the passage let out, and he was too big to fit in the spot, so...

He hit the second landing and found Blade watching over the level, perched on the small sofa where they'd sat with dead Elke earlier. The big man stood when he spotted Declan.

"Everything okay?" he asked.

Declan shook his head. "Princess isn't in her room, and Charlotte went through a secret staircase in the wall. Did you see anyone moving on this level?"

Blade stalled as he processed Declan's information and shook his head.

"I haven't seen anyone. What do you want me to do?" he asked.

Declan pointed down the hall.

"First room in. That's where the staircase is. Stand outside there and keep your ears open. If you hear anything like Charlotte calling for help, do whatever you need to do. The wall access will be on the right, near the baseboard in that room. It's a flap big enough for an enormous rabbit or my wife to fit through."

Blade nodded. "On it."

He stationed himself in front of the room, and Declan trotted to ground level. He checked the front door for signs of someone coming or going. It didn't seem anyone had. He heard rain steadily falling, and no wet footprints were inside the house. Intruders would have been hard-pressed to sneak inside without getting the floor wet.

He turned and took a moment to get his bearings.

The kitchen.

Charlotte was right. That had to be where the hidden stairs let out.

He strode in that direction.

"Charlotte?" he called as he moved.

No response. He didn't hear anything. He gritted his teeth.

She should have reached ground level by now.

He entered the kitchen and turned to the wall to find the hidden door. Instead, he found himself staring at an oven.

Something banged against the wall, and the oven shuddered.

"Charlotte?"

"The door is stuck," came her muffled response from inside the wall.

"Hold on, I'm coming," he called back.

He frowned. Princess didn't come that way if the exit sat behind a stove.

That answered *that* question but begged others. Namely—how did she get out of her room while he was on guard? It would be incredible luck for her to run out of her room and straight down the stairs while he was inspecting Charlotte's rabbit invasion. On top of that, Blade would have had to miss her, too.

Unlikely, but possible.

"Hello?" called Charlotte's voice again.

He returned to his oven problem.

"Sorry—two seconds."

He bent to put his weight against the stove and noticed

scratches on the wooden floor at his feet. Linear scratches that lined up with the oven's feet.

Someone had shifted the oven before—*in front of the staircase door.*

That meant it was possible Princess had come that way and then shifted the oven over the door afterward—

"Take your time," called Charlotte. "It's *totally* easy to breathe in here."

He pushed the oven back to its original position.

"You're clear," he called.

Charlotte's foot popped through the swinging section of wall, followed by the other. The door was identical in size and shape to the one in their room. He had no idea why someone would turn servant access doors into rabbit doors, but people were strange. Little surprised him these days.

He bent to assist Charlotte as she shimmied through, pulling her by her feet once she'd gotten as far as her thighs.

When the makeshift door released, it swung both ways like a saloon door—perfect for rabbit access.

"Careful, you'll clip my nose off," she said as he slid her out.

She sneezed.

"Dusty in there?"

"Dark, cramped, *and* dusty. It's the trifecta," she said, turning off the flashlight. "But it's not as dusty as it should have been."

"What does that mean?"

"Footprints. There were bare footprints in the dust. It was hard to see them at first because it looked like the rabbits were exploring recently, too, but there were a couple of spots where the tracks were less rabbit and more human bare feet."

Declan nodded. "So she *did* come that way."

"Good chance. The size of the footprints would fit Princess just fine."

"Did you see anything else?" he asked, helping her up.

She sneezed again.

"Some old candy wrappers and an old can that looked like it had been there for decades. It was full of cigarette butts."

"Like someone had been sneaking them in the hidden

staircase? A teenage girl, maybe?"

She nodded. "That's what I was thinking."

"I have something interesting to report, too," he said. "Whoever came through there pushed the stove in front of the door once they got out."

"That's why I couldn't get out?"

"Yep."

"Like they didn't want anyone to find the door?"

"That's what I'm guessing. Do you remember where the stove was when we brought Elke in?"

She shook her head.

"No. Stuffing a dead body into the freezer had my attention."

He nodded. "Mine too. Bindy might be able to tell us. Then we'd know if Princess came through and then shifted the oven or if the oven always sits in front of the door."

"Does it matter?"

He shrugged. "If she shifted it before bed, it shows forethought. It means she always meant to sneak out. "

Charlotte chuckled. "It's hard to imagine her with *forethought* last night, but I guess anything is possible."

Outside, the storm howled, and Declan frowned.

"We've got to find her. She *has* to be in the house. She wouldn't go out in a storm like this. Why would anyone?"

Charlotte shrugged. "To beat a murder rap?"

Declan laughed. "*A murder rap.* Listen to you. You sound like some grizzled old gumshoe."

She giggled.

Declan put his hands on his hips and hung his head in thought.

"If she killed Elke and then ran out in the middle of a storm with no phone and no car, she'd look *incredibly* guilty."

"You mean once we tell the cops, and she's the only one missing."

"Exactly. She'd have to keep running forever, and somehow, I don't think Princess Christmas of Palm Beach is ready to live in obscurity."

Charlotte nodded. "No. Even if she reinvented herself, it couldn't last long. One video post and people would notice her resemblance to her former famous self."

Declan walked to the freezer to check that Bindy had added the padlock. It hung there, as promised. No one would stumble on the body, so that was one less thing to worry about.

"If she planned to move Elke, it looks like she didn't get in."

Charlotte nodded. "That's something, I guess. Let's make a sweep of the first floor."

They split around the center stairs, moving from room to room, checking every spot big enough to hide a person. Like the foyer, the area near the back door was dry. While it was hard to see through the driving rain, Declan didn't see any evidence that anyone had gone outside onto the porch or into the muddy yard.

He met Charlotte halfway around in the sitting room.

"Nothing," he reported as he entered.

She raised her finger to her lips and motioned to a sofa where Munch lay sleeping with a blanket over him.

"I guess it was too stormy to go to his room above the barn," she whispered as they headed back through the library.

"See anything besides Munch?" asked Declan.

"No. Did you check the rabbit hutch?"

He shook his head. "*No*, but that's a good idea. Maybe someone went in there, spooked them, and that's why one was trying to snuggle up with you."

Charlotte scoffed. "It can't be because I'm *snuggly*?"

"That too. Naturally."

They checked the hutch but found nothing except three munching rabbits. The fourth was either still in their room or somewhere on the stairs in between.

"I thought we were on to something there for a second," said Charlotte.

They heard footsteps and turned to see Mariska approaching, rubbing at her sleepy eyes. She wore a long-sleeve tee shirt with a kitten on the front that said *Walter Mitty the Skinny Kitty*. Charlotte had no idea what that meant, but she knew better than to ask.

"You're up," said Mariska. "Is there coffee?"

"We've got bigger things to worry about than fresh coffee," said Charlotte.

"Not as far as she's concerned," said Darla, appearing behind Mariska. She wore a short-sleeved tee shirt with a rollerskating bunny and otter on the front that said, *This Bun...and the Otter One.*

This made more sense than Mariska's shirt—but not much.

Charlotte glanced at Declan, and he gave her a look that said, *this is all you.*

Mariska squinted at her.

"Did you wear that yesterday?" she asked, wrinkling her nose.

Charlotte looked down at her shirt. "Yes. I slept in my clothes."

"Why?"

"Because there might be a *killer* roaming the halls. Somehow, getting comfy didn't seem like a high priority."

Darla nodded. "Good thinking. Girls always get killed in their jammies in the movies."

Charlotte sighed.

"Listen—We need your help. We'll wake up Bindy, but we need everyone else awake ASAP, too."

"You want us to knock on doors?" asked Darla.

"Without *coffee?*" asked Mariska.

"*Yes.* Knock on doors. I don't care if they actually get *up*—I just need to know if anyone is missing."

"*Missing?*" echoed Mariska.

"Princess wasn't in her room. We don't know where she is. We need to find her, and we need to know if anyone else is missing."

Mariska yawned. "Okay, just as soon as I get my coffee—"

Charlotte shook her head. "*Now*, Mariska. Someone could be getting *murdered* as we speak."

Mariska frowned. "Oh. *Fine.*"

She turned and bumped into Darla, who had her eyes closed while cracking her neck side to side.

"Watch it," muttered Darla, catching herself against the wall.

Mariska shoved her back toward the stairs as Darla slapped at her to stop the manhandling.

"We have to go wake everyone up," hissed Mariska.

"I'm *going*," snapped Darla.

"You can skip the third floor," Charlotte called after them as they slap-fought their way to the stairs.

"They really need coffee," noted Declan.

She nodded.

"I'll go to the third floor and talk to Bindy. You relieve Blade."

Declan nodded. "You know, you could have let them get their coffee. I could have easily knocked on the second-floor doors."

Charlotte shook her head.

"It's better to give them busywork. *Believe me.*"

CHAPTER TWENTY-TWO

Charlotte and Declan trudged up the stairs to the second landing, where Blade stood at the window watching the storm. He heard them coming and turned as they arrived at the top of the stairs.

"You're okay?" said Blade to Charlotte. "You were in the wall?"

"You were *what*?" asked Darla from the hall, her fist hovering, ready to knock on a guest's bedroom door.

Charlotte held up a hand to stop the questions. She needed to get to Bindy.

"Long story. I'll let Declan tell you," she said.

She avoided Declan's eyes and jogged up the stairs. She knocked on Bindy's door, and the innkeeper answered, looking showered and dressed, her usually spikey hair flat on her head.

"I was just coming down," she said. "I need to get breakfast on. I overslept."

Charlotte realized how hungry she was and tried not to think about it.

"We've got a problem. Princess is missing."

Bindy straightened. "*Missing*? You mean you think she left? I'm not surprised—"

This struck Charlotte as odd.

"You're *not*?"

Bindy frowned.

"I mean because she obviously hated it here, but you're right—

to leave in this storm..." She hooked her mouth to the right. "She doesn't seem like the trudging through the mud type, does she?"

"No. That wouldn't be very *princessy*," agreed Charlotte. "Do you know about the hidden staircases in the walls?"

Bindy barked a laugh. "As of *yesterday*. Brendan told me."

Charlotte hadn't expected that answer.

"*Brendan*?" she echoed.

"Yeah—he interviewed Elke for his book, so I guess he got the info from her. He's been peppering me with trivia about the house and the area. I'm going to have to hire him to write my website."

Charlotte nodded. Now, they had three people who knew about the staircases—Princess, Bindy, and Brendan.

"What about Munch? Does *he* know about the staircases?"

"I suppose he does. He's been here forever."

Bindy leaned into her room to grab a squirt of mousse for her hair as Charlotte grimaced. That made four people who knew, and maybe that wasn't all.

"This is sort of an odd question, but was anyone in the room with you when Brendan told you about the staircases?"

Bindy scratched at her chin.

"*Yes*. Strella was with him. Oh, and Iko was on the sofa having a meltdown over some orange juice she'd sloshed on the cushion. I practically had to hug her to get her to calm down."

Charlotte chuckled.

"She's a little high-strung."

Bindy grinned. "Ya think? Anyway, that's everyone, I think."

Charlotte sighed.

That means everyone knew about the stairs.

Her group were the only people who *hadn't* known about them.

"Why are you so curious about those stairs?" asked Bindy.

"We think Princess might have used them to sneak out of her room last night."

Bindy scowled. "Wait—you think she used the staircase in the *wall*? How did she get to it? I assumed they were closed up."

"They're not. There are flaps hidden in the walls."

Bindy gaped. "*Flaps*? How did I not see them?"

"They're camouflaged pretty well. We had a rabbit come into

the room. That's how we knew about it."

"A *rabbit*?" Bindy slapped her hand to her head. "You are blowing my mind. That explains how those little buggers keep showing up upstairs. I thought they were hopping up the main stairs but never caught them doing it. I was starting to worry about things just appearing around here—rabbits, dolls—"

Charlotte nodded. "Speaking of dolls, we found one hidden in the wall called *Princess Christmas*—"

"*Another* doll?" Bindy shook her head. "I'm tellin' ya. As soon as this rain lets up, I'm taking all those dolls to the nearest Kindergarten—or incinerator."

"Sounds like a plan to me," muttered Charlotte.

Bindy stepped into the hall and closed her door.

"But wait, you said this one was called *Princess Christmas*? Like Princess herself?"

"That's what the sash said."

"Is it her doll? Did she bring it with her and leave it in the wall? Is that why you think she went that way?"

"No, it was covered in dust. It's been there a long time."

Bindy pulled her hand down her face.

"This is too much. We might have to start from the beginning. What exactly makes you think Princess is *missing*? You're saying you looked *everywhere,* and she's *nowhere*?"

"She's not in her room or any of the common areas. We're knocking on doors now. That's why I'm up here, to clear this floor."

Bindy's mouth rounded into a perfect O.

"*Ooooh.* I get it. You're thinking if she ran away in the middle of the night."

Charlotte nodded. "That's what we're thinking. We found a letter Elke wrote to a family member, begging for money to save this place."

Bindy poked at the ground.

"Save *this* place? How long ago? Is that why she was jerking me around on the signatures?"

"I don't know. It was a draft in a journal—it could be old, but we also found a Palm Beach address, which made us think she might have been writing to Princess."

Bindy's teeth gritted.

"Princess was here to stop the sale?"

"I don't know."

Bindy's expression pinched as if she were thinking.

"Maybe that's why she finally gave me the paperwork—because Princess said *no*," she said. "Though I don't know why Princess would come all the way here just to say *no*."

"Me neither, but there's a lot of evidence piling up that those two have a history. We have a locket with a picture of Elke and a girl who looks like Princess. I heard them arguing—though I can't tell you what it was about. Princess knew about the staircases as if she'd been here before."

"So, you think that Princess killed Elke?"

"I don't know for sure, but I *do* think she's Elke's daughter or *some* relation."

Bindy sighed. "I guess it's possible. I'm starting to think you'd need a dump truck to carry everything I don't know about this place."

"Who else is on this floor?" asked Charlotte.

Bindy pointed to the rooms as she went through the list.

"Your whole group, me, Princess, and Elke. The other rooms are full of Elke's things or in the process of being redone."

"Okay, then this floor is cleared of *people*. Let's check the empty rooms. If Princess knows her way around this place, she might have gone into one of those."

Bindy nodded. "I'll go get the keys—"

"You don't have to. I have something that will work," said Charlotte, pulling the lockpicks from her pocket.

Bindy's eyes widened. "Look at you."

They moved to the handful of other rooms and popped the locks one after the next. Princess wasn't hiding in any of them. Two of the three were chock full of junk, and one was empty and freshly painted. Charlotte noticed the last junk-filled room had a few square feet of space that seemed less dusty than the rest of the floor and pointed to it.

"Do you know what was here?" she asked.

Bindy considered the spot and shook her head.

"Something Elke already threw out, I guess."

Charlotte nodded. That made sense. All that mattered now was Princess. If she was still in the house, she wasn't on the third floor.

There remained a last, thinner door with no lock. Charlotte assumed it was a closet but opened it to discover steep stairs leading up.

"This goes to the attic?" she asked, though the answer seemed obvious.

Bindy nodded. "Do you want to check up there?"

"Not really," said Charlotte with a thin smile. "But I suppose we should. In theory, it wouldn't be a bad hiding spot to wait out the storm."

"Doesn't hurt to look," agreed Bindy, starting up the steep stairs.

Charlotte followed, turning her feet sideways to crab up the skinny stairs.

Thanks to the twenty-foot turret they'd seen from the outside, the attic felt airier than any other spot in the house. Charlotte's attention shot up as lightning lit the room.

Bindy flipped on a light, and the rest of the attic appeared.

"That's better," she said.

Piles of junk and furniture filled the sprawling space. Boxes marked as decorations for every holiday lined one wall. Charlotte spotted footprints in the dust leading toward a large chest.

Bindy noticed her attention.

"That's where I put the dolls. I left them in trash bags on that chest," she explained.

Charlotte made a note to look for the trash bags. Whoever re-piled the dolls in her room had to have done *something* with the bags eventually.

She returned her focus to the dusty floor.

"That means some of these footprints belong to the person who brought them down," she said, crouching to take a better look.

The dust wasn't deep, and the footprints weren't clean. She couldn't make out anything useful, though she could tell both Bindy and the other visitor had been wearing shoes. She didn't see the familiar toe pattern of bare feet that she'd seen on the hidden stairs.

She sneezed and noticed some of the footprints veering to another path. Someone had shuffled their feet, perhaps to hide the size and shape of their shoes, but they couldn't avoid disturbing the dust. The new path led to an open, empty paper box. Next to it sat a lid with an oval of see-through plastic in its center. Writing curved around the top—*Wedding Preservation Box.*

"The wedding gown from here is missing," she said.

Bindy peered down at the box.

"I don't know anything about that. I don't remember seeing a wedding gown, but I didn't spend much time in here."

Charlotte ran her fingers along the inside of the box. It felt clean. It hadn't been lying open like that for long.

"Someone came up here to get those dolls and take a wedding gown?" she said, mostly to herself.

Bindy shrugged. "I dunno. I only know I came up here to get rid of those dolls. They were *everywhere*, and I didn't want to be *that* bed and breakfast, y'know?"

Charlotte nodded.

She knew. She still couldn't believe she ended up with a worst-case doll scenario despite Bindy's best efforts to *avoid* being cliché. Now, she had a missing wedding gown somewhere—maybe some Mrs. Haversham situation brewing.

Nah.

Not creepy *at all.*

CHAPTER TWENTY-THREE

Bindy closed the attic door, and they took the main stairs to the second floor to find Declan and Blade waiting for them on the landing.

"Where are Darla and Mariska?" asked Charlotte.

"They went downstairs to make coffee," said Blade.

Bindy groaned.

"*Ugh*, I'm so behind. Excuse me."

She headed down the stairs.

"How'd it go?" asked Declan.

Charlotte shrugged. "We checked all the rooms and the attic. Everything seems pretty normal except for a missing wedding gown," reported Charlotte.

Declan scowled. "A wedding gown?"

"There's an empty box in the attic. You haven't seen a wedding gown floating around anywhere, have you? Maybe on a ghost or a skeleton?"

Declan smirked. "Ah, *no*."

"How about the guests on this floor? Everyone good?"

He nodded. "We're missing Strella, but Brendan said she already went downstairs. Everyone else is accounted for."

"Was Strella with him when he woke up?" she asked as they headed downstairs.

"Yes. I asked, though he looked at me like I was crazy. No one saw Princess either."

Charlotte frowned. She still found it hard to believe Princess went out in the storm, but then, desperate people did desperate things.

"What about Bindy? Anything new with her?" asked Declan.

Charlotte shook her head. "I can tell you she knew about the hidden stairs, but it turns out everyone does. While sharing the house's history, Brendan told everyone about them."

"Except us?" asked Blade.

She nodded. "None of us were there at that point. I guess that's when we were on our way to the freezer."

He grunted at the memory.

When they hit the lower level, Charlotte left the boys to make a loop around the downstairs and found Strella back in the parlor with the VHS. She had one of the tapes she'd recorded playing. Charlotte stopped to watch Strella talk about her stay at the inn in less than glowing terms.

She looked behind her, happy to find Bindy wasn't watching.

At least she could check Strella off her list. Everyone was officially accounted for except Princess.

Declan entered to watch Strella on television and side-eyed Charlotte.

"I see you found her," he muttered.

She nodded. "Which is good because, in a perfect world, I'd like to keep dead and missing people to one a day if possible," she murmured back to him.

Charlotte eyed the sofa pillow behind which she'd hidden the Christmas pageant tape. It didn't seem like Strella would ever stop watching herself. There wasn't anything else to distract her with, either.

With Princess missing, she decided she couldn't wait any longer to view that tape.

"Would you mind if I played a tape on there?" asked Charlotte.

Strella scowled at her as she popped her latest tape out.

"Now?"

Charlotte nodded. "It won't take long."

Strella huffed.

"I guess. Go ahead. I think I'm done messing with this thing. I can't believe people used to use these things to *post.*"

Charlotte's brow furrowed.

"They didn't use them to *post—*"

Strella blinked at her, and Charlotte decided to drop it.

Never mind.

While Strella tucked away her own tape for safekeeping, Charlotte reached behind the pillow to grab the hidden tape and popped it into the machine.

The images sputtered to life, starting at such an awkward moment that Charlotte checked to make sure it couldn't rewind a little more.

It couldn't.

The person holding the camera had left it on while walking through a crowd. Jiggling legs and wobbling floor filled the first minute.

"Wow, did this one win an Oscar? Very artsy," teased Strella.

Finally, the camera angle raised to focus on what looked like a school auditorium stage. Six smiling girls in their late teens stood posed in red and green princess-like dresses.

The camera panned up to a large banner announcing the reason for the event: *The Princess Christmas Pagent.*

"Princess Christmas... like... *Princess*?" asked Strella, suddenly interested.

A mustachioed man in a tuxedo stood at the corner of the stage, speaking into a microphone. His voice was faint, and Charlotte leaned to turn up the television.

"In third place..."

A drumroll started—Charlotte couldn't tell if it was a recording or if a drummer stood somewhere off-stage and out of frame. The drumming stuttered and then picked up again, wildly off-beat.

That answered that question.

"Deena Perez!"

The camera bobbled as the person holding it attempted to film and clap simultaneously. Charlotte noted the camera operator's long red nails and thin fingers.

Definitely a woman.

Darla and Mariska wandered in.

"Whatcha watching?" asked Mariska.

"Do we have cable now?" asked Darla.

Charlotte paused the film and shook her head.

"It's from a box of old VHS tapes Strella found."

"Real riveting stuff," said Strella.

"Oh, hit play, this is adorable," said Mariska.

Charlotte did.

On the blurry screen, one of the girls in a red dress with green lace trim stepped forward to accept a small bouquet and an equally small trophy from a woman, who moved in from offscreen.

The girl returned to her place in line with a frozen smile on her face.

The announcer continued.

"In second place, Lina Zeitz!"

Mariska perked. "Zeitz? Wasn't Zeitz the name on all the gravestones out back?"

Darla nodded. "It was."

No one stepped forward, but Charlotte heard the person holding the camera cheering louder.

"Yay, Lina!"

The announcer looked annoyed. He turned to look at the line of girls.

"Come get your crown, *Lina*," he growled.

Apparently, he'd forgotten a microphone can pick up voices speaking through gritted teeth.

The camera zoomed in on the face of a girl. She had her lips pressed tight and eyes squinted down to tiny, angry holes.

"Uh-oh. That one is *not* happy," said Strella.

"That's the girl from the locket," said Declan.

Charlotte agreed. "I think the person holding the camera is Elke."

"Come get your crown," urged the announcer again.

The girl shook her head.

"I don't *want* that crown," she said.

"But you won—"

"I didn't *win*." The girl yelled the words at the announcer, her hands curling into fists. "I don't want that *little* crown. I want the *big* one."

She sprinted forward and snatched a larger crown from a pillow near the announcer.

"Hey!" he screamed, trying to grab her.

She dodged away as a pair of ladies jumped on stage and all but tackled her. They wrestled, tugging at the crown in her hands as she thrashed.

"I won. *I'm* the princess!" she screeched.

Strella covered her mouth with her hand, laughing.

"Wow, that girl is a *really* sore loser. This is *hilarious*," she said.

One of the ladies tumbled back with the crown in her hand as Lina lost her grip. The girl lunged after it, only to be blocked by the other woman who jerked the sleeve of her gown. Lina twisted, and the fabric tore away.

Free again, she ran to the edge of the stage and stared directly at the camera.

"This is *your* fault. This is because you won't let them *fix me*."

She pointed at a large brown splotch on her forehead. It looked like the half-moon of an irregular-shaped chocolate chip cookie. The other half disappeared into her hairline.

"Birthmark," mumbled Charlotte.

Near the girl, a young man about her age struggled to climb onto the stage.

"*Lina—*" he called to her.

He flopped like a landed fish onto the stage and clambered to his feet to stumble toward Lina. He grabbed her arm, but she yanked it away from him.

"Get away from me, *Owen*," she snapped. The announcer grabbed the young man and pulled him out of frame.

"Lina, *no*," screamed the woman holding the camera. As she lowered the lens, it twisted, and the group in the parlor caught a brief glimpse of the woman holding it.

"That's definitely a young Elke," said Charlotte.

Declan nodded. "Sure looks like her. Looks like the woman in the photo, too."

"And the locket," agreed Charlotte.

"Elke knew Princess when she was little?" asked Strella, brow furrowed. "Where are they, anyway?"

"They're under the weather," said Charlotte.

"Oh." Strella's nose wrinkled. "I hope they don't get us all sick."

Declan leaned to speak softly in Charlotte's ear.

"I'm sure we don't have what Elke has," he murmured.

She elbowed him.

On the television screen, the camera turned back to the stage just as Charlotte hit pause. The movie froze on a tight shot of the girl, her birthmark in full view.

"Princess doesn't have a birthmark," whispered Declan.

Charlotte shook her head.

"No, but those things can be removed."

She sniffed as the smell of bacon wafted into the room. She saw Munch in the dining room setting the table.

Bindy had started cooking.

"This inspired me. I need to do another," said Strella, popping out the pageant video.

Charlotte reached for it and then let Strella put it aside. She'd seen all she needed to see.

Princess Daria Dalca, direct descendant of Prince Nicholas of Romania, AKA *Princess Christmas*—was actually Lina Zeitz of Middle of Nowhere, Florida.

They needed to find her.

Right after breakfast.

CHAPTER TWENTY-FOUR

Blade followed his nose into the kitchen to find Bindy and Munch making breakfast.

"That smells like heaven. Can I help?" he asked.

Bindy looked up at him and grinned.

"Sure. Could you fill those chafing dishes with eggs, bacon, sausage, and little pancakes?"

Blade gave her a salute. "Can do, ma'am."

She tittered.

"Please don't call me *ma'am*. I feel old enough as it is."

Blade found a large spoon and moved eggs from a large pan into the first dish.

"What made you buy this place, anyway?" asked Blade as the eggs piled.

She shrugged. "I dunno. I'd told my real estate agent I wanted to buy a business that was kind of *remote*." She chuckled at the memory. "To find a successful business in the middle of nowhere is a tall order, eh? I didn't think she'd find anything, but next thing I know, she's telling me this place might be for sale."

"So, you didn't *ask* for a bed and breakfast?"

She shook her head. "No. Not specifically. I was thinking more of a *farm*, but as soon as I saw this place, I knew I had to have it. It's pretty *outback* in its own way, eh? I grew up with rabbits—it seemed like fate. Especially when I saw how big those suckers are."

Munch stacked plates and silverware in his arms and headed to the dining room to finish setting the table. Blade moved on to the sausages and bacon, popping one of the small sausages in his mouth as he shifted them.

"I saw that," teased Bindy.

He snickered.

She wiped her hands on her apron and glanced at the walk-in freezer as she moved to flip the pancakes. Spatula in hand, she did a double take.

"What's wrong?" Blade asked, seeing her quizzical expression.

She scowled.

"The *lock*," she said.

She pointed, and he followed her finger to the padlock on the walk-in freezer.

It hung open.

"That should be locked," he said.

"I *know*. I'm the one who locked it," said Bindy.

"You didn't open it?" he asked.

She shook her head, and he frowned.

That's bad.

"Who else knows the combination?" he asked.

"It's not a combo. It's a key," she said.

"Where do you keep the key?"

"In the drawer." She motioned to a nearby drawer and winced. "Not that great a hiding spot, I guess. It's in the back, though. You'd have to be looking for it."

Blade moved his last bunch of tiny sausages and put down the spoon. He moved closer to Bindy and lowered his voice to a whisper.

"We better see if someone went inside," he said.

She nodded, her eyebrows slanted with clear anxiety.

Blade put a hand on her shoulder.

"Maybe Munch opened it to look for breakfast stuff?" he suggested.

She gasped and then covered her mouth with her hand to whisper through her fingers.

"You're *right*. I didn't think to tell him to stay away. He *might* know where the key is. It was Elke's lock."

They glanced to the dining room, where Munch continued to set places, oblivious to the drama unfolding in the kitchen.

"If it was him and he did go in, he must not have seen her, right?" she said. "I mean, he doesn't talk, but he lets me know things in his way. He would have mentioned seeing Elke *dead*."

She whispered the last word so softly that Blade could barely hear her.

He noticed she still hadn't started moving to the freezer.

"I guess we better check it out," he prompted again.

She nodded and seemed to realize he was waiting for her.

"Oh. *Right*." She took his hand. "Come with me?"

He nodded. "I'm right here."

They walked to the door together.

Bindy placed her fingers on the handle and looked over her shoulder to ensure no one was coming.

With a jerk, she opened the heavy door.

Blade felt the rush of cold air chill his body.

In unison, they gasped.

They didn't need to check behind the buckets. Elke wasn't even the most interesting thing in the freezer anymore.

In the center of the frosty floor lay Princess Christmas, eyes closed, wearing a green gown with red trim. The dress seemed small for her, and one sleeve hung at an angle, torn. A crown rested against the top of her head. Her arms crossed against her chest.

She looked like a holiday version of Sleeping Beauty, waiting for her prince to arrive.

Princess's trademark cherry red lipstick radiated against her pale skin. Crimson smeared her frosted cheeks.

She looked like a doll.

She looked very *dead*.

"Not another one," said Bindy, rushing into the freezer.

Blade followed.

Bindy knelt beside Princess and shook her hard enough to set her crown rolling. It spun across the floor and collapsed like a flicked penny.

"She's freezing. *Frozen* even," Bindy said, looking up at Blade.

He agreed. "She's been here a while."

He noticed a frozen pork loin lying nearby and shuffled to inspect it.

"There's blood on this," he said.

"You think someone killed her with a pork loin?" she asked.

He shrugged. "It *would* make a handy club."

Blade heard a click behind him, but before he could turn to see what it was, the lights went out, plunging them into darkness.

He realized what the click had been.

The door shutting.

"Oh no," said Bindy. "I forgot to tell you to prop open the door. I got so flustered—"

Blade rose and felt his way to the door. His fingers searched for an emergency release. He thought he found it, but when he pulled, nothing happened. He tried pushing and twisting, but still, nothing.

"There has to be a way to open this?" he said.

"Naur, that's just it," said Bindy, a defeated, disembodied voice in the darkness. "The release broke off years ago. Elke warned me. She wasn't happy about the sale and wasn't chatty with me, but this was one of the few things she warned me about. *Make sure you always prop open the freezer door,* she said. *At that temperature, you'll be dead in two hours.*"

She imitated Elke's sour tone, which sounded funny with her Australian accent. Blade couldn't see, but he suspected she was shaking a finger at him as she mimicked the woman.

"Munch has to be back soon," said Blade, pounding on the door. "We'll be good."

He heard Bindy behind him rubbing her arms.

"It's freezing," she said. "And we're trapped with two dead bodies. None of this is good."

Her voice seemed higher off the ground. She'd stood.

It *was* cold. Blade was surprised at how quickly the chill had seeped into his bones. If Princess hadn't been dead when she first hit the floor of the freezer, she still couldn't have survived for long.

"The cold will kill us in a couple of hours, but on the upside, we probably have enough air for ten to fourteen," said Bindy.

Blade rubbed his arms. "You're in a good mood for a human popsicle."

She laughed. "Strangely, I felt better the second I couldn't see the bodies around me anymore."

He pounded on the door again and felt Bindy arrive at his side.

"*Munch!*" she yelled.

They continued to pound as the minutes ticked by.

"I'm *so* cold," said Bindy, sounding less jolly.

"Come here," said Blade.

He felt her fingers touch his chest and he wrapped his arms around her.

"We can share body heat," he murmured. "If you're okay with it. I guess I should have asked—"

"No, good on ya," she said, pressing against him.

"Any better?" he asked.

"Better," she said.

He heard her giggle.

"What's funny?" he asked.

"Growing up in Northern Australia, you never dream someday you'll freeze to death."

"Someone will find us," he said, pounding again with one arm.

She joined him and then rested against him.

"There's something you should know," she said.

In the dark, Blade grimaced at the comment. Nothing good ever started with *there's something you should know*. She would probably tell him that she had a husband in Australia or didn't like him the way he liked her.

"What?" he asked, against his better judgment.

She sighed.

"Munch is a little deaf."

CHAPTER TWENTY-FIVE

The closer Charlotte got to the kitchen, the more the delicious scent of bacon she'd noticed earlier went wrong. It didn't smell like breakfast food anymore. It smelled more like a fire.

"Something's burning," said Declan, echoing her thoughts.

"You're crushing my dreams. I was trying to pretend I didn't smell that," she admitted.

A cloud lingered at the entrance to the kitchen. They spotted a smoking pan, and Declan rushed to remove it from the stove.

"Where is everyone?" asked Charlotte.

She leaned her head into the dining room to find the table set and Munch nowhere in sight.

"Did something happen? Munch is gone, too. He was setting the table when I saw him. Please tell me we didn't lose two more people."

"If we did, we're going to have to consider black holes and hellgates as possibilities," said Declan. "Nobody could bump off this many people under our noses."

Charlotte snorted. "Have you *never* seen a horror movie? There are about a hundred Christmas horror movies. *Silent Night, Violent Night, Krampus—*"

He held up a hand. "Okay, Miss Rotten Tomatoes, but assuming *Krampus* didn't kill them, *where is everybody?*"

They heard a deep pounding noise, and both turned toward the walk-in freezer.

Charlotte's eyes widened.

"Did that come from *there*?" she asked, pointing at the freezer.

"I think so," he said.

She scowled, listening for another sign.

"Not Elke…? We couldn't have put her in there *alive*?"

"No…" He bit his lower lip. "But that being said, you win. This is *definitely* a Christmas horror movie."

Charlotte thought about the burning bacon and gasped.

"*Bindy*. She must have locked herself in."

Charlotte rushed to the freezer door.

"Please don't be Elke," she whispered under her breath.

She jerked the handle and hauled open the door. Blade and Bindy spilled into the kitchen, shivering.

"Oh my God, are you okay? How did you end up in *there*?" asked Charlotte.

Blade pointed into the freezer, and Charlotte peered inside.

She'd been so shocked to see Bindy and Blade that she hadn't even noticed the dead woman wearing a Christmas gown on the floor behind them.

"What happened?" asked Declan.

"We noticed the padlock was open," said Bindy, barely able to speak. Her teeth were chattering so hard. "We went to check, and Princess—"

A violent shiver ran through her body, stopping her mid-sentence.

Blade picked up where she left off.

"The door closed on us. The emergency release is broken."

"Jeez, lucky we came in," said Charlotte. "Lucky your bacon was burning."

Bindy glanced at the pan and frowned. "Great. It stinks in here."

"You must have just missed the fire alarm going off."

Bindy looked up at the fire alarm on the ceiling. Charlotte followed her gaze and noticed no light blinking.

"Elke had fallen a little behind on the maintenance. I'll add *change alarm batteries* to my list," said Bindy.

"Right after we cross off *stop people from dying*," muttered Charlotte.

"I'll fix that freezer for you before we go," said Blade.

Bindy smiled at him. "You can do that?"

He sniffed, chest puffing. "I'm pretty handy."

Charlotte couldn't help but snicker at his peacocking, but she needed to get back to the dead woman in the freezer.

"Hey, Handyman, what can you tell us about Princess?"

Blade cleared his throat. "I think someone killed her with a pork loin."

"With a *pork loin*?" echoed Declan.

Bindy nodded. "Go ahead in. You'll see. We'll watch the door."

Blade pointed. "There's a pork loin on the ground there. Next to her head. You'll see."

Charlotte and Declan walked inside the freezer.

"Boy, it's a good thing we checked on the kitchen. It is *freezing* in here," said Charlotte, wrapping her arms around herself.

"I think that's the point," said Declan, crouching beside the frozen pork loin lying near the body. "Blade's right. There's blood all over one end of this."

"And blood on and around her head," said Charlotte, pointing.

She spotted the crown nearby.

"They knocked her crown right off," she said, motioning to it.

"That was resting against her head when we came in," said Bindy, sticking her head inside. "It fell off and rolled over there."

Declan frowned. "No way to tell if she was already dead or if she froze to death while unconscious. The end result is the same."

Charlotte's attention drew to a belt around the center of the gown, split dark red threads with silver Christmas icons spaced evenly across it.

"Look," she said, pointing to the belt. "The mark on Elke's neck had two strands, and the face looked a lot like the little Santa on this belt—"

Declan nodded. "Does that mean *she* killed Elke? While in *costume*?"

"Seems unlikely she killed Elke, and then someone killed *her*, right? It's probably more likely one person killed them both, but why? We're not even close to a motive. In fact, with Princess dead, we lost our best suspect for Elke."

Declan frowned. "This underscores our killer is still *here*. We can throw out the window any theories about a madman swinging by to kill Elke and then leaving."

Charlotte looked down at Princess.

"Whoever did this took their time posing her. She didn't fall this perfectly, and—"

She stood and searched the shelves until she spotted what she was looking for.

"Her *clothes*," she said, moving aside a large package of salmon filets and motioning to a silk sleeping shirt and a robe piled in the corner.

"So someone lured her down here, hit her on the head, and *then* changed her into this gown to pose her as Princess Christmas?"

"And left Elke's murder weapon behind. It had to be that belt," said Charlotte.

She tilted her head as she looked at Princess. Her dress seemed to be bursting at the seams.

"That dress is too small for her, and look at the torn sleeve," said Charlotte. "This is the same gown the angry second-place winner was wearing."

"So Princess is Sore-Loser Lina, and she's definitely related to Elke," said Declan.

Charlotte motioned to Princess's bare feet.

"Her daughter, I bet, and it must be Princess's barefoot prints I saw on the hidden stairs. She grew up here, so she knew about the passageway."

She leaned down to squint at Princess's dress.

"I don't see where that little ruby I found could have come from, though."

Declan grimaced. "I'm not surprised. I wouldn't think she'd wear that dress down here unless it was a very specific—and *creepy*—request."

"You think the killer put it on her? Here?"

He nodded.

She gasped. "The wedding gown preservation box up in the attic. It wasn't a wedding gown. It was *this dress*."

She inspected the woman's hairline, holding the flashlight over her temple.

"There's some slight scarring here."

"The birthmark? She had it removed?"

Charlotte nodded. "Princess usually wore full makeup but came downstairs for this clandestine meeting without it."

Declan scowled.

"Her lips are red. And her cheeks—"

Charlotte nodded. "I was just thinking that. *This* isn't her makeup. Someone put the lipstick on her and put color on her cheeks for this Princess pose. I mean, look at those cheeks. She didn't do *that*."

"It's pretty garish," Declan agreed.

"Princess was all about her Palm Beach image, but she came down without makeup."

Declan shrugged. "It was the middle of the night."

"*True*, but I think she'd still have fixed her face unless she was in a hurry or didn't care what the person she was meeting thought of her—which maybe tells us something right there."

Declan pulled at his chin like he did when he was thinking.

"Do you think the person who killed her knew Elke was in here?" he asked.

"They must have, right? Seems like too much of a coincidence otherwise."

Charlotte turned to inspect the buckets. Someone had moved one of the buckets to reveal Elke's face.

"If they didn't know before, and this *is* some weird coincidence, they know now," she added.

"Maybe they used Elke as bait to get Princess down here," suggested Declan.

Charlotte pointed at him.

"*Yes*. That tracks. It would be the easiest way to hurry her into the freezer."

"Unless they hit her on the head first and then dragged her in here, but why would you use a frozen pork loin unless it happened to be handy? Plus, no blood trail..."

Charlotte nodded and rubbed her arms.

"That's a good point. You don't *plan* to kill someone with a pork loin, so that leads to it being a spur-of-the-moment decision. But they had the dress with them...?"

"We need to find who stands to inherit with Elke and Princess gone. We need to find her will. *And* we need to get the heck out of this freezer."

Bindy and Blade awaited them in the kitchen, looking a little less blue and chattery now that they'd had some time to warm up.

It never took long to warm up in Florida, even in December.

"How do you think someone opened your padlock?" asked Charlotte as they closed the freezer.

Bindy cast her eyes down for a moment, projecting her regret.

"I had the key in the drawer. It was *stupid*. I didn't think anyone would be looking for it. In hindsight, I should have made it a little harder to find."

"Who might look in that drawer or have seen you put the key there?" asked Declan.

Bindy glanced over her shoulder to ensure they were alone in the kitchen.

"Maybe Munch?" she whispered. "I don't know. Anyone could have been looking. What do we do now?"

Charlotte's stomach growled.

"Let's try and keep things as normal as possible."

"Are you sure?" asked Bindy.

"No. But we need a second to think."

Declan nodded. "On the upside, our pool of suspects has dropped by one."

Bindy snorted. "Boy, you are glass-half-full, aren't you?"

A massive clap of thunder shook the house. The lights turned off, and the steady hum of an electrified house ended abruptly.

A deep silence settled over the room.

"Maybe less glass-half-full now," said Declan into the gloom.

CHAPTER TWENTY-SIX

Bindy opened the shades to let in whatever sunlight penetrated the heavy cloud cover as guests gathered at the big table for breakfast. There was enough light for eating, but Charlotte dreaded having no electricity once the meal ended. The day would be bad enough. Staying in a house with a murderer overnight with no electricity sounded like a nightmare.

They had no electricity and *two* dead bodies. Things had gotten decidedly worse in less than twenty-four hours.

Twelve hours ago, she didn't even think that was possible.

The storm needed to *go*. If it calmed down, they could send someone out for help. Probably Declan. He was in shape and could jog until he found a phone. Blade could stay as muscle.

She had it worked out—*if the lightning ever stopped.*

Or maybe it was time to blow up the time lock safe.

Before sitting for breakfast, she found Mariska and Darla and pulled them aside.

"I have something to tell you, but don't gasp," she said.

Mariska covered her mouth with both hands.

"That looks a lot less suspicious. *Perfect*," drawled Darla.

Charlotte decided to talk fast.

"Princess is dead," she said.

Mariska gasped behind her hands.

Charlotte and Darla looked at her.

"Sorry," she said, the word muffled.

"How? Where is she?" whispered Darla.

Charlotte nodded toward the kitchen. "She's in the freezer."

"You put her in there too?" asked Mariska.

"No, that's where we found her. Just do me a favor and try to avoid talking about her. We'll eat breakfast and then check out her room. We want things to seem as normal as possible."

"So people don't panic," said Mariska. "I wish you hadn't told me. Now *I'm* starting to panic."

"It's more than panic. We don't want to tip off the killer that we *know*. We need every advantage we can manage."

"It's one of *us*," muttered Darla, as if she'd left herself on the suspect list.

She squinted at the table as people gathered. Mariska looked the most worried, and Charlotte touched her arm to break her from her doom spiral.

"We'll be *fine*. There's a reason those two were targeted—the person doing this probably isn't working his or her way through the whole group. It had something to do with them."

"*Probably*," echoed Mariska.

Charlotte patted her. "We just need to wait a little longer. Though, we *might* have to run for it before tonight."

"I hate running," muttered Mariska.

They moved to the table and took seats while Blade, Bindy, and Munch brought out the chafing dishes and other food. Charlotte ate some lukewarm bacon that hadn't been burned, eyeing the others at the table.

Which one of you is a murderer?

Munch sat a pitcher of orange juice near her, and she watched him return to the kitchen.

Hm. Munch.

Where had *he* been when they looked for him earlier? He'd stepped away from setting the table. Had he run to the bathroom? Run another errand? Or was he covering his tracks once he saw Bindy and Blade enter the freezer?

Maybe the freezer door hadn't closed on its own.

Munch knew the most about the house. He probably knew about the hidden stairs and maybe saw where Bindy put the padlock key.

Strella, on the other hand, seemed like a long shot. She was too wrapped up in herself to take the time to kill anyone. Of course, she *did* seem jealous of Princess's media empire.

Brendan was writing a book on the house. Was the place *really* that interesting, or was he here for a different reason? He knew about the hidden stairs before anyone else did.

"Brendan," said Charlotte. "What made you decide to write a book about this place?"

The man looked up from his eggs and smiled.

"It's not just about this house. It's about this area of Florida."

"Do history books sell?"

He shook his head while he finished swallowing a bite of toast.

"Oh, it isn't nonfiction," he said.

"Brendan's writing a *novel*," explained Strella, beaming. "I'm going to help him market it."

"Like a sweeping historical saga?" asked Charlotte.

He shook his head. "No, it's a thriller."

"A murder mystery?" asked Darla before Charlotte could get the same question out of her mouth.

He shrugged. "More or less, but dark."

The word *dark* caught Charlotte's attention. After all, what was darker than killing someone in a freezer and dressing them up like a teenage Christmas princess?

"Can you tell us about the plot?" she asked.

Brendan lowered his fork and leaned back in his chair as if mulling the question.

"I can't really," he said finally. "It isn't done, and I haven't worked out all the details yet."

Charlotte nodded, defeated, unable to find a way to turn his book description into a sudden confession.

"Do you think the lights will come on before tonight?" asked Iko to no one in particular, effectively changing the subject.

"Considering the size of this storm, there are probably thousands of people without power. I wouldn't bet on it," said Declan.

Iko pouted. "It's going to get warm in here."

Charlotte could see her stressing.

"The universe will solve itself," she said.

Iko's attention shot to her, and she nodded.

"Yes. *Yes*." She pressed her palms together and bowed her head to start mumbling.

"*The universe is all-knowing. The universe is all-knowing...*"

Strella rolled her eyes and then scowled.

"Princess and Elke are still sick?" she asked.

Charlotte nodded. "I guess so."

She scanned the table for reactions, hoping the killer would find this conversation irresistibly funny.

No one reacted except Iko, who dropped her head and changed her chanting.

"*I don't want the flu. I don't want the flu...*"

Charlotte leaned to Declan, who sat mopping the last of his egg with cold toast.

"If you're done, let's go through Princess's room," she whispered as the others broke into several different conversations.

Declan nodded, and they excused themselves. When they attempted to carry their plates to the kitchen, Munch appeared to take them.

"Thank you," they said, handing them over.

Munch nodded and disappeared back into the kitchen.

They headed upstairs.

"I don't think Iko could kill two people—between her size and her nerves, I don't think she'd have the power to choke Elke or beat Princess with pork," mused Charlotte as they climbed the stairs.

Declan bobbed a shoulder.

"I don't disagree, but the whole Nervous Nelly thing might be an act to throw us off."

Charlotte nodded. That was true. She'd been hoping he'd agree, and she'd feel more comfortable about crossing Iko off her list.

They went to Princess's room on the third floor to find it unlocked. Declan pushed open the door.

"Someone made the bed," said Charlotte. "Maybe this is where Munch went while Bindy and Blade were in the freezer."

Charlotte opened the closet and pulled out a suitcase. Princess had shoes and miscellaneous clothing inside. In a side pocket, she found a folded piece of paper—a printed photo of a baby in blue overalls sitting between two giant rabbits. The photo looked old. Whoever the baby was, he was a grown man now.

"Look at this," she said, holding it out for Declan to take it.

"A baby?" he looked at her. "*Her* baby?"

"I don't know, but what if we combine Elke's letter with that photo?"

His jaw fell open. "Elke was blackmailing her over a secret baby? Princess ran away to reinvent herself, leaving the boy with Elke?"

"That's what I'm thinking. The blackmail was enough to get Princess here, but she didn't give in. She refused to give Elke the money to save the inn, and that's why Elke finally signed the paperwork for Bindy. She was out of options."

Declan studied the photo of the baby.

"Are you thinking what I'm thinking?"

She nodded. "It has to be Munch. He must be Princess's *son*."

"That would make him next in line for an inheritance. Maybe Princess killed Elke to shut her up, and Munch killed Princess for revenge?"

Charlotte hefted the case back into the closet.

"*Or,* Munch could have killed them both. He might hate them both."

Declan's brow furrowed.

"I could see hating Princess for abandoning him, but why hate Elke? Because she was selling? Leaving him behind?"

Charlotte shrugged. "Who knows? People can always find a way to hate the people who raised them. *Familiarity breeds contempt* and all that."

Declan chuckled. "I know when Seamus showed up, I wanted to kill him after about three days."

"Seamus is special that way."

Declan held up the baby photo. "We need to find Munch. I'll take this. We might need it to show him so he knows we *know*."

Charlotte agreed, and they continued to root through Princess's room, looking for anything else that might be helpful.

They found nothing.

"We should stop by Elke's room again and see if we can find a will?"

Declan nodded, and they headed that way. They pulled open every drawer and opened every shoebox in Elke's closet but found nothing.

Charlotte sighed. "This is hopeless. She's got her stuff packed and ready to go somewhere. She's living like a guest."

Declan agreed as they wandered back into the hall. He glanced into their room.

"Should we spot-check under the dolls? Make sure they haven't killed anyone else?"

Charlotte rolled her eyes.

"Very funny, and *no*. I honestly don't want to know. Let's go find Munch."

Downstairs, they found Brendan and Strella still at the table, lazily picking over their food. She didn't blame them—there wasn't any reason to rush or anywhere to go.

In the parlor, she saw Iko rearranging the decorations on the Christmas tree. The tinsel seemed much more linear than it had before.

She heard dishes clanking and glanced into the kitchen to see Bindy and Blade washing up. No electricity meant no dishwasher.

"Have you seen Munch?" she asked Brendan and Strella as Declan grabbed an apple.

Brendan motioned to the back yard.

"He went out to his place," he said.

Charlotte stopped. She hadn't expected them to have an answer. She'd only asked for the heck of it on her way to the kitchen.

"He went *outside*? *Why*?" she asked, turning to look out the window. It was still raining, but not as hard as earlier. Maybe the end was in sight, and they could make a break for the main road soon.

Maybe Munch already did.

She didn't see anyone outside.

Brendan shrugged. "I dunno. Your friends went with him,

though."

"Our friends?" asked Declan, sounding as alarmed as Charlotte felt.

"Melissa and Debbie," said Strella.

"Mariska and Darla?" asked Charlotte.

Strella shrugged. "Whatever. Remind me to interview them later for a post. They're *hilarious*."

Brendan nodded. "That's a good idea. Old people are *funny*."

Charlotte's eyes popped wide as she turned to Declan.

"Why would they go outside with Munch?"

Declan shook his head. "I don't know."

"I think he wanted to show them something," said Brendan.

"*Kittens*. He has kittens," said Strella.

"Thanks," said Charlotte, spinning on her heel and tugging Declan into the parlor.

"Kittens make good bait," she whispered to him as they moved. "He *lured* them out there."

"Like Princess to the freezer," said Declan as they dashed for the back door.

CHAPTER TWENTY-SEVEN

Twenty minutes earlier.

As Darla and Mariska helped Munch clear the table after breakfast, one of the giant rabbits hopped into the room. Munch bent to move it to the parlor, which struck Darla as funny.

"Are you worried we'll trip over it?" she asked.

Munch nodded, and she laughed.

"I think they're safe. That would be like not noticing an elephant in the room."

She was struck by how gentle Munch was with the animal. He seemed like a sweet kid. It was a shame he couldn't speak.

"Do you take care of the rabbits?" she asked.

Munch looked to see if she was talking to him and then nodded. Something about the look in his eyes said he wished he could tell her more.

"You like animals?" she asked.

He nodded enthusiastically.

"Do you have any other pets?"

He nodded again, growing even more animated. He mimicked licking his hand and then curling his fingers over his ear.

His mime caught Mariska's attention, and she stopped what she was doing to watch him.

"Ooh, I love charades. Do you have a *cat*?" she guessed.

He nodded and then held his hands close together, implying something small.

"A *kitten*?" asked Darla.

He nodded and made a peace sign.

"You have *two* kittens?" asked Mariska.

He nodded.

Mariska squealed with delight.

"Where are they? Are they here?"

He pointed out back.

The ladies turned and looked out the back window at the barn.

"At your place? You live over the barn, right?"

He nodded, pointed to them, himself, and then out back.

"You want to show us the kittens?" asked Mariska.

He winced and wiggled his fingers to imitate rain. The three of them walked to the back door to inspect the situation. The rain had lightened considerably.

"I think we're getting hit by bands of weather, but we're in between now," said Darla. "Maybe we can run out to see the kittens and be back before it gets bad again?"

Munch nodded and headed out the back door, motioning for them to follow.

They did.

Darla pointed out puddles as they walked, knowing Mariska wasn't always the *steadiest* person on uneven terrain.

"Stick to the path. It's less muddy," she warned.

"I *know*," said Mariska as her foot slipped off the side of a stone and splashed.

Darla shook her head.

Munch broke into a jog, and the ladies did their best to pick up the pace. While the rain wasn't as bad as it had been earlier, it was still miserable, and they didn't want to be in it for longer than they needed to be.

They reached the barn, and Munch hauled the sliding door open to let them inside.

Darla gasped.

The inside of the barn looked like a giant Christmas parade.

"Oh my stars," said Mariska, eyes wide with wonder.

Munch left the large door open to provide light and grinned, clearly proud of his Christmas wonderland. White and red ribbons wrapped every post, making them look like giant candy canes. Unlit lights in every color draped from the rafters and garlands ran back and forth along the walls. An enormous Christmas tree at the back had enough tinsel and decorations for three trees.

Every spare inch of wall sported a sign or decoration from decades of Christmas at the inn. Tin caroling elves, Santa faces, reindeer—no classic holiday character had been overlooked.

Mariska shook the rain from her hair.

"This must be amazing when the electricity is on. All these *lights*," she said.

Darla nodded, pulling her attention from the decorations long enough to notice the left wall of the barn. There hung a collection of machetes, hatches, butcher knives, a rusty scythe, and other tools dangling from pegs like the worst Christmas decorations *ever*.

She scowled.

"Um..."

Except for the festive tinsel running along the top of the pegboard, it looked like a serial killer's toolbox had exploded against the wall.

She tugged on Mariska's shirt.

"Um..."

"Look at those elves—" said Mariska, pointing in the other direction.

"Um—*Mariska?*"

Annoyed to have her sleeve tugged, Mariska finally turned.

"What is it?"

Darla pointed to the Wall of Pointy Things.

Mariska turned that way.

Her chin dropped an inch.

"We're out here alone with him," Darla reminded her. "And two people are *dead*."

Mariska swallowed. "We maybe didn't think this out."

Darla noticed a dark stain on the ground below a dangling hook. She held her arm against her body to stop herself from pointing at it. Mariska was better off not seeing it.

"That is just occurring to me," she said.

She looked to see where Munch had gone. He was halfway up a set of stairs that ran along the right wall to a small enclosed room on the barn's second level.

"Do you think he killed Elke and Princess?" asked Darla.

Mariska shook her head. "I don't know. I'm not feeling good about it right now, though."

"No. We really should have told someone we were coming out here. But *kittens*—"

Munch cleared his throat, and the two of them looked up the stairs to find him at his door, motioning to them to follow.

"Should we run back to the house?" asked Mariska.

Darla considered their options. They *could* do that, but it felt rude. Also, if Munch *was* up to something, maybe they could find evidence to take back to Charlotte and Declan.

"Let's just stick together," said Darla, taking Mariska's hand. "Maybe we can find a clue."

"Us *dead* in his room would be a *great* clue," said Mariska.

Darla headed for the stairs.

"I hope there are *kittens*, at least," Mariska said behind her.

When they reached the top of the stairs, Munch let them through his door into a tiny apartment on the second level. He walked in and opened the windows to let in more light. As he did, their eyes dropped to a pile of clothing on the floor to their right— whites, stained with red.

"Is that *blood*?" asked Mariska, loud enough for Munch to hear.

He turned and saw her staring in horror at the pile. Scurrying over, he grabbed the pile and moved toward a closed door, looking flustered. He held up a finger, asking them to wait, and disappeared inside the room, closing the door behind him.

Darla and Mariska exchanged a look.

"We're not crazy, right? That did look like blood?" asked Darla.

"It *definitely* looked like blood," said Mariska. "Do you think anyone can hear us scream from up here?"

Darla stared at the closed door.

"Where did he go?"

"I assume that's his bedroom," said Mariska.

"No, I get that, but *why* did he go in there? I mean, was it to hide the bloody clothes we already saw? Why did he close the door? Is that where he keeps his other butcher knives?"

"I don't know. I'm hoping that's where he keeps the kittens," murmured Mariska.

Darla found her attention drawn to the kitchen.

"Nevermind. That's not where he keeps the knives," she said.

"How do you know?"

She pointed into the tiny kitchen.

"Because *that's* where he keeps the knives."

A large collection of knives clung to a magnetic strip over the stove. They ranged from a butcher's cleaver to a small paring knife.

"Does that seem like a *lot* of knives to you?" asked Darla.

"Why does he need that big butcher thing?" asked Mariska.

Darla glanced at the bedroom door to ensure Munch wasn't on his way, then hustled to the kitchen. She took the smallest knife off the strip.

"What are you doing?" hissed Mariska.

"I'm keeping this one for a while. Just in case," she said, slipping it into her pocket.

Mariska grabbed her arm as she scanned the room.

"I don't see any kitten stuff," she noted.

"Me neither. Hey, look at this—"

Darla moved to a corkboard hanging on the wall over a small desk. The only things that fit in the tiny apartment were the desk, a table with two chairs, an old loveseat, and a console supporting a modest flat-screen television.

Mariska walked over and peered at the corkboard. Black and white, seemingly home-developed photographs of Elke covered the face of it. Every shot featured Elke posing somewhere on the property—pushing a gerbera daisy into a planter, serving food, making a bed. Giant rabbits were the only other living things in any of the photos.

"Seems a little obsessive, doesn't it?" muttered Mariska as she studied the photos.

Darla scoffed.

"Ya *think*?"

She leaned in to admire how the morning light glowed behind

Elke as she drank a steaming beverage from a large mug on her porch.

"He's really good, though," she said.

Mariska nodded. "He really is."

Darla's eyes dropped to another pile of photos on the desk, but these images appeared printed from the Internet. She recognized the woman in each of them.

"These are all of *Princess*," she whispered, a creeping dread crawling up her spine.

"Oh *no*," said Mariska. "I only know one thing those two women have in common."

Darla picked up a printout that, stylistically, looked more like the photos on the corkboard. In it, Princess wore the same clothes she'd been wearing the day they arrived. In the background, she spotted Brendan and Strella.

She held it up for Mariska to see.

"This one is new. He must have taken this photo yesterday."

"I guess that's when he shifted from obsessing over Elke to obsessing over Princess," said Mariska breathlessly. "I'm thinking this is all the evidence we need. We should go get Charlotte and Declan—"

Mariska turned to move. Before Darla could follow, Munch's bedroom door jerked open. He appeared at the threshold, a kitten hanging from each hand.

The smile on his face melted when he heard them yip with surprise.

They stood with their hands on their hearts, panting.

"You scared us," said Darla.

"*Kittens*," said Mariska.

Darla turned her head from Munch's view to speak directly into Mariska's ear.

"Never mind the *kittens*. We have to *go*," she whispered through gritted teeth.

She took a few steps and grabbed the knob of the front door.

It didn't turn.

Panicking, Darla felt for the knife in her shorts pocket, her fingers curling around the handle.

She turned to face Munch and forced a tight smile.

"The, uh, door here is stuck?" she said.

He stared back at her, brow furrowed, a kitten still dangling in each hand.

"You, uh, really do have kittens?" Darla added in the cheeriest voice she could muster.

He tucked the kittens into one arm and closed the bedroom door behind him. When he walked toward them, Mariska held up a palm to stop him.

"Do you mind if I ask you a question?" she asked.

He blinked at her, waiting.

Mariska pointed.

"Why did you have a pile of bloody clothes here?" she asked.

Darla grimaced.

"Maybe we shouldn't ask him questions like that until we figure out how to open his door," she mumbled.

"You have a *knife*," Mariska said back to her in what, in her head, was probably a whisper.

There was no way Munch didn't hear.

Darla scoffed.

"What am I going to do? *Pare* him to death?"

Munch waved his free hand at them, shaking his head. He walked to the kitchen and opened the top of his old refrigerator. Darla assumed that was the freezer.

She imagined that's where he kept the best parts of his victims. The *trophies*.

He motioned for them to look inside.

"Oh *hell* no," said Darla.

When the ladies didn't move, he rolled his eyes and pulled out a brown paper-wrapped package. He walked it over to them and held it up so they could read the writing on the outside.

Someone had scrawled *Deer Loin* in red ink.

"Deer loin?" Darla read aloud.

Growing up in Tennessee, she'd seen many similar packages. There'd been a time when her own freezer burst with identical packages.

She didn't remember which husband was the hunter—one of

them.

"You hunt?" she asked.

He pretended to hold a gun as best he could with an arm full of kittens and then shook his head. He mimed chopping something and nodded.

"Oh, you don't *hunt*, but you dress deer?"

He nodded and pointed downstairs.

"Down there." Darla's mouth fell open, and she nodded. "Oooh, I get it."

She turned to Mariska.

"All those knives and the hook—he breaks down deer for hunters."

"Oh," said Mariska. "*Yuck.*"

She pointed to the corkboard.

"What about the photos? Why do you have so many photos of Elke?"

Tired of being held, the kittens mewed. Munch motioned to hand them to Mariska, and after a hesitation, she took them both.

"It can't hurt to take them," she mumbled to Darla as Munch returned the package to the freezer.

"Well, it *can* if now his hands are free to grab all the knives," hissed Darla. "Apparently, he chops things up all the time, remember?"

Munch moved to the photos and away from the knives.

It made Darla feel a little better—a step in the right direction. *Literally.*

One of the tiny tabbies climbed Mariska's shoulder, and she lost all interest in the possibility of being murdered.

"So *cute*," she cooed.

Munch opened a deep drawer. He pulled out an old camera and held it up for them to see.

"You take photos with that?" asked Darla.

He nodded and handed her a brochure for The Timeless Inn, urging her to open it. She released her grip on the knife in her pocket, took the brochure, and found many of the photos from the corkboard featured inside.

"*Oh.*" Darla looked at Mariska. "He took marketing photos for

Elke. Those are all for this brochure."

"But what about *Princess*?" asked Mariska, pointing to the pile of Princess on the table.

Darla held up the photo of Princess she'd taken.

"Why so many photos of Princess?" she asked.

His expression contorted, and his lip began to quiver.

Darla didn't love that she'd upset him.

That could lead to bad things.

She wasn't sure how to feel. He looked sad, which made her sad. On the other hand, *why* was he sad? Because Princess was dead?

He wouldn't know she was dead unless he killed her...

"What's wrong?" asked Mariska, noticing his distress. Immediately, her attention returned to the kittens tumbling around in her arms.

"Oh, they are so *precious*," she giggled.

Darla glared at her.

"Could you maybe pay more attention to what's happening here with the people?"

Mariska looked up as the kitten on her shoulder tried to climb the side of her head.

"Sorry."

Munch moved to the desk and picked up a pad of paper. He found a pen and wrote something. He stared at what he'd written as if he were having second thoughts about sharing it and then held it up for them to read.

"What does it say?" asked Darla, squinting.

It says, "My mother," read Mariska with a kitten's toes on the bridge of her nose.

Darla gaped at Munch.

"Princess is your *mother*?"

Munch nodded.

"Princess was, er, *is* his *mother*," said Darla.

She looked to find Mariska dangling one of the kittens in front of her face.

"Look at those little *eyes*," she said.

Darla smacked her arm.

"Ow," said Mariska, glaring at her.

"Did you hear what I said? Princess is his *mother*."
"I know, I read—"
Her eyes widened.
"*Oh*."

CHAPTER TWENTY-EIGHT

Frank took a sip from a water bottle as he sat in his wise man robes in Bob's front yard. As excited as they were to *start* Thief Watch Whiskey Party, the group had grown tired of drinking some time ago. It was two o'clock in the morning.

Bob had fallen asleep, his chin on his chest, snoring.

"I don't think our fish will bite tonight," said Seamus.

"Doesn't look like it," agreed Frank.

He was surprised they'd lasted as long as they did. They'd had so much activity earlier in the evening between the sleepwalker and Pete that it seemed impossible the plan wouldn't work.

Seamus stood and stretched. "I'm going to walk over to Jackie's and sleep there," he announced.

Frank scowled. "Won't she kill you for waking her up in the middle of the night?"

Seamus shrugged.

"I know where she keeps the key."

Frank nodded. "Right. I'll be over later to identify your body."

Seamus chuckled as he wandered away, holding up his hand as a goodbye.

Frank turned his attention to Bob.

"*Bob*," he said, shaking him.

Bob opened his red-rimmed eyes.

"Hm?"

"Go inside. We're done."

Bob looked around, confused, and then realized where he was.

"Did we catch him?" he asked.

"No."

Frank stood and stuck out a hand to help him to his feet.

"Bed sounds like a good idea," said Bob.

"You want the glasses?" asked Frank, motioning to their collection of whiskey tumblers.

Bob grunted.

Frank leaned over to pluck the empty whiskey bottle from the manger.

"At least take this so it doesn't look like Baby Jesus has a drinking problem."

Bob took the bottle and shuffled up his driveway to the house, crunching cookies and plate shards with every other step.

Frank started down the street to his own house. When he opened the door, Turbo, their miniature Dachsund, came running from the bedroom to say hello.

"You want to go out?" he asked.

Turbo danced, and after removing his wiseman costume, he clipped the leash to the dog's collar. Outside, he enjoyed the quiet of the neighborhood. There wasn't much of a moon, but plenty of stars. It had been a while since he was last outside so late at night. He'd forgotten how pretty it could be.

Frank walked around the block and noticed a bright light glowing down the street. He stopped to stare while Turbo sniffed a patch of grass. He couldn't imagine the source. It wasn't the clubhouse or the overheads around the tennis courts. It seemed too bright to be Christmas decorations. It looked like an alien spacecraft was beaming someone up, though he doubted that was it.

He grunted.

But who knows around this crazy place?

He continued in that direction and realized he was heading toward grumpy Zac's house. Zac *had* complained that the neighbor's decorations were out of control.

Could *that* be what he saw?

He hadn't seen many decorations at the neighbor's—some lights around the frame of the house and a couple of reindeer in the yard. Hardly anything to get upset about.

He assumed Zac was just being *Zac*.

As he moved closer, it became clear the bright glow *was* Zac's neighbor. The light came from the fenced *back* yard, which was strange.

Why would someone put decorations where no one could see them?

He reached the house and picked Turbo up to tuck the tiny dog under his arm. He didn't see any cameras on the front of the house.

Meh.

He'd take a peek.

If the owner had a problem with him snooping around, he could always claim he was investigating Zac's complaint. Zac would back him up.

He'd be *tickled*.

Frank opened the unlocked gate on the fence and poked his head into the back yard. He had to squint because the place was so bright. Someone had run rows of string lights along the inside of the six-foot fence surrounding the property's back yard. Most were plain old lights—some larger, some more fairy-light size—but some were unique, like the row of smiling pineapples.

One was *very* interesting.

Flamingos wearing Santa hat lights.

Funny lights.

Stolen lights.

He entered and walked along the side of the house to take in the glory of the whole yard.

His jaw dropped.

Santa rode a dinosaur.

A glowing labradoodle stood wrapped in lights.

There was his own Grinch, stealing a *different* tree.

Funny Christmas decorations covered the entire yard. In addition to larger pieces like the inflatable dinosaur, smaller characters created dioramas. A Santa climbing the fence had a dog nipping at his heels. A snowman reached for where his head had been with stick arms while nearby a collection of naughty elves carried his head away.

There was no doubt Frank had found his thief.

They'd spent all night hoping to trick this guy, and the whole time, he was brazenly displaying his stolen items a couple of blocks away.

"Hello?" said a voice.

Frank turned to find an elderly man behind him. In his arms, he had the pants-dropping Santa from Bob's yard.

"I was admiring your collection," said Frank.

The man sighed.

"You're Sheriff Frank, aren't you?" he asked.

Frank nodded. "And you are?"

"John."

"It's nice to meet you, John. Though I'm not sure you're happy to see me."

The man's shoulders slumped a little farther.

"You got me. I've been stealing them."

Frank smiled.

That was easy.

"We've had reports," he said. "I've been looking for you."

The man nodded. "I figured you'd find me eventually. I was hoping it would be *after* Christmas, though."

Frank looked at the back yard and then at the man. He couldn't figure out why this old guy would do all that.

"Why would you steal so many decorations?" he asked.

The man set down the Santa.

"My wife. Florence."

He walked past Frank into the yard, and Frank followed. Just past the house, he stopped and turned to point at one of the windows.

"She's dying, there, in that room. Cancer."

Frank frowned. Just the word *cancer* made his stomach a little wobbly. His oncoming hangover didn't help.

"I'm sorry to hear that," he said.

John nodded. "Florence loves Christmas. They say she won't last until then, but she's trying. She wants one last Christmas."

By the light of the decorations, Frank saw the man's lip start to quiver.

"She's in terrible pain," he said, his voice almost a whisper. "I bought her one decoration—that Santa climbing over the fence with the dog grabbing at him—and she *laughed*. I hadn't heard her laugh in a while."

He wiped his eyes, seemingly too overcome to finish his story.

"So you got more."

He nodded. "One a day. I open the curtains every night, and she looks for the new decoration. I couldn't buy them fast enough, and we don't have the money. Fixed income."

Frank nodded.

The man bit his lip and locked his gaze on Frank's.

"Do you get it?" he asked. "She'll make it to Christmas if I keep finding her new decorations to make her laugh. It's what gets her through the night."

Frank motioned to the drawer-dropping Santa. "That one belongs to my friend Bob," he said.

John looked at him and started to hand it over. Frank shook his head.

"You keep it," he said. "Do you remember where you got them all?"

John patted his pocket. "I have a list."

"You'll take them back after—Christmas?"

John nodded. "I *will*."

He nodded and pointed to the Grinch.

"That one's mine."

John grinned. "She liked that one."

"It's a good one," he said.

Frank smiled and turned to go. He paused and turned back.

"How about I help you get enough until Christmas? What is it? Ten days?"

"Nine."

"*Nine*. I'll touch base with you tomorrow, and we'll figure it out. I don't want you stealing anymore."

The man wiped a tear away.

"Thank you."

CHAPTER TWENTY-NINE

The Outback Inn

Dark clouds rolled in as Charlotte and Declan bolted out the backdoor into the rain. They beelined for the open barn door.

Charlotte's mouth fell open as she scanned the decorated barn.

"It looks like Christmas threw up in here," she said.

Her gaze fell on the festively framed cutting tools dangling from the wall. She pointed.

"*Except...*"

They exchanged a look, and Charlotte turned to the stairs, running up to what she assumed was Munch's room.

"*Mariska?*" she called.

"*Darla?*" yelled Declan as they ran for the stairs.

They'd only hit the second step when the door at the top opened, and Mariska peered down at them.

"What are you doing here?" she asked.

"What do you think we're doing here? We're looking for *you*," said Charlotte.

"Kittens," said Mariska, holding up a gray tabby.

Another kitten tumbled around the ground at Mariska's feet as she nudged it away from the stairs.

"Are you okay?" asked Declan.

"We're *fine*," said Mariska. "Which is more than I can say for Munch."

Charlotte and Declan reached the top and entered the small

apartment. Inside, Darla sat on a small loveseat with her arm around a teary-eyed Munch.

"What's going on?" asked Declan.

Darla handed a pad of paper up to Charlotte.

"This is his side of the conversation we just had. It should explain everything," she said.

Charlotte and Declan huddled together to read.

She's my mother.

She left. She doesn't want me.

I looked everywhere.

Charlotte felt dread in the pit of her stomach.

"*He* wrote this?" she asked.

Mariska nodded. "When we asked him why he had pictures of Princess."

"I think Elke talked to Princess about him. Now she's disappeared, and he thinks it's his fault. He thinks she ran away to avoid him."

"I don't feel great about telling him that's not the case," Declan murmured to Charlotte.

"Me neither."

She grimaced, picturing the bodies in the freezer. That wasn't a sight she wanted Munch to see.

She looked at the teary-eyed young man and wondered if maybe he knew—if not about Princess, maybe about Elke?

She leaned to Mariska.

"Did you tell him? About either of them?" she asked in her ear.

Mariska shook her head.

Charlotte sat beside Munch. She heard thunder in the distance and counted the seconds. She didn't get far. The worst of the storm was closing in on them again.

She handed Munch the pad of paper and pen.

"Munch, can I ask you a question?"

He took the pad and nodded.

"Do you know where Elke is?"

He frowned and looked down.

"We know, so don't be afraid to tell us. Do *you* know where she is?"

Munch stared at the pad, the pen hovering over it, and Charlotte held her breath. If he knew Elke was in the freezer, it increased the odds he'd killed Princess. He might confess to one, not realizing it set him up for the other.

"Go ahead and let us know."

He chewed his lip and wrote two words.

Your room.

Charlotte's eyes widened.

"You think she's in *our* room?"

She glanced at Declan, whose eyes had also saucered with surprise.

"Is she—" Charlotte tried to best way to phrase her question. "—hidden in our room?"

He nodded and wrote *dolls.*

"She's hidden under the dolls?"

He nodded.

"How do you know she's there?"

He pointed to his chest.

"You put her there?"

He nodded.

"Was she alive?"

He scowled and shook his head.

"Did you kill her?" asked Declan.

Charlotte winced. That question, while necessary, seemed *really* direct. She'd been winding her way there.

Munch shook his head harder, looking alarmed.

"It's okay. We didn't think you did," said Charlotte, trying to calm the young man. "So Elke was dead when you found her? When you hid her there?"

His lip began to quiver, but he nodded.

"Why did you hide her?"

He leaned forward and picked up a photo of Princess.

"To protect Princess? Princess killed her?"

He bobbed his head from side to side, and his tight expression implied he'd thought so. Charlotte wanted to be sure she was reading him correctly, though.

"Did you see who killed Elke?" she asked.

He shook his head.

"But you thought it might be Princess because they were arguing?"

He nodded and placed a palm on his chest.

Arguing over him.

Charlotte felt tears welling in her own eyes. The boy looked *so* sad. As far as he knew, his birth mother had killed the only mother he ever knew and then ran away, abandoning him.

That would be tough for anyone to work through.

Charlotte wanted to make him feel better, but as far as they knew, he was right. All she could do was keep him distracted until help came.

"Hey—let's go back to the house, huh?" she suggested. "The storm is getting worse. We should get to the main house before we're stuck here."

He looked at her, and she thought of one thing she could share that might help. *Maybe.* For a little while.

"What if I told you I knew for a fact that Princess didn't abandon you?" she asked.

She glanced at Declan. He seemed uneasy about the direction the conversation had taken.

Munch scowled as if he didn't believe her.

"I can't tell you how I know, but I know. Okay?"

He wiped his eyes and nodded.

She stood. "You have a lot of decorations downstairs. Did you do all that?"

He nodded.

"You did a great job. Do you love Christmas?"

He nodded again.

"Do you do it every year?"

His eyes cast downward, and she knew that had been the wrong question. He *didn't* do it every year—he'd done it to impress Princess. She could feel it in her bones.

His mother hadn't responded to it like he'd hoped she would.

She shifted the topic again.

"I have an idea—what if we went back to the house and did something Christmassy?"

Munch's scowl released another notch. She had his attention.

"We could decorate," suggested Mariska.

He looked at her. He liked that idea.

"What if we did a Secret Santa?" asked Charlotte. "Everyone will make one gift to give—we can use things around the inn."

Munch nodded his head as if he had ideas. He stood, eager to get back to the house.

Charlotte gave Darla a hand as she rose from the loveseat.

"Let's get back," she said.

"It might be safer here," murmured Darla in her ear as she stood. "We know the killer isn't us, and I don't think it's him."

Charlotte chuckled.

"You're probably right—but we can't leave Blade or the others to the wolves."

"I'm bringing the kittens," announced Mariska, rushing down the stairs before anyone could stop her.

CHAPTER THIRTY

The group made it back to the main house, wet but safe. Mariska showed the kittens to the others amongst a lot of oohing and aahing.

"There you are," said Bindy, approaching. "I was starting to wonder where everybody went."

"We were visiting Munch's kittens. We brought them back here," said Charlotte.

Bindy nodded and gave Charlotte a look that said she'd worried they'd been killed. The woman looked flustered and tired. A couple of murders could rattle even a seemingly unflappable Australian.

Charlotte knew how she felt. She was exhausted. She couldn't remember the last time she wanted a weekend to be over so badly. She'd have to take Mariska on vacation as a thank you—maybe to the middle of the Everglades without mosquito spray or the middle of Death Valley in August.

Bindy watched the kittens tumble around on the floor. She smiled as if the sight of them were a tiny vacation from her life.

"Elke had warned me about the critters Munch occasionally comes home with. I'm glad it's only kittens this time," she said.

Her expression drooped, and she ran her hand over her hair.

"Is he entirely my responsibility now?" she asked quietly.

Charlotte offered her a tight smile. She understood how Bindy could feel a sense of duty toward the young man. He wasn't the sort of person who could just pack up and find some other job. The inn was his *home*.

Bindy was also probably wondering if staying at the inn was feasible for *her*. Losing two people on opening weekend wasn't exactly a marketing dream.

Charlotte remembered their idea for distracting the guests and decided it might get Bindy's mind off her problems, too.

"Do you have anything people could use to make little Christmas ornaments? We could do it as a Secret Santa to kill time?" She leaned close to add, "It'll also keep people close. It's hard to keep an eye on them if they hole up in their rooms."

Bindy's brow knitted. "It's funny you should mention that. Elke was pretty crafty. She's got a closet full of stuff. I'll go get it."

She wandered off, and Declan sidled up to Charlotte.

"What do you think about Munch?" he asked.

"That poor kid is heartbroken," said Charlotte. "Do you remember when he, Princess, and Elke headed out to the barn at the beginning of the treasure hunt?"

"Kind of. I wasn't really looking for future murder victims at the time."

Charlotte chuckled. "Fair enough. From what I could tell, Munch was trying to get Princess to go to the barn. Elke followed them. The three of them headed back there, where I suspect Munch tried to win his absentee mother's love with his Christmas Wonderland. It didn't work. Princess left in a huff, fought with Elke, and everyone started disappearing."

"The kid's had a tougher weekend than we did."

Charlotte nodded. "I don't think he could fake that sadness." She paused and added, "Though, maybe no one should go to the barn with him alone."

"You mean like Mariska and Darla just did."

"Right. Exactly like that." She grinned and sighed. "The argument I heard between Elke and Princess makes more sense now."

"They were fighting over Munch."

Charlotte nodded. "I bet Elke was furious that Princess was cruel to Munch, and Princess was furious at Elke for putting her in that position."

"So, Princess had plenty of motive to kill Elke—she was using the boy to blackmail her."

Charlotte noticed Strella looking at them.

"I think someone's eavesdropping on us. Let's go into the other room," she mumbled.

She wandered away, and Declan followed.

"Who was it?" he asked when they were alone in the little library.

"Strella. It felt like she was trying too hard to listen."

Declan sat on the library's reading couch.

"Munch said he hid Elke, but did he bring the dolls from the attic? Or were they already there?"

Charlotte winced. "That means he took the gown, too? And we know where that showed up."

"Oh. Right. Hm. Munch still makes a good suspect. Princess might have killed Elke, but she didn't conk herself on the skull with a pork loin."

"No. It's still possible Munch killed one or both. He's been wronged by both—but, like I said, I don't think he has the skills to lie to us and stage Princess's murder. I mean, he buried Elke under a bunch of dolls. Who does that? That thought process seems more childlike than that of a sophisticated psychopath."

Declan smirked. "I don't know. Children can be pretty good liars."

Charlotte sat beside him and rested her head on Declan's shoulder. The lack of sleep from the night before had started catching up to her.

"I'm *tired.*"

She felt his head nod against hers as she closed her eyes.

"Me too," he said.

"Everyone in the sitting room!"

Declan and Charlotte jumped as Bindy's voice bellowed through the house.

"She's like a human bullhorn," grumbled Charlotte.

Declan stood and stretched. "This *vacation* is never going to end."

"Time for Secret Santa!" added Bindy.

Declan put out a hand for her to take. Charlotte's eyes felt heavy. A big part of her wanted to curl up on the sofa and sleep until Sunday. *Forget the killer.*

Heck, murder me next. I could use the rest.

She sighed.

Time to get back to work.

She grabbed his hand and rose to her feet.

"When we get home, I'm going to sleep *forever*," she said as they walked toward the sitting room.

He put an arm around her and kissed the side of her head.

"I'll be right there with you and Abby, too. She'd love that."

They entered the sitting room, where Bindy had gathered a collection of crafting materials that would put a kindergarten teacher to shame.

Charlotte stood at the entrance to the room and leaned against the wall, afraid if she sat she'd fall asleep. She heard someone sniff behind her and turned to spot Strella headed her way.

The woman's eyes were red and glassy. When she noticed Charlotte looking, she turned away and wiped at her makeup.

"Are you okay?" asked Charlotte.

"Hm?" Strella glanced at her. "Yes. I'm *fine*."

Charlotte rolled off the wall to block Strella before she entered the sitting room.

"You don't look fine," she said.

Strella huffed. "It's *stupid*. Brendan and I had a fight. Not a big deal."

Charlotte winced. She certainly hadn't meant to pry into Strella's love life.

"Oh. I'm sorry—"

"He's really invested in my career, but I think I'm letting him down," she said.

Charlotte nodded. She hadn't planned to ask about the argument, but judging by the earnest way Strella stared into her eyes, she'd been sucked into the drama.

"Why would you think that?" she asked.

It seemed like the polite thing to ask.

Strella rubbed her eye. "Because my influencer career isn't taking off like we'd hoped. I know I seem amazing, but this is *really* hard."

She paused to wait for Charlotte's reaction.

"Uh-huh," she said.

Strella continued with a stomp of her foot.

"We got some traction, but it doesn't help that I don't have my *phone*. These two days are going to *kill* me."

Strella waited for her input.

"Um, you can't take all the blame," said Charlotte. "Getting followers is as much luck as effort. Some people have tried a *thousand* angles to hit it big online before they found the strategy that worked."

Strella gaped at her as if she were the only person who had ever understood her.

"I *know*, right? That's what I keep telling him." She took a deep breath and let it go. "Between you and me, I think he was hoping to get some insight from Princess —but now she's sick, and he's mad I didn't talk to her sooner."

"She didn't seem that approachable before," muttered Charlotte.

"Before?"

Charlotte realized what she'd said.

"Before she was sick," she explained.

Strella laughed nervously. "Oh, you're talking about that little exchange between us at the dinner table last night. That was nothing. She was getting sick, you know? *Everyone* is cranky when they're getting sick."

"Right. Absolutely."

Charlotte decided it was probably time to end this conversation.

"So, Secret Santa is starting—"

"Do you think I should knock on the door?" asked Strella, cutting short her attempt to change the subject.

Charlotte didn't understand her question.

"What door?"

"*Princess's.*"

"*No!*" said Charlotte quickly.

Strella's head cocked with surprise at her panicked response.

Charlotte held up her hands. "I mean, like *you* said, she won't be receptive to questions if she feels bad."

Strella nodded. "I guess..."

"Maybe you can catch her on the way out tomorrow?'

Strella perked.

"That's a good idea."

Her attention wandered to her thoughts, and, without another word, she walked into the sitting room and sat.

Charlotte huffed a sigh.

Whew.

She reentered the room, and Declan glanced at her. She rolled her eyes.

"Everybody here?" asked Bindy.

Charlotte scanned the room.

Brendan was still missing—

"Excuse me," said Brendan, brushing past her. He walked in and stood next to Strella's chair. He put a hand on her shoulder, and she smiled up at him.

He smiled back.

It seemed their tiff had ended without a death.

Charlotte gave a tiny fist pump.

Whee. Progress.

Bindy clapped her hands together.

"Alright—hello, everybody. I have here a bunch of fun crafting stuff. Scissors, glitter, construction paper, ribbons. You name it, I have it."

She motioned to the pile of items on the table and then picked up a coffee can.

"In this can, I have slips of paper with everyone's name. I need each of you to pick a slip of paper—that name is your Secret Santa person. You make them a craft you think they would like."

"Like this vacation wasn't bad enough," muttered Strella, loud enough for the room to hear.

Bindy cleared her throat and stuck the can out at Blade.

"You start," she said.

Blade reached in and took a strip of paper. He looked at it. A flash of disappointment crossed his expression.

"Don't tell anyone who you have," warned Bindy as she moved

the can to Mariska.

She made her way around the room until everyone had a name.

Charlotte leaned to Declan.

"I'll let you see mine if you let me see yours."

He snorted a laugh.

"*Never.*"

When Bindy had made the rounds, she returned to the crafting table.

"You can use any of this stuff or whatever you find. Though, don't steal or ruin any of the inn's stuff."

Everyone sat staring at her.

"Go ahead now. Start," she urged them.

No one looked thrilled, but they picked through the craft table collection. As Iko leaned to grab a ball of multicolored yarn, a necklace swung out from her blouse. It was gold with alternating red and green stones spaced an inch apart. Very Christmassy. Red, green, red, green—

Blank.

Charlotte leaned forward.

Hold on.

Iko's necklace was missing a *red* stone.

Charlotte reached into her pocket and pulled out the small red gemstone she'd found on the hidden stairs. Her attention bounced from the stone in her hand to Iko's necklace.

It looked like a perfect fit.

"Iko," she said.

Iko looked at her. "Hm?"

Charlotte motioned to her. "I like your necklace."

Iko looked down and touched her jewelry.

"Thank you. It's silly. It's my holiday necklace."

"Are you missing a stone from it?"

"A stone?"

Iko dropped the yarn in her hand and reached behind her neck to unclasp the necklace. She laid it across her hand and spotted the blank spot.

"Oh *no*," she said, looking like she might burst into tears.

Charlotte held out the stone she'd found in her palm for Iko to see.

"Is this it?"

Iko gasped.

"It is! Where did you find it?"

"On the ground."

Iko pinched the stone between her fingers and picked up a tube of permanent glue from the table.

"You're a *life*saver," she said. "The stones are fake, but I love this necklace. It belonged to an aunt of mine. She wore it every year."

Charlotte nodded and stepped back to stand by Declan.

"Is that the stone you found in the hidden stairs?" asked Declan.

She nodded, the smile still frozen to her face.

"Yep."

"So we're going upstairs to check Iko's room?"

She nodded.

"Yep."

CHAPTER THIRTY-ONE

Charlotte and Declan were about to peel off to check Iko's room when Blade approached. He looked down at his massive foot and toed the end of a throw rug's fringe.

"Who did you get for Secret Santa?" he asked.

"I thought it was called *Secret* Santa," said Declan.

"Hold on, I think I know where this is going..." Charlotte smirked and held up the strip of paper she'd pulled from the coffee can. "You're looking for this one, aren't you?"

Blade read the word on her paper, and his expression lit even as his cheeks flushed red.

She knew why. Her note said *Bindy*.

He held up his own slip.

"Want to switch?" he asked.

She handed over her strip, grinning.

"Sure."

Blade's said *Iko*. She showed Declan.

"What a coincidence," he murmured.

She nodded. "And easy. I'll make an ornament that looks like the all-knowing universe."

With a nod, Blade headed for the crafting supplies.

"Do you think we should warn him again?" asked Charlotte. "He's getting more smitten."

Declan shook his head.

"*Nah*. I don't think Bindy's our killer, and even if she is, good luck getting one over on Blade."

Charlotte snickered. "We're going to have to stop bringing him on cases. He keeps falling in love with our clients."

"This wasn't supposed to be a case," Declan reminded her.

"*True.* We're just lucky this way." She patted his leg. "Okay, I'm headed to Iko's. Wait here and keep an eye out for me."

While the others cut construction paper and glued ribbons—reluctantly or otherwise—Declan took a spot where he could keep an eye on everyone, and Charlotte ran to the second floor to Iko's room.

As expected, she found Iko's door locked. Luckily, she'd taken to carrying around her lock picks. This had stopped being a vacation a long time ago, sometime after the *first murder*. Plus, she had a lot of room in her pockets without that pesky phone.

She poked the picks into the door, popped the lock almost as quickly as if she'd had a key, and slipped inside Iko's room, closing the door behind her. The space was neat, and the bed made. A suitcase sat on a collapsable luggage rack against the wall, and she ruffled through the clothes inside, finding nothing unusual. The case was full—like her, Iko didn't move clothes into drawers or closets for a short stay, preferring to use the luggage as a makeshift bureau.

She noticed Iko had her own bathroom and suffered a flash of jealousy.

Fancy.

Iko must have upgraded.

People who won *free* rooms didn't get the *best* room.

She moved to the small but clean bathroom to shuffle through Iko's makeup case. Inside, she found the usual items and a pair of something she hadn't expected.

Surgical gloves.

Charlotte scowled as she unballed them. They didn't have blood or anything *murdery* on them.

Why would Iko have gloves? To hide fingerprints? Or were her reasons less nefarious? Did she dye her hair? Plenty of older ladies in Pineapple Port dyed their hair, and she knew those kits came with surgical gloves in them.

But who went on vacation to dye their hair?

She checked the trash, but it was empty. If she did have a hair-coloring box, Munch might have swept through and cleaned it up by now—

"Incoming!"

Charlotte whirled at the sound of Declan's voice booming up the stairs.

Iko's coming.

She stuffed the gloves back into the makeup case and zipped it shut. Hustling to the door, she put her ear against it and heard footsteps outside in the hall.

She grimaced.

Too late to get away.

"They're working on the room. They should be done in a second," she heard Declan say. His voice was closer now. He'd followed Iko up the stairs.

"I just have to grab something," said Iko.

The knob jiggled.

"So, you're going inside your room?" asked Declan, *way* too loudly.

Charlotte winced. Clearly, he was sending her a warning, which she appreciated, but Iko had to think he was *crazy*.

Charlotte scanned the room. There was nowhere to hide. Sure, she could dip behind the bed or hop in the closet, but it would look worse if Iko found her hiding.

Let's go the other way.

She took a deep breath and threw open the door.

Iko gasped. She stood with keys in her hand, the signature bunny charm dangling between her fingers.

She scowled.

"What are you doing in my room?" she asked.

"We've been retained to search for a stolen item," said Charlotte.

Declan stood behind Iko, and Charlotte saw his eyebrows rise at her lie.

He silently lipped the word *sorry*.

"A stolen item?" echoed Iko. "You think I *stole* something?"

Charlotte shook her head.

"No. We're searching all the rooms."

Iko's eyes flashed with anger.

"I didn't *steal* anything," she said through gritted teeth.

This was a new Iko. Charlotte hadn't seen the nervous woman angry before.

"I'm sorry," she said. "I'm done searching. We apologize for any inconvenience."

Iko stepped back to let her exit and went into her room. She turned at the threshold to face them.

"I'm going to ask Bindy about this. This isn't right," she said.

She dropped her gaze to the floor and shook her head.

"This vacation was supposed to help me unwind. It's done the complete *opposite*."

She slammed the door shut.

"I hear you," muttered Charlotte.

"Sorry," said Declan, out loud this time.

She shrugged as they wandered to the stairs.

"No biggie. It's fine. I didn't find anything anyway, except gloves. I'm still trying to figure that one out."

"Gloves?"

She nodded. "Surgical gloves. She had a pair balled up in her makeup bag. It's a little suspicious. She's uptight but not a *germaphobe*. Have you noticed her acting like she's afraid to touch things?"

He shook his head. "No."

"People use surgical gloves when they dye their hair, but vacation is a weird place to do it. That's something you'd do *before* you went somewhere."

"Plus, she has gray around her temples," noted Declan. "If she dyed here, she did a terrible job."

"I noticed that just now in the hall. So, right—I don't know what the gloves are about."

"What now?" he asked.

She shrugged. "I guess we should go make our gifts while we think about our next move."

They strolled back to the sitting room to work on their Secret Santa gifts with the others. Charlotte knelt in front of the table with the supplies. Nearby, Mariska sat busily coloring folded paper with magic markers.

"There you are. Do you want to know who I picked?" asked Mariska coyly.

Charlotte looked at the ornament in Mariska's hand, spotting a dog that looked suspiciously like her Abby.

"I wouldn't want to ruin the surprise," she said.

Darla leaned in.

"You know her head will *explode* if you don't let her tell you."

Mariska scoffed. "I wasn't going to tell her anyway. *I* can keep a secret."

At this, Charlotte and Darla laughed. Mariska scowled and returned to her coloring, twisting her body to hide her work.

Iko appeared and, after shooting a look at Charlotte, marched to where Bindy sat working on a gift.

"Did you hire people to look through my room?" she asked.

Bindy scowled. *"What?"*

Charlotte leaned toward Declan.

"We forgot to tell Bindy what we told Iko," she whispered.

He grimaced. *"Whoops."*

Charlotte needed to intervene *quickly*.

"She found me in her room," she said to Bindy. "I was looking for that *missing* item."

Bindy froze, her mind clearly whirring as she tried to piece together what was happening. Charlotte flashed her eyes at her when Iko wasn't looking—the international symbol for *play along.*

"That missing—*oh*," Bindy said after a pause. "Right. I apologize, Iko. She was looking for the, uh—"

Bindy looked at Charlotte, who bobbed one shoulder.

"—*thing*," she finished.

Iko crossed her arms against her chest.

"So she *was* doing something for you?"

Bindy nodded. "Yep. Yepper."

Iko huffed. "Well, I don't like people poking around my room."

Bindy held up a hand to show she understood.

"Yeah, nah. I'm sorry. In fact, we, ah, we found it, actually, so that's that."

She glanced at Charlotte, silently asking if her comment

worked.

Charlotte nodded.

Sure.

Iko grunted and returned to the window seat where she'd been working on her Secret Santa. She squeezed glue on a sheet of construction paper and sprinkled it with glitter. As she did, her frown relaxed until she was almost smiling.

The woman had been *desperate* for ways to forget her destress. Who knew glitter worked?

Bindy leaned to Charlotte.

"Is there something I should know?"

Charlotte shook her head. "False alarm. Probably."

Bindy frowned and leaned back.

Charlotte and Declan returned to their gifts, watching the other guests as they moved in and out of the room.

"Should we follow her?" asked Declan pointing to Strella with his eyes. She was the first to wander off.

Charlotte shook her head. "Nah. Part of me says *yes*, but if we follow every time someone goes to the bathroom, it'll look pretty strange."

Declan agreed.

Charlotte concentrated on Iko's ornament. She had to make it *especially* good so Iko would forgive her for snooping around her room.

After a bit, her morning coffee caught up to her, and it was her turn for a pit stop.

"I'll be right back," she said, standing.

Declan nodded without looking up from his ornament, and she headed to the third floor. Even if they didn't have a *private* bathroom and had to use the one in the hall, she felt she should use it on *her* floor. It also gave her a reason to wander and see if anything was happening.

She used the bathroom and opened her room door to peek inside on the way back. The dolls were still there, sitting in their spots like a bunch of little psychopaths—

She eyed them and hung in the doorway a moment.

Wait a second...

She'd put the dolls in a particular order to make sure she could tell if someone moved them around.

"Blonde, brunette, blonde, *blonde*."

She pointed at the last blonde.

"You're not in the right place."

She took a deep breath. It wasn't just *moved*. It was *swapped*.

It couldn't have been a visiting rabbit.

Did the killer come back to check on Elke?

Or was the universe messing with her?

She bit her lip as she thought of another option.

Is a new body under here?

She'd seen everyone downstairs, but people came and went.

Had someone not come back?

She rested her hand on the offending doll's head.

On three...

She counted to herself, bracing for what she might find.

One, two—three!

Wincing, she jerked away the doll.

Pillows.

All she found beneath it were the pillows she'd used to plump the pile.

No *body*.

Whew.

She replaced the blonde doll and wondered if she'd screwed up.

Did someone move the dolls, or did I mess up my own pattern?

Something clattered in the wall, and her head snapped that way.

She froze, listening.

Someone cursed.

The words were muffled, but she was sure she'd heard it.

Someone's in the hidden staircase.

She moved to the flap in the wall and pushed aside a particularly creepy old doll to clear the way.

She smelled something strange. Even stranger than the old doll now glaring at her with its cracked face.

Smoke?

Charlotte opened the flap.

CHAPTER THIRTY-TWO

Charlotte didn't need her flashlight to check the stairs this time. As soon as she opened the access flap in the wall, she saw a light glowing inside. The smell of smoke grew stronger. She crawled into the hidden staircase as silently as possible to peer over the edge of the steps leading down.

Five or six steps below her, a slight figure with dark hair sat perched on a step next to the coffee can, much like the one she'd passed earlier on the other staircase. The woman had a large flashlight sitting beside her, shining its beam upward like a makeshift lamp. Charlotte recognized it as one of the flashlights Bindy had scattered around the house to help them with the blackout.

She also recognized the woman.

"Iko?"

Iko gasped and turned to see her at the top of the stairs.

She stamped her cigarette dead on the step.

She wore surgical gloves.

"What are you doing in here?" she asked.

"What are *you* doing in here?" responded Charlotte.

Iko's shoulders slumped. She looked about as miserable as Charlotte had ever seen her, and for the little time she'd known the woman, there had been a lot of highs and lows.

"I'm sneaking a smoke," she admitted.

Charlotte crawled the rest of the way in to take a more

comfortable seat on the top step.

"Why here? You could go out on the porch on whatever side of the building the storm isn't hitting."

Iko frowned. "Because I don't smoke."

Charlotte arched an eyebrow, and Iko sighed.

"The thing is, I'm *telling* myself I don't smoke, but the *stress*. It's hard to quit. For some reason, hiding in here makes me feel like I'm hiding it from myself." She rolled her eyes. "I know it doesn't make any sense."

"How did you find this place?"

"Brendan told Bindy about it, and I realized my room was along the inner wall. I checked and found this little door. I sneaked in, saw cigarettes in this can, and—" She tilted her head back. "I had an emergency pack in my luggage, and here I am."

"That almost doesn't seem fair."

Iko chuckled. "I know. That's what I was thinking. It's like the universe *wants me to smoke*."

"This is where I found your red stone," admitted Charlotte.

"It is?" Iko's mouth made a silent O. "That makes sense. In fact, I was sitting here playing with my necklace when you showed up. Thank you again for that."

"No problem. Just dumb luck."

Iko cast her gaze downward.

"Sorry if I was mean about you in the room, but—"

Charlotte shook her head. "No. I get it. We should have told you."

"What were you looking for? What went missing?"

Charlotte didn't answer directly but padded a few more lies onto their already flimsy, spur-of-the-moment excuse.

"It was nothing. Bindy misplaced something. It wasn't stolen."

She motioned to Iko in an attempt to change the subject.

"The gloves are to protect your hands from smoke?"

The woman nodded. "I hate it when my fingers smell like cigarettes."

She offered Charlotte a sheepish grin.

"I won't tell anyone," said Charlotte.

Iko nodded. "It doesn't matter. No one cares if I smoke except me, and I'm not really fooling myself."

Charlotte motioned to the little door.

"I'm going to head out."

Iko waved. "See you."

Charlotte slid back into the bedroom and brushed herself off. She scowled at the dolls.

"Don't move," she told them, shaking a finger at them like they were misbehaving children.

She left. At least, her interaction with Iko explained the gloves. They didn't seem so suspicious now.

She headed down the main stairs, rearranging the list of suspects in her head as she walked. When she hit the second landing, she heard a door shut, and the noise snapped her from her thoughts. She spotted Brendan leaving his room with a black and white composition notebook in his hand.

She nodded a hello. "Hey."

"Do you want to check my room?" he asked.

She stopped, struck by the oddity of his comment.

Is that the worst pickup line ever?

"What?" she asked.

He sniffed. "I heard you were looking for something missing. Do you want to check my room?"

She shook her head and groaned a little inside.

This lie won't die.

"No, we found it," she said, deciding that would be the party line.

"What was it?" he asked before she could proceed downstairs.

She turned to answer this new question and stopped breathing for a second.

The corners of Brendan's mouth curled but fell short of a smile.

A tiny shiver ran down her spine.

Something isn't right.

Brendan's shoulders relaxed, and his head cocked slightly to the right as he awaited her answer.

Charlotte swallowed.

He looks casual, but...

She realized the problem was his *attention*—his laser focus on her—as if he were trying to see *through* her. No wrinkles radiated beside his brown eyes. The contrast among his body language, expression, and gaze felt like she was looking at a mask—one he'd worn to hide his *other* face.

The one that owned those eyes.

She hemmed. She didn't want to name the imaginary thing they'd been looking for in Iko's room. That would just be one more lie that she, Declan, and Bindy would have to keep straight. But if they didn't the killer would know they were hiding something. They would guess they were on to them.

"Um, nothing. Just a misunderstanding," she said, forcing herself to shrug.

No worries, as Bindy would say.

Brendan nodded and crossed his arms with the notebook pressed against his chest.

"Gotcha. Well, if you do need to look in there, feel free. I left it open."

"Okay. Thanks."

He motioned for her to head down the stairs, and she hesitated. The hair on her neck stood up. Her body wouldn't let her walk in front of him down those steep stairs.

Nope, it said. *Let him go first.*

"Go ahead. I forgot something," she said, returning to the stairs leading *up*.

He passed her and trotted downstairs. She paused and saw him glance up.

Is he looking to see if I headed for his room?

She waved. He flashed a smile and kept going.

Charlotte waited.

When she was sure he was gone, she turned to look down the hall at Brendan and Strella's room.

Should I search their room?

It felt like he *wanted* her to.

Why?

Because he was so sure there was nothing in there? Because he thought that would take him off her list of imaginary suspects?

Does he know this is about *murder* and not some missing

object?

Heck with it.

She hustled to Brendan's room and placed her hand on the knob, hesitating again.

Why does this feel like a trap?

How could it be? She couldn't think of a way Brendan could have booby-trapped the room. If she thought gloves were an odd thing to bring on a vacation, a pound of C-4 explosives would be even stranger.

She shook it off.

I'm being silly.

She turned the knob, and it moved with ease. As promised, he *had* left it open.

Charlotte let herself inside and shut the door behind her.

The room was similar to hers. No attached bathroom. No dolls, either, which was a selling point.

She moved as quickly as she could, checking their suitcase, behind the pillows, under the bed, and in the drawers of a small bureau. She didn't find anything odd at all.

Hm.

He was right. Nothing to hide.

She left and headed downstairs, still feeling unsettled.

In the sitting room, she sat next to Declan and picked up her ornament to get back to work. Everyone was in that room or nearby. Blade worked in the library, hiding his art from Bindy. Strella and Brendan had shifted to the parlor, where she heard them giggling. Whatever problems they'd had were over.

Maybe she'd *imagined* Brendan's menace? The place was making her crazy. She'd probably think Mariska was the killer by the time they got out of there.

"You were gone a while," said Declan. "I was about to send out a search team."

She nodded. "I found Iko on the hidden stairs sneaking a smoke. She uses the gloves to keep her hands from smelling like cigarettes."

"The *gloves*," he said. "And that's why her necklace gem was there."

She nodded.

"Well, that answers that," he said.

"I also ran into Brendan on the second floor."

Declan tilted his head to look through the library and into the parlor.

"And?"

She shrugged. "Nothing, I guess. It looked like he was getting a notebook from his room. He told me to go ahead and search it."

"The notebook?"

She snorted a laugh. "No, his *room*. He overheard Iko telling Bindy about us and wanted me to know his room was open to scrutiny."

"Okay..." Declan looked at her. "Why do you look like that? Was there a problem? Did you check his room?"

"I did, and there was nothing, but..."

She winced, wondering if it was worth mentioning.

"What?" he prompted.

She sighed. "I don't know. He creeped me out."

Declan puffed. "How? Did he say something?"

"No, calm down," she said, tittering at his flash of machismo. "I don't know. He—*I don't know*. I feel like he's hiding something."

He grunted. "Maybe it's about how he acted at dinner."

She scowled. "Dinner?"

"When Princess tore into Strella he didn't stand up for her. He just watched. Almost *amused*."

Charlotte frowned. She'd almost forgotten about that. It *had* bothered her at the time.

"You noticed that, huh?"

He nodded. "It made me uncomfortable. Poor Strella's a nightmare in her own right, but she looked like she wanted to slide under the table."

"They *were* fighting earlier, too," said Charlotte. "but being a bad boyfriend doesn't make you a murderer."

Declan nodded. "Most of the time."

She laughed. "Most of the time."

Charlotte went back to work on her ornament. She'd started with dark paper and used glitter to make stars. She cut a round piece of yellow construction paper for the moon. It wasn't looking half bad.

She was almost done when she heard banging somewhere upstairs.

She cocked her head. "Did you hear that?"

Declan looked up.

They heard steps on the stairs, and a moment later, Brendan burst into the room.

"Has anyone seen Strella?" he asked.

"She was in the parlor with you?" said Declan.

Brendan huffed and ran his hand through his hair. "I know, but she went upstairs. She took so long that I went looking for her. I can't find her anywhere."

Bindy stood and shot a panicked look at Charlotte and Declan.

"She has to be here *somewhere*," she said.

Charlotte turned her back to the others to whisper to Declan.

"Rock, paper, scissors?" she asked.

"For what?"

She frowned.

"For who's checking the freezer."

CHAPTER THIRTY-THREE

"You checked your room?" Bindy asked Brendan.

Bindy radiated with stress. Charlotte knew she'd barely been holding it together with *two* people dead. A third, and she'd be on the next plane to Australia.

"Not exactly. Our bedroom door is locked, though," said a frantic Brendan.

This caught Charlotte's attention. She was sure she hadn't locked the door he'd left open for her.

"I was hoping you have a master key?" he said.

"Where's *your* key?" asked Bindy.

He rolled his eyes. "Strella had it."

"Oh," Bindy looked relieved. "So she *must* be in there?"

"I *guess*, but I knocked on the door, and she didn't answer."

"Maybe she's asleep," suggested Charlotte.

Brendan frowned. "I banged pretty loud."

"That's what we heard," murmured Declan.

Charlotte nodded.

"I'll get the master key from Munch," said Bindy.

Charlotte looked around and realized she hadn't seen Munch in a while. She'd been concentrating so hard on the guests that she'd forgotten about him.

Hm.

Darla stood and moved toward Charlotte.

"What do you want us to do?" she asked.

Charlotte took a moment to decide the best way to use their resources. She glanced into the library, where Blade remained working on his art with the tip of his tongue poking from the corner of his mouth.

He could stay there for now.

Charlotte turned her attention to Darla.

"You two stay here and keep eyes on the others. If something happens, at least, we'll be able to account for everyone."

"Got it. You can count on us."

Charlotte grinned. "I know."

They turned to look at Mariska, who wasn't paying attention *at all*. She held a kitten over her head, talking to the dangling animal in a baby voice.

"Are yous the cutest? The teeniest, tiniest, cutiest cutie pie in the whole world?"

Darla and Charlotte exchanged a look.

"Well, you can count on *me*," said Darla.

"I've got Brendan," said Declan.

"I'll take Bindy," said Charlotte.

Bindy strode off, and Charlotte followed.

"Where do you think Munch is?" asked Charlotte, jogging to catch up.

"He's usually in the kitchen." She side-eyed Charlotte. "Strella better be in that room, or I'll *scream*. I'm a pretty cool cat, but I can't handle this anymore."

Charlotte agreed. Finding Strella alive was more important than maybe Bindy realized. There was an argument to be made about why someone might kill both Elke and Princess. She didn't know what it was, but their lives were intertwined.

If *Strella* turned up dead, it meant someone was targeting *anyone*, not just Elke's family.

She realized they might need a whole new plan. If Strella was dead they'd need to get everyone in one room and *stay there* until eleven, when the phones became available again. No more worrying about people panicking. It would be much more important to keep people *safe*.

The question was, how would they force everyone to stay in

one place? What if the killer freaked out? What if he or she had a gun?

"Do you have a gun on the premises?" asked Charlotte.

Bindy looked at her, alarmed.

"Why?"

"Just in case?"

Bindy sighed. "I do, but it's in the time lock safe."

Charlotte put her hand on her head.

That *stupid* safe.

So much for that idea.

They walked into the kitchen, where Munch sat, eating leftovers at the small kitchen table. He looked up as they entered.

"Munch, I need your master key," said Bindy.

He nodded and stood to pull the key off the collection of keys he had clipped to the belt loop of his cargo shorts.

"Have you seen anyone in here?" asked Charlotte.

Munch shook his head.

"Have you been in here long? For the last half hour?"

He shook his head and held up a hand with his fingers splayed.

"Only five minutes?" Charlotte grimaced. "Tell you what—can you stay here and guard this room?"

Munch nodded, though he looked understandably confused.

Bindy looked at Charlotte.

"Just in case there's a pattern," explained Charlotte with a glance at the locked freezer.

Bindy frowned.

They went to the center stairs, where Declan and Brendan stood waiting. Together, the four headed to the second floor, and Bindy opened Brendan's door with Munch's master key.

The room was empty.

It looked the same as Charlotte remembered, except for a piece of paper on the bureau. That hadn't been there before.

Brendan saw her looking at it and picked it up. He read to himself and then looked at them, his brow furrowed.

"It's a *confession*," he said, looking stunned.

No one said anything. Charlotte knew what they were thinking. She almost forgot Brendan *wouldn't* know what they were thinking.

"For what?" she asked.

Brendan shook his head.

"It says she *killed* someone?" he said. "What is she talking about? How is that possible?"

He handed the lined paper to Charlotte. Someone had ripped the sheet from a book. Creases across the face of it implied it had been folded to about the size of a credit card. She read the ragged scrawl aloud.

"I hate her. I killed her. Forgive me."

"There's no signature, and it doesn't say *who* she killed," she said.

Brendan motioned to the note. "I can tell you that's Strella's handwriting—it's wobbly but definitely hers."

"But why would she kill someone?" asked Declan. "And *who*?"

Brendan put his hands on his hips. "If I had to guess, I'd say Princess. I know she felt threatened by her success, and then there was that thing between them at dinner. It might have pushed her over the edge."

"Pushed her to *murder*?" asked Charlotte, her tone implying how unlikely she found his theory.

Something rippled across his expression. He seemed annoyed she'd questioned him but recovered quickly, biting his lip with worry.

"I know it seems crazy, but we should check on Princess to be sure, right?"

Charlotte looked at the paper again.

Even if Strella had snapped and killed Princess, why would she kill Elke? And why would she kill Elke *first*?

She handed the paper back to Brendan. He took it and crossed his arms against his chest with the paper tucked there, much like the way he'd tucked away the notebook.

The notebook.

Charlotte leaned over to Declan.

"Go check Princess's room. I'll be right back," she murmured to him, making to go down the hall.

Brendan stomped his foot. "Let's *go*. What is there to talk about? This is a nightmare. We have to check on Princess."

"And find Strella," said Charlotte.

Brendan rolled his eyes. "Yes, of course, *and* find Strella."

Charlotte left them behind to hurry down the hall.

"Where is she going? Is she checking?" she heard Brendan asking behind her.

She kept moving. She jogged downstairs and entered the parlor.

She needed to find it.

The notebook.

Strella's confession was written on a sheet pulled from the black and white composition book she'd seen in Brendan's hand. Everything said that's where the paper came from—from the type of lines on the paper to the torn edge.

The note hadn't been on the bureau when she checked his room. He'd taken the book to the parlor to work on the ornaments.

That meant Strella wrote a confession in the parlor, tore it out, took it to the bedroom, left it on the bureau, and then disappeared?

It was too strange.

If Strella *really* confessed, why would she confess to one murder and not two? Why would she suddenly write the note in Brendan's notebook and run it to the room?

Charlotte wanted that *book*. She didn't know if it would tell her anything, but everything inside her said she needed to find it.

The problem was that the notebook could be in Brendan and Strella's bedroom, the parlor, or anywhere in between.

She didn't like Strella as the killer.

There was another option.

What if *Brendan,* with his crazy eyes, wrote the note and kept it in his pocket until it was time to plant it?

What if he wrote it after killing Elke and didn't update it after Princess?

She'd worried the room-searching lie might panic the killer, and maybe it did. So, perhaps Brendan had decided the time had come to frame Strella. He wanted them to find that note, but he didn't want them to see that notebook. He carried it with him to protect it.

Why? What was in the notebook?

Charlotte hoped it would explain everything.

She burst into the parlor and scanned the room. The book wasn't clearly visible anywhere.

Dammit.

She took a deep breath and looked again, more carefully.

If I was going to hide a book in here...maybe without Strella noticing...

Her gaze fell on the sofa where she'd stuffed the VHS tape. A tan rabbit sat there now, its face partially tucked in the end cushion.

Cushions are a handy place to hide things in a hurry...

Shooing aside the bunny, Charlotte felt behind the cushion. Her eyes widened as her fingers hit something thin, flat, and solid.

The notebook.

The composition book had been stuffed between the arm and the seat cushion, right where she'd hidden the VHS tape.

She pulled it out. The top edge of the book looked as if something had been chewing on it.

She looked at the rabbit.

Seems she wasn't the first to find it. Animals always knew when something was *different*. The rabbit knew that book wasn't usually there. That meant it was fair game for munching.

Her pet dog, Abby, had a similar theory as a puppy.

Charlotte flipped through the book, moving to the window to use what dreary light it provided. Outside, the rain had eased but remained steady. She realized she hadn't heard thunder in a while.

Things are looking up.

She tilted the book to look at the pages at an angle. Maybe she could find the impression of the confession on the blank pages. Maybe there were damning drafts?

Halfway through the book, she found a pencil drawing of Princess Christmas. It was *good*. There was no doubt who it was. She flipped to the next page to find another. Then another. Then *another*. In each sketch, Princess wore a different outfit—a gown, a bikini, a teddy. One of the more sweetly themed images was labeled *Lina*. In it, Princess was only a girl.

One image featured Princess staring lovingly at a man who looked a *lot* like Brendan with more muscles and a decidedly sharper jawline…clearly an idealized portrait.

It was labeled, *Owen+Lina.*

Charlotte scowled.

Owen?

On the VHS tape, young Lina called the boy coming to rescue her on stage *Owen.*

Get away from me, Owen!

Was Brendan *Owen*? Was he still obsessed with Princess?

And had he reinvented himself, too?

She needed to tell Declan—

"Give me my book."

Charlotte whirled to find Brendan staring at her from the doorway to the foyer.

His hand balled into a fist.

CHAPTER THIRTY-FOUR

Yesterday

Brendan lowered his head to stare at the table. From the corner of his eye, he watched Princess. The way her mouth moved when she talked. She never smiled, which was funny—he followed her on all her social media platforms, and other than some sultry selfies, she was *always* smiling.

That was her brand, after all.

Christmas was *happy*.

Not here. She didn't smile *here*.

Her gaze had passed over him once or twice. He was no one to her.

She didn't recognize him.

He wasn't sure how he felt about that. In one way, it was good—he'd worked hard to become her *type*. On the other hand, he believed she'd have recognized her true love in any form.

It probably didn't help that he'd introduced himself as Brendan. He'd changed his name a couple of times over the years. Brendan, his current choice, meant *Prince* in Irish. He had a beard now—he was a *man* now. The last time she'd seen him, he was seventeen.

Maybe she didn't recognize him, but he hadn't forgotten *her*.

Maybe he'd pushed her memory aside for a *while*, but he remembered the day she showed up in his online feeds. This person—*Princess Christmas*—was his Lina—married to some millionaire and living the life she deserved.

Thinking her lost to him, he tried to recreate her with Strella—but Strella was no Princess Christmas. He knew now she never would be. He'd tried to help Strella raise her online profile, and she did *okay*—

Pathetic compared to Princess.

Then, it finally happened.

Princess got a divorce.

She made a few questionable moves after that—dating schmucks, cheesy reality shows—

It was beneath her.

She needed his help.

That was when everything made sense.

He found the purpose he'd been missing.

The purpose he'd forgotten.

He'd visited the Timeless Inn earlier on to talk to Elke, hoping to gain access to Princess, but Elke was no help. He kept in touch, pretending to research his novel, and just when he was ready to give up, Elke told him Princess was coming.

Finally.

He booked a room, and now, here he was, sitting at the same table with Princess.

He could barely breathe.

He was thrilled, but Princess didn't seem happy to be home. She kept glaring at her mother. He assumed she was afraid people would find out Elke was her mother. Online, Lina pretended to be from royalty. It would destroy her social status if people found out she'd grown up in an old bed-and-breakfast farmhouse in the middle of nowhere.

He wouldn't let that happen—

He snapped from his thoughts as Bindy addressed the group.

"—I've arranged a little treasure hunt ..."

Brendan nodded.

This is perfect.

While the others were looking for eggs, he'd get Princess alone.

He took a deep breath and braced himself to talk to her—

That's when Princess headed for the house.

Dammit. Where is she going?

He was about to go after her when the mute kid, Munch, stopped her. A moment later, Elke came out, and the three of them talked. Elke was more animated than he'd ever seen her.

He tensed.

Something's going on.

Princess seemed *exasperated*.

The three returned to the pergola area—and kept walking to the barn.

Why?

"Where do you want to start?" asked Strella, buzzing in his ear like a mosquito.

"Hm?"

"The treasure hunt. Where do you want to start?"

He scowled. "We have to do it separately. You heard the lady."

Strella rolled her eyes. "We don't have to do everything she says."

He twisted his body to ensure only she saw his expression.

"*Go do it yourself*," he said through gritted teeth.

She blanched and stepped away.

Brendan huffed and then took a deep breath to calm his agitation.

He didn't have time for Strella and her BS. Her brattiness was what he'd liked about her—what reminded him of Princess—but she was *such* a pale imitation.

A sad little girl.

She wasn't a *princess*.

He wandered toward the barn, but before he could get far, the door slid open, and Princess stormed out. She swung wide around him to head toward the side of the house. Elke went in the back door. Munch remained in the barn.

Brendan felt a panic run through him.

She's leaving.

Maybe she'd found a way to call a car? It would be like her to hide a phone somewhere. She was clever.

He strode as fast as he could without drawing attention, walking around the *opposite* side of the house from where he'd seen

Princess go.

He'd cut her off in the parking lot out front.

He rushed to beat her so he could arrive in time to look *casual* like he'd been there all along, but she was nowhere to be found when he arrived.

Where—?

He heard voices.

Princess.

He headed toward her side of the house.

She was talking to someone there. She'd never made it to the front.

"How *dare* you blackmail me. You're my *mother*," he heard her say.

"You're leaving me no choice—"

That voice was Elke. He was sure of it.

Princess huffed. "I don't know who you think you are. I knew I shouldn't have come here."

"You can't just leave—it isn't right—"

"*Get off me.* You've got a lot of nerve if you think I would do anything for *you*."

He heard a door slam and peeked around the corner. The women were gone. He flexed to go after them, but another woman suddenly appeared at the opposite corner.

The detective lady.

He threw himself back against the front of the inn and gritted his teeth.

Dammit.

Never mind.

It didn't matter.

Now he knew how Elke had got Princess to show up. She was blackmailing her own daughter—threatening to tell the world who she really was, no doubt.

He jogged around the building and entered the back door but saw no one. He checked the lower level, finding no one but a man— the husband of the woman he'd seen on the porch. He was checking under cushions for eggs like an idiot.

Brendan sneered. He didn't like that guy. He was tall and

handsome, and Princess had looked at him. He knew she fell for that sort of thing because she didn't have *him* to show her what a *quality* man was like.

A man with *depth*.

He needed to hurry.

He jogged up the stairs to the third floor where he knew Princess was staying.

At the top, he turned left to go to Princess's room and stopped.

Princess is upset.

Was now a bad time to talk to her?

Her world was in chaos. He could help—but how could he *make* her understand that? He wasn't rich. He couldn't be her next multi-millionaire. But he *could* make her rich using her own talents. He'd accomplished so much with Strella in such a short time.

Unfortunately, using Strella as an example didn't make a *great* case for him. Obviously, she didn't have Princess's natural star power. Princess would have to understand that, but still... he needed *more*.

What else can I offer her?

He could protect her. He'd die for her—

His hand was still hovering over Princess's door, ready to knock, when he heard crying behind the bedroom door across the hall.

He turned and, through the crack of the partially open door, saw Elke sitting on the side of the bed. Her face was in her hands.

That's when it hit him.

Elke's blackmailing her.

He could end *that*.

Princess would be grateful.

He grinned.

That's it.

He knocked on Elke's door, and the woman looked up.

"What do you want?" she asked.

"I need to talk to you," he said.

She shook her head. "Talk to Bindy. It's her place now."

She stood and tried to close the door.

He blocked it with his foot.

She scowled. "What are you doing?"

"Stop blackmailing Princess," he said.

"What?" It took her a moment to shake away the shock. "Who do you think you are? That's none of your business."

He shook his head.

"That's where you're wrong."

He reached for her—he wanted to shake her—scare her—but she slapped at his hand and sucked in a breath to scream.

No!

He couldn't let her scream.

It would ruin *everything*.

He grabbed her by her shirt and jerked her toward him. He put his arm around her throat. She wrestled to break free.

She was strong for an old lady.

He fell back across the hall, hauling her with him, until his back hit the wall. He twisted and pushed her through the door into Princess's old bedroom. In the corner sat Princess's dolls piled like a pyramid.

The site of all those doll eyes watching him cost him his concentration. Elke twisted and almost broke free. He snapped out of his shock just in time.

They fell on the floor together with a *thud*.

That's when he spotted something familiar. Red lace, sticking out from under the dolls—it was the dress Lina wore at that ill-fated Princess Christmas Pageant.

What is it doing under there?

He reached into the pile with the hand not wrapped around Elke's throat and pulled the first thing he felt. A strap? It gave way, and he looked at the thing in his hand. He recognized the charms along the length of it.

He'd whipped the belt from Princess's dress.

That'll work.

He wrapped those strong threads around Elke's throat and pulled with all his might.

It took a minute, but she stopped thrashing.

He released his grip on the belt and moved away. He leaned against the back of the bed, staring at the dead woman.

That's one way to end the blackmail.

He hadn't planned to kill her, but it was okay. It solved Princess's problem.

She'd always hated her mother anyway.

Now, he had to show Princess what he'd done. The lengths to which he'd go for her.

How much I love her.

He propped Elke against the dolls and got up.

His eyes fell on the dress again.

He reached out and ran his fingertips across the fabric.

He knew one thing.

He had to have it.

He gathered up the dress and took it with him. He jogged downstairs and hid it in his closet. As he came out of the room, planning to look for Princess, suddenly, she appeared on the second-floor landing.

Like a *vision.*

"Princess?" he said.

She ignored him and approached the stairs leading down.

"Were you in your room?" he asked.

She stopped.

"What?"

"Your bedroom. Your *old* bedroom. Are you coming from there?"

Princess flinched. Her scowl etched deeper. She squinted at him.

"What are you talking about?" she asked.

He moved closer. He smiled.

She hadn't seen the body.

"I have a surprise to show you," he said.

She eyed him up and down.

"Go away, *loser,*" she said.

It felt like someone had stabbed him.

She started down the stairs, and he watched her go, too stunned to move.

He felt *sick.*

He took a deep breath.

Calm down. She didn't mean it.

He glanced upstairs and thought about Elke's body.

Leave her there.

Someone will find her.

Then she'll know what I did for her.

That night...

Brendan nodded.

Now, it made more sense.

Princess wasn't staying in her old room.

Once he realized that, he slipped a note under her door telling her to meet him in the kitchen using the stairs no one knew about. She wasn't staying in her old room—the one attached to the stairs where they used to sneak smokes as kids—but the room she *was* in for the weekend had hidden stairs of its own.

In the note, he told her he knew everything. Told her he could help. Teased he had a secret.

She'd *have* to come.

Now, sitting in the kitchen, waiting, twirling the padlock key around his fingers, he'd found himself in a weird place. Half-euphoric, half-terrified.

The detective couple, ironically, were staying in Princess's old room, but for some reason, they'd hidden Elke's body in the freezer. They'd had the two old ladies keep a lookout, but he'd seen enough to figure it out.

The question was, *why?*

Why would they hide the body and not tell anyone?

He heard a noise near the stove.

He'd moved it to reveal the hatch in the wall and clear a path for Princess, and now her adorable bare feet were popping through the little door.

He almost died of happiness.

"Let me help you," he said, rushing to her.

"Don't touch me, *freak*," she snarled from inside the wall.

He winced and stepped back.

He needed to earn her trust. He knew that.

She shimmied into the kitchen and stood to brush herself off.

"How do you know about these doors?" she asked.

He hemmed. He wasn't ready for the big reveal yet.

"Um, I've been here for weeks with your mother, working on this book—"

"My *mother*?" she said, but the energy seemed to drain from her as soon as she said it. Like she didn't have the strength to pretend anymore.

She didn't *have* to pretend anymore. She'd know that soon.

"You're a real princess," he said.

"You just said you know she's my mother," she muttered.

"I know she's blackmailing you, too."

"That's what you said in the note." Princess's eyes widened. "And you're blackmailing me, too? Is that what this is?"

He held up his hands.

"No. *No*. The opposite. I'm here to save you."

She scoffed. "Save me? *Please*. I think we all know what you want, creep."

She turned to go.

"Elke is here," he said quickly.

She paused. "What?"

"Elke. She's in the freezer."

Her expression went slack.

"What do you mean *she's in the freezer*?"

He smiled. "I'll show you."

Brendan opened the freezer door and propped one of the kitchen chairs in front of it to keep it from closing.

"In here," he said.

Princess peered inside.

"I don't see anything."

He went inside and pushed a bucket aside with his foot, exposing Elke's dead face.

Princess took another step inside and bent to get a better view.

She sucked in a breath.

"She's *dead*?" she asked.

He nodded. "She won't blackmail you anymore."

She gaped at him.

"*You* killed her?"

He nodded. "I did it for *you*."

She slapped her hands to her chest.

"For *me*? What are you talking about? I didn't ask you to *kill* her."

"No, but she was blackmailing you. I heard you talking—"

"I know, but—you *killed* her?"

She was really hung up on that one point.

"It was the only way you could keep your secret safe," he said.

She blinked at him, speechless.

Speechless *with gratitude*, he imagined, but he could tell she hadn't seen *him* yet.

He reached onto the shelf where he'd hidden the original Princess Christmas dress and held it up for her to see.

"Remember this?" he asked.

Her jaw fell open. "My dress—?"

He nodded. "It's your Princess Christmas dress."

"I know what it is. I built a whole persona around it," she spat. "The question is, why does some mother-murdering rando have it?"

He tucked his chin.

Ouch.

"Don't you know who I am yet?" he asked.

She shook her head slowly, wrapping her arms around her body. The cold was getting to her in her silky robe.

She started to leave again.

"I don't know, and I don't care. I—"

"I'll tell them *you* did it," he said, rushing the words. He didn't want to threaten her, but she had to stop trying to *leave*.

She couldn't go until she saw how much he loved her.

"It's me," he said. "Owen."

"Owen?" She gasped. "*Owen Tinsdale*?"

He nodded.

She squinted at him.

"You don't look like Owen. Your nose—"

He touched his face.

"I had some work done."

She laughed and raised her hand to her forehead.

"Oh, that's just *perfect*," she said.

He scowled. Something the way she said it. He didn't understand her tone.

"I—what do you mean?" he asked.

She sighed. "She wasn't blackmailing me about where I grew up, idiot. She was blackmailing me about *Munch*."

"Munch?"

"He's our son."

"*Our*—" Brendan gaped. His knees felt weak. He put his hand on the shelf to keep from falling and almost slipped when his hand landed on a rolling pork loin. He recovered and left his hand resting beside it.

He sucked in a ragged breath as warm tears rushed to rim his chilly eyes.

"*Our* son?" he repeated in a whisper. "Why didn't you tell me?"

She laughed.

"Oh, *right*. Like I'm going to stay here, like some trapped teenage mother."

"But—"

She raised a hand to cut him off.

"Mom sent me to her sister's. She said my aunt wanted to adopt him, and I *had* to do the right thing. As soon as I had him, I ran away. I had a *life* ahead of me."

He placed his hand against his chest.

"But *we* could have had a life—"

She laughed again. He'd heard her laugh on so many videos.

Her laugh had never sounded like this before.

Her video laughs were like a melody.

This laugh made him *mad*.

Princess sighed.

"There was no *we*, Owen. You caught me at a weak moment, and I paid for it. I didn't want to be tied to you. You would have been an *anchor*. You would have *sunk my life*."

Brendan's jaw clenched.

"Does he know I'm his father?" he asked.

"*No*. She *just* told him I'm his mother. This weekend, before I showed up. It's funny—out in the barn, she told me nobody knows what happened to you."

She snorted a laugh.

"I told her you probably offed yourself," she added.

Brendan's hand moved over the pork loin again. He gripped it.

"Kid's just like you, too," said Princess, continuing.

"What do you mean?"

"He's not all *there*," she said, tapping the side of her head.

She rolled her eyes.

"Talk about making the right decision—"

Brendan's vision went white.

He didn't hear the rest of her sentence.

Instead, he swung the pork loin, hitting her *hard* on the side of her skull.

Princess spun and bounced off the opposite shelves to collapse in a heap.

"Not laughing now?" he asked, standing over her, breathing the sharp air. "We could have had a *life*. We could have been a *family*."

His fingers relaxed, and the frozen pork loin clattered to the ground.

What have I done?

He reached for her and then retracted his hand.

No.

She was too far gone. That was obvious. She wasn't *his* princess anymore.

She wouldn't be anyone else's, either.

But, as mad and hurt as he was, he couldn't leave her like this.

In a *pile*.

He crouched and rolled her on her back.

She was still breathing.

"*I loved you*," he said as he arranged her neatly.

She moaned but didn't speak. He laid the dress over her.

It didn't look right.

He took his time undressing her, pulling the dress over her head. She remained limp.

The dress *almost* fit.

She'd had her breasts enhanced. He couldn't get the back zipped. He did his best and gave up. While dressing her, he found an old lipstick in the folds and put it aside. A plastic crown hung from a pinned ribbon at the back, and he arranged it against her head.

"You were my princess," he whispered as he applied the lipstick.

Her lip twitched.

He added color to her cheeks and stuffed her pajamas on the shelf behind some frozen salmon filets.

Finally, he crossed her arms against her chest and stepped back.

He smiled down at his work.

It was good.

She looked like a princess.

CHAPTER THIRTY-FIVE

Pineapple Port

Frank knocked on Bob's door at ten o'clock in the morning. His friend answered, looking tired.

No shock there.

"I know who the thief is," said Frank.

"Yeah? Did you get him?" asked Bob.

Frank bobbed his head from side to side.

"Yes and no. It's a long story. Let me in."

Bob grunted and walked into the kitchen. Frank smelled fresh coffee.

"I'll take a cup," he said.

Bob nodded and poured him one.

"I can't promise how good it is. Mariska usually makes it," said Bob, handing him a steaming mug. He sat on the stool next to him at the kitchen island. "Okay, tell me the story."

They both lifted their mugs and took a sip. Bob winced. Frank let his mouthful slip back into the mug.

"What did you make this with? Gasoline?" he asked.

"I think I got the recipe wrong," muttered Bob.

"I'd say so."

"Tell me the story anyway."

Frank took a deep breath and told Bob what happened during his walk with Turbo—about the man, the stolen decorations, and the dying wife.

Bob gaped at him when he finished.

"Sad, isn't it?" prompted Frank. "Damn near broke my heart."

Bob scratched the side of his face as if he were trying to work out something.

"Are you saying he stole my bare-bottomed Santa after we sat there all night watching for him?" he asked.

Frank scowled.

"*That's* what you took away from that story?"

"Yes—" Bob shook his head. "I mean, *no*, it's a sad story, don't get me wrong. I just can't believe we sat there all night, and he took it in the end anyway."

Frank shrugged. "He did. He'll return it after Christmas or— you know."

Bob grunted. "Not much use to me *after* Christmas."

"Oh, shut up. You know Mariska wouldn't let you leave that tacky thing in the yard anyway."

Bob grunted. "Probably not." He cracked his neck. "So, what are we doing today?"

Frank pulled his phone out and looked to see if anyone had called. No one had. He'd called Darla that morning, but she didn't answer again.

"Call Mariska," he said.

"Why?"

"Because I've called Darla and Charlotte, and no one is answering. Something's wrong."

Bob shrugged and got up to find his phone. He dialed and held it to his ear before lowering it.

"Voicemail," he said.

Frank shook his head. "I don't like it."

Bob looked at his phone.

"It is weird," he said. "Usually, she'd call me by now."

Frank huffed a sigh.

"How about you and I drive to that bed and breakfast?"

Bob's nose wrinkled, and he turned to stare at the cup of coffee beside him.

"Deal. If you buy me breakfast first."

Frank sighed.

"You are the *cheapest* bastard."

CHAPTER THIRTY-SIX

Charlotte stood in the parlor with the notebook in her hand, her gaze locked with Brendan's. He had the same look she remembered from the hallway upstairs.

It was as if something had snapped in his head.

Probably the staple that held that mask in place.

Now, that *other* Brendan, the one he'd tried to hide from her earlier, didn't want to stay in the shadows anymore.

Maybe that is Owen.

She braced for what she knew was coming.

Brendan launched at her.

He'd kept his hands low to grab the book from her hands, and she swung as hard as she could at his face with a closed fist. Her knuckles cracked into his cheek.

It *hurt*.

It maybe hurt her more than it hurt him because it only stopped him for a split second.

Brendan's head was knocked sideways. A second later, he refocused on her.

His eyes held a new fire now.

She had one thought.

Run.

She tried.

She didn't get far.

He grabbed her by her shirt and hooked her with his arm, placing her head in the crook of his elbow before she could scream.

As she struggled against him, she heard footsteps running on the stairs.

So did Brendan.

He jerked her toward the back door to get away. She fought to keep from going, but he was too strong, and the pressure on her windpipe was too steady.

He pulled her outside and down the porch steps. As the rain pelted her face, she saw a flash of Declan inside the house.

"Charlotte!"

He appeared on the porch as Brendan pulled her toward the barn.

Charlotte didn't know where they were going, but she remembered the things on the barn wall.

The *sharp* things.

She did not want to go there.

"Stay back, or I'll kill her," Brendan roared.

His grip on Charlotte's throat grew tighter, and she clawed at his arm, praying her windpipe wouldn't crack.

"What's going on?" said Mariska as she and Darla ran into the parlor.

They'd heard a commotion, and they weren't alone. Blade was a step ahead of them.

It was crazy, but Mariska thought she'd heard Charlotte *scream.*

"The door's open," said Darla, running through the back door.

Outside, the storm raged—the sound of rain on the porch's roof almost deafening.

"That Brendan guy has Charlotte," said Mariska, pointing.

Declan was in the yard, stalking after the man and Charlotte. His hands were in the air as if trying to calm Brendan down.

Blade jogged into the rain after him, and Declan glanced over his shoulder. He motioned for Blade to stay back.

The big man slowed.

"We have to help," said Darla.

Mariska nodded, a rising sense of panic making her stomach churn.

She considered their possibilities. They could walk out behind Blade and Declan, but that wouldn't help anyone. If there was a way to get around *behind* Brendan—

"Around the pergola," she said. "We'll go around and through the little graveyard. That will put us on the other side of him."

"What good will that do?" asked Darla.

"He won't see us coming. We can *surprise* him."

Darla grimaced. "Okay. I'm in."

The ladies hurried into the rain, running far around the pergola so they could pass unnoticed by Brendan. Brendan moved slowly. Charlotte wasn't making it easy for him.

By the time they reached the back of the graveyard, they were both soaked.

Darla stepped over the low fence and held out a hand to assist Mariska. They stayed low, weaving between the gravestones as they approached the front.

"He's still coming," said Darla. "He's going to walk right past us soon. We'll be back where we started, behind Declan."

Mariska watched as Declan took another step toward Brendan. It seemed as though Brendan would continue past the barn.

"He didn't go *into* the barn," she said.

"He'd be trapped," noted Darla.

It was a good point. Mariska couldn't imagine what Brendan's plan was. That made her nervous. Eventually, he'd get desperate.

They crouched behind a small above-ground mausoleum just behind the entrance to the graveyard. Brendan stopped in front of them, wrestling to keep Charlotte still.

Mariska thought she saw Declan's hand move at his side.

Was he motioning to them?

He'd seen them.

He was telling them to stay down.

"Declan sees us," she reported.

Darla nodded, rain dripping from the tip of her nose.

Suddenly, Declan sprinted toward the barn, forcing Brendan to turn to face him.

That put his back to the graveyard.

Brendan yelled something at Declan, but Mariska couldn't make out the words.

"Why did he do that?" asked Darla.

"I don't know, to keep him from seeing us, maybe?"

"Declan thinks this was a bad idea," said Darla.

Mariska frowned. "Or, maybe he's thinking we can distract Brendan. If he turns to look at us, Declan might be able to run at him."

"Ah, that's a good idea," said Darla. "Should we scream at him?"

Mariska chewed her lip. They only had one shot at this. Her eye drew to a round river rock sitting on the ground beside them.

Hm.

"I'll *cornhole* him," said Mariska.

Darla's eyes saucered as her attention whipped to Mariska.

"*What*? It sounded like you said you're going to *cornhole* him."

Mariska grimaced. "I *did.*"

She picked up the rock and showed it to Darla.

Darla's mouth made a perfect O.

"Oooh, you're going to throw it like a cornhole bag? At *him*?"

Mariska nodded. "We won the Pineapple Port cornhole tournament for a reason."

Darla rolled her eyes. "Yeah, to get the *prizes*. Are you sure this is our best option?"

Mariska stepped up.

"Yes."

She focused on Brendan's back and took a deep breath.

You can do this.

She gritted her teeth.

"*Nobody* hurts my baby Charlotte."

She swung back her arm and *tossed.*

"There's nowhere to go," Declan called to Brendan. "*Let her go.*"

"Go back to the house, and I will," Brendan called through the rain.

Declan shook his head and took another step.

"I can't do that."

Brendan gave Charlotte a jerk.

"You will if you don't want me to break her *neck.*"

Declan stopped. As he did, he caught movement from the corner of his eye—somewhere in the graveyard.

He turned his head slightly so as not to alert Brendan and tensed.

Oh no.

Mariska and Darla were in the graveyard, sneaking up on the man.

Brendan would see them any second.

He had to do something.

He took a deep breath and *sprinted* to the left toward the barn. He reached the side wall and turned to find Brendan facing him, his back to the graveyard.

He'd turned.

Just like Declan hoped he would.

"One more move like that, and I swear I'll kill her," screamed Brendan.

Declan raised his hands and took a step forward. Maybe he could force Brendan back against the graveyard, or the women could distract him long enough for him to get to Charlotte.

It was inevitable they'd make their presence known at some point.

He'd have to be ready.

"Don't come another step closer, I *swear*," said Brendan when he was ten feet away.

Brendan was screaming now. *Crazed.* He jerked at Charlotte's neck, and Declan saw her fight for air.

His thoughts grew dark.

"Hurt her, and I promise you won't survive the day," he roared.

"Who cares? Who cares now?" said Brendan, but Declan could see his hold had loosened.

Declan saw Mariska rise up behind Brendan. She had something in her hand.

What is she doing?

She swung her arm back like—

Declan's mouth fell open an inch.

—like she's playing cornhole?

Before he could react, Mariska's arm slingshotted forward.

He couldn't see what she threw, but suddenly, Brendan barked with surprise.

His head spun to look behind him.

Declan saw his chance.

He sprinted forward and snatched Brendan's forearm to keep it from tightening on Charlotte.

Brendan panicked and tore himself back and away.

"Take her!" he screamed, shoving Charlotte forward at Declan as he moved.

Charlotte stumbled forward, and Declan released Brendan's arm to catch her.

Brendan sprinted away, headed for whatever lay beyond the barn.

"Are you okay?" Declan asked Charlotte, wiping away the hair stuck to her wet face.

She nodded, coughing but breathing.

With her safe in his arms, Declan glanced at Brendan's retreating form in time to see a black beast rush out from the side of the barn and tackle him.

Declan gasped.

What the—

"Oooooh!" screamed one of the ladies in the graveyard.

"Oooooh!" came a collective moan from the direction of the house.

Declan turned to see the rest of the guests had gathered on the porch to watch the drama unfold.

They, too, had seen Brendan struck like a tackling dummy, but he still didn't know what hit him.

Mariska and Darla ran up to dote on Charlotte.

"Are you okay, honey?" asked Mariska.

"Take her to the house," said Declan.

They nodded and headed that way, cooing over his wife as if she were a little girl, who'd skinned her knee on the playground.

Declan jogged to Brendan to find *Munch* holding Brendan's face against the ground.

Munch had been the mysterious tackler.

"If I hold him, will you get me rope?" Declan asked.

Munch switched places with Declan. He moved to run toward the barn and then stopped. He stood in the rain, staring down at Brendan.

Somewhere, thunder clapped, and light flashed across the boy's angry expression.

"What's wrong?" Declan asked when the young man didn't move.

Munch pointed down at Brendan.

"He killed Momma?" he said in a strange halting staccato.

Declan nodded.

"But you got him," he said.

Munch smiled and pounded his chest.

"Me."

CHAPTER THIRTY-SEVEN

"Are you okay, Miss Charlotte?" asked Blade.

Walking back to the house, Charlotte, Darla, and Mariska reached Blade, who'd been on his way out to help Declan.

Soaking wet, Blade looked even bigger, his goofy teeshirt stuck to his massive body, his mustache drooping even farther than usual.

"I'm fine," she said, though she had to clear her throat.

She whooped as Blade suddenly bent and scooped her into his arms.

"That's good, Blade, you take her," said Mariska.

Charlotte put her arms around Blade's neck and noticed two new but familiar faces in the crowd on the porch awaiting them. She squinted, worried that she'd suffered some kind of brain damage from lack of oxygen.

Is that Frank and Bob?

Sheriff Frank came off the porch to shadow Blade as he neared the house.

"Are you okay?" he asked.

She nodded as Blade ushered her through the group to the parlor and placed her on the sofa.

As Charlotte sat up, she spotted Strella staring shyly across the room. She'd never seen the young woman so *demure*.

She pointed at her and looked at Bindy, searching for an explanation.

"We found her in the freezer. Cold but unharmed," said Bindy. "Brendan tried to make it look like she'd locked herself in there.

Regret over the murders."

Charlotte gaped, and Bindy sniffed before continuing.

"Yeah, luckily, it hit me we should look in there sooner rather than later, or she would have been a goner."

Charlotte nodded in enthusiastic agreement.

Bindy pointed to her. "Are you okay?"

Charlotte rubbed her throat.

"I will be," she said, her voice feeling stronger.

"What in the name of Sam Hill is going on here?" asked Frank.

"I'll explain it to you, but for now, you really have to get the police out here," croaked Charlotte.

"I *am* the police," he growled.

"Not for this county, and you're not state homicide," said Darla.

Frank's eyes bulged.

"*Homicide*? Who's dead?"

"Brendan will be if you leave him with Declan after what he did to our Charlotte," muttered Mariska.

"No one you know," said Darla, patting Frank on the shoulder. "That man Declan and Munch are bringing in killed two women."

Frank gaped at her.

"*Two women*? And you didn't even call me?"

"The phones are all in the time-lock safe," said Bindy.

Frank rubbed his temples.

"Someone will have to sit me down and explain all this to me," he said, pulling out his phone. "Where are the bodies?"

"They're in the freezer," said Bindy.

Frank looked like his head was going to explode.

"Why is everybody in the *freezer*?"

He looked at his phone. "I can't get any reception. Let me go use the unit in the cruiser."

He paused, looking at the stuffed Christmas otter decoration in the corner.

"Hey, can I borrow that funny little guy for a little while?" Frank asked. "Week or two?"

Bindy shrugged. "You're here to save our butts. Sure."

Frank nodded and headed out.

He left as Declan entered with Munch and Brendan. He'd tied Brendan's hands and then wrapped more rope around him, cocooning him like a spider. He had a sock stuffed in his mouth.

He wasn't going anywhere.

Declan pushed Brendan into a chair and spotted Strella.

"You're *alive*," he said.

She rolled her eyes. "Alive to keep my terrible boyfriend streak going for another half a century."

Frank returned.

"They're on the way. I've got ambulances, homicide, the works."

"We need *everything*," said Iko. "Mostly, I need a cigarette. I'm not even *pretending* I don't smoke for the rest of this weekend. I deserve that."

She wandered off.

"You're a hero, Munch," said Bindy, putting her arm around him.

"He spoke, too," said Declan.

Bindy gasped. "Really? That's *wonderful!*"

Munch blushed.

Bindy smirked at Blade.

"You were wonderful, too," she said.

"Aw, I didn't do anything," said Blade.

She eyed him. "We should get you out of those wet clothes."

Blade smirked and looked away.

Charlotte looked at the old clock on the wall. It was getting late. It would take at *least* four hours to review everything with the police. The safe would open by then, and they could reclaim their phones and *go home*.

The lights flickered and came on.

The group cheered.

"Everything is looking up," said Darla.

Bindy nodded and rubbed her hands together.

"So—I can count on you all for good testimonials, right?"

Declan and Charlotte sat curled on the sofa together, glasses of eggnog in hand. The long weekend had been a *long* weekend. They'd taken showers, gotten into comfy clothes, and decided to decompress a little before throwing themselves into bed. They'd picked up Abby after dropping off Mariska, and the dog had inserted herself into the crook of Charlotte's tucked legs. She flopped her furry chin on her mother's thigh.

"She's happy to have Mommy home," noted Declan.

Charlotte smiled. "Seems like it."

He sighed. "Hey, *now* can we agree no more Mariska trips?"

"You can't say they're *dull*."

"No. *Dull* isn't the word."

Charlotte laid her head on his shoulder, and he leaned his cheek against her hair.

"You scared me today," he murmured.

"Scared you?"

"*Brendan* grabbing you like that."

"Oh." She chuckled. "He scared me, too."

He put a hand on her leg. "Can we add these things to our New Year's resolution list?"

"I didn't know we had a resolution list."

"We do now. No *more* Mariska vacations and no more almost getting killed."

She shrugged. "Sounds easy enough."

She noticed his empty glass.

"Do you want another eggnog?"

He shook his head. "I'm shifting to wine. I'll get it—you can't disturb Abby's pillow. You want one?"

She nodded and handed him her glass.

"Sure. I'll shift to wine before I put on a hundred pounds of *nog*."

He walked to the kitchen, and Charlotte petted Abby until she realized the room seemed unusually quiet. She turned to find

Declan—not in the kitchen—but standing at the front window.

"What are you doing? Looking for snow?" she asked. "It might be a while."

He shook his head.

"You know that funny little yard decoration you set up with all the Christmas puppies rolling around in the garland?"

"Yes?"

He turned. "It's missing."

Charlotte sat up.

"What?"

~~ THE END ~~

Thank you for reading! If you enjoyed this book, please go to Amazon and review!

ABOUT THE AUTHOR

USA Today and *Wall Street Journal* bestselling author Amy Vansant is also the founder of AuthorsXP.com – a website for authors (marketing) and readers (free/deal books!).

Amy lives in Jupiter, Florida, with her muse/husband and a goony Bordoodle named Archer.

Books by Amy Vansant

Pineapple Port Mysteries
Funny, clean & full of unforgettable characters
Shee McQueen Mystery-Thrillers
Action-packed, fun, romantic mystery-thrillers
Kilty Urban Fantasy/Romantic Suspense
Action-packed romantic suspense/urban fantasy
Romantic Comedies
Classic romantic romps
The Magicatory
Middle-grade fantasy

Made in the USA
Coppell, TX
19 June 2025